JAGGED LITTLE SCAR

Micheala Lynn

Bella
BOOKS
2014

PUBLISHER'S NOTE

About the Author

Micheala Lynn divides her passions between writing, playing a wide variety of music, mountain biking, snuggling with her partner of many years on cold Michigan nights and home schooling their daughter. When not at her desk, she can be spotted on the local mountain biking trails or at a Renaissance faire speaking Old English and performing on the Scottish smallpipes. Her degrees include English Literature and Language, Anthropology and a master's in Creative Writing, all from Central Michigan University. Find out more at www.MichealaLynn.com.

Dedication

In memory of Mike Werstler, the best dad anyone could
ever have.

To my partner, Kate, who has taught me both to live and
love, not in spite of the scars but because of them.

CHAPTER ONE

"Girl, it's about time you got out and did something." Cheryl threw her arm around Sam as they walked along the line of vendors, pulling her close and laughing.

Sam crossed her arms and grumbled. If it were up to her, she'd much rather be at home, working on her computers, but Cheryl, her best friend since college, had bugged her all week until she finally gave in. She had just landed a new job to create a huge corporate website and she couldn't get her mind off it. Even without that, she'd much rather be working instead of being dragged around Pride.

"Yeah, Sam. There's much more to life than sitting in front of a computer." Angi, Cheryl's partner of five years, now chimed in, seemingly reading her mind. "And a little sun certainly wouldn't hurt, either. Good God girl, you're starting to look like a vampire." Given their propensity for dressing alike and sporting the same hairstyle—long on top and shaved on the sides and back—Angi and Cheryl were often mistaken for sisters instead of partners but that didn't stop them from being the most adorable lesbian couple Sam had ever seen.

"Yeah, whatever." Sam hid a small grin. She couldn't deny that it had turned out to be a lovely afternoon. All week, the weatherman had been predicting rain and she had kept her fingers crossed for just that. Yet, as she looked up, there wasn't a cloud in the sky. Well, that was just her luck. She hadn't been to Lansing Pride in three years, not since she and Jennifer, her ex, had come. Since then, she really hadn't had much interest in anything but her work.

Still grumping to herself, she wiped back the sweat beading on her forehead and trickling into her eyes. Already it was hot and it was barely noon. If the feel of the sun on her skin were any indication, she was probably going to end up with a wicked sunburn to boot. Just what she needed. She continued to grumble under her breath when Cheryl quickly tugged her to the left, nearly ripping her off her feet. "Hey, watch it."

"Oh, come on. I want to check this out." Cheryl beelined up to a vendor selling hats and T-shirts. In the background, music drifted over the festivities from the live bands on stage. While Cheryl and Angi checked out the shirts, Sam ran a finger over a black cap with a barbwire rainbow embroidered on the front. The black would certainly look great with her fiery shoulder-length red hair and with a little luck, it might even keep her from getting too scorched under the sun. Besides, if she had to be there, she might as well have something to show for it. But when she flipped it over, she nearly choked. "You've got to be shitting me. Thirty-five dollars? For a cap?"

"That would look really good on you."

She whipped around, her chest tightening. "Excuse me?"

A woman with tousled brown hair and mirrored sunglasses smiled at her. "I was just saying that cap would look really good on you—especially with your red hair." She tilted her head as if getting a better look at her.

"Um…thanks." She had been out of the lesbian scene for so long, she wasn't sure how to respond to such an obvious flirtation. Running away came to mind. She shot a quick glance toward Cheryl and Angi but they were still busy looking through shirts. With no help there, all she was left with was biting her lip and spinning the cap around in her hands, hoping upon hope that her new friend would quickly lose interest and move on.

"Well, I'd better get going." The woman leaned in closer and then let out a laugh as Sam contorted her body in what looked like some bizarre yoga position to keep the same distance between them. She lowered her voice. "I'd buy the cap, though." Then with a wink, she walked away.

Still spinning the cap around in her hands, Sam watched as the woman walked out of sight.

"Hey, she was cute." Cheryl threw an arm around her shoulders. "What did she want?"

"She was just being nice. Said this cap looked good with my hair." Sam held it up to emphasize the point. She tried to sound casual but her hands were still shaking.

"Wow. You should have asked her out. It's been like how long?"

"Oh, yeah, right. Believe me, that's the last thing I need." Sam avoided Cheryl's gaze as she pulled her wallet from her back pocket and paid for her cap.

"Boy, Sam, you're a bright ray of sunshine today. You know what you need? You need to get laid." Cheryl poked her in the ribs.

Sam let out a loud snort and rolled her eyes. "Oh, like I'm just going to find someone out of the blue here and get laid."

"What better place to meet someone?" Angi waved an arm at the large crowd milling between the vendors. "Look—hot girls everywhere."

"Well, like I've said a hundred times, I'm not interested in meeting anyone right now." Her friends certainly meant well but since breaking up with Jennifer over a year ago, she had sworn off all romance—who needed all that heartache anyway? She had been with Jennifer for nearly three years and everything had seemed to be good. That was until she came home and found her in bed, *their* bed, with some woman she had picked up at the local coffee house. As if that weren't bad enough, Jennifer blamed her for the affair—if she had known how to pleasure a partner, she wouldn't have had to find it somewhere else, thank you very much. Grinding her teeth, she tried to push the memory away. No, she certainly didn't want to go through that again anytime soon.

"I just worry about you, Sam." Cheryl once more wrapped her arm around her waist. "I want you to be happy."

Sam pulled her hair into a ponytail and fed it through the back of her new cap. "I am happy." At Cheryl's look of utter disbelief, she stomped her foot. "Really, I am."

Cheryl pulled her in closer, hugging her tight. "Okay, okay. Just keep an open mind. You never know when the right person will just appear and sweep you off your feet."

Angi burst out laughing. "Yeah, like you did?"

"What?" Cheryl slapped a hand to her chest, doing her best to look innocent. "I swept you off your feet."

"Knocking someone flat on her back is not sweeping her off her feet." Angi wagged a finger at her.

"I didn't knock you flat on your back."

"You knocked me down on my butt—that's bad enough."

"Well, I was in a hurry. At least I helped you up."

"Not until *after* you got your coffee. Only then did you look down and go, 'oh geez, are you okay, miss?'" Angi wrinkled her nose at Cheryl.

"Oh, I wasn't that bad. Besides, I really needed that coffee."

By now, Sam was laughing so much, her sides hurt and tears ran down her lightly-freckled cheeks. She had heard this story more times than she could remember but each time it subtly changed. A detail here. A detail there. Cheryl and Angi were constantly reinventing their first encounter, but it always amused her. They never seemed to tire of each other.

Angi stood up on her toes and wrapped her arms around Cheryl. "Well, you certainly got my attention." She gave Cheryl a tender kiss.

"Mmmm." Cheryl had her eyes closed. "I'm so glad I ran you down."

Sam turned away, letting out a soft sigh. If only she could find what they had. Was that too much to ask? Apparently with Jennifer it had been. Maybe she was destined to always be alone.

Then again, maybe Cheryl was right—the right person would just appear and sweep her off her feet.

"Hey, where you at?" Cheryl waved her hand in front of Sam's face. "You're like a million miles away."

Sam blinked twice and then giggled. "Just lost in thought as usual."

"Wow, I guess." Cheryl took Sam's hand in one and Angi's in the other. "Well, come on. Why don't we get something to eat? I'm pretty hungry."

"Now, that sounds good." Angi swung her and Cheryl's arm back and forth, swaying as they walked.

At the mention of food, Sam's stomach gave a massive growl. Other than a banana and coffee, her usual breakfast of champions, she hadn't eaten all day. "So, what do they have here that's good?"

Cheryl skipped a couple of steps. "I saw a booth selling Thai food. That's what I'm having."

"Oh, that sounds good. I haven't had Thai in forever." Angi licked her lips, making a big scene of it.

"Yeah, that actually sounds really good." Sam couldn't remember the last time she had eaten Thai either—probably with Angi and Cheryl. Left to her own devices, she lived on Ramen noodles and TV dinners. Granted, she *was* a computer geek.

* * *

"Hey, Jodi, there you are." Kat stepped around the far side of the enclosed trailer hitched to the back of Jodi's Ford Escape. "I've been looking everywhere for you."

Jodi sat on top of her large Fender amp, strumming her guitar lightly, eyes closed. At the sound of Kat's voice, she slowly lifted her head and gave her a wry smile. She had been hoping no one would find her until the show. With her little pixie bob haircut and super petite build, Kat seemed small and delicate, almost childlike. However, her fiery personality would fit someone three times her size.

Kat looked up at Jodi and gave her a bright smile. "Why don't you come and walk around with us. Terra and Lynn want to check things out. There are a lot of cool vendors here today."

Jodi merely shook her head and glanced down at her feet. Just the thought of walking around in a crowd of people made her stomach churn. She'd much rather sit back behind the trailer, alone with her guitar.

"Oh, come on. It'll be fun." Kat grabbed her by the hand, trying to pull her off the amp. "Besides, it will do you some good to get out instead of sitting back here and sulking."

Jodi yanked her hand back. "No." She mouthed the word, barely more than a whisper. Kat may only be trying to help but she wished she'd leave her alone. She wished everyone would leave her alone.

Kat peered up into Jodi's eyes as she hung her head. "Sweetie, are you okay? I'm worried about you."

"I'm fine." Again, she breathed out the words, her lips moving but no sound coming out.

Kat let out a long sigh, her shoulders falling. "Jodi, I just want to see you happy, girl."

Her eyes now began to sting and she quickly turned away, staring off into the distance. She wanted nothing more than to be happy too but she just didn't see how that would ever be possible. How could she go out there with all those people walking about? She couldn't even stand to be around herself. Finally, she lowered her head and began to fingerpick a simple chord progression, concentrating on the movements of her fingers, hoping to keep away the tears that threatened to spill.

Kat let out another deep breath and patted Jodi lightly on the leg. "Okay. I'll leave you be, but I sure wish you'd come with us." She stood and peered down one last time before she shook her head again and slowly walked away.

Once Kat was out of sight, Jodi ground her palm to her eye, quashing away a tear. She hated feeling like this. Three years— not a day went by that she wasn't reminded of that terrible accident. It just wasn't fair. Why did a drunk have to blow through a red light and wreck her life? Why did she have to lose her voice, the one thing besides her guitar playing that meant the most to her. Why did she have to have deep, jagged scars up and down her body as if someone had chiseled away her flesh? She couldn't count on both hands the number of skin grafts she had endured and for what? She still looked like a slasher film reject. And what about the endless counseling sessions? *You just need to work through the stages of grief—you have to accept this is your new normal.* What a joke. Couldn't they see? She would *never* be normal again. How was that for fair?

Again she closed her eyes and slowly plucked through one of the ballads she had written. It was a new song, written since her accident. That was how she had come to think of her life— before her accident and after her accident. She didn't play her songs from before her accident. It was too painful a reminder of everything she had lost. At first, she had thought her music career was over. How could she ever face a crowd again after what had happened? But she couldn't give up her music. She could still play the guitar. At least that hadn't been taken away. Another tear spilled down her cheek as she continued strumming her guitar, feeling the notes wrap around her like a warm, comfortable blanket, shutting out everyone and everything.

* * *

With a Styrofoam bowl of Pad Thai in one hand and a glass of Thai iced tea in the other, Sam scurried to keep up with Angi and Cheryl, weaving her way through the small groups dotted across the hillside along the Grand River. Finally, they found an empty spot and kicked back in a small circle. Music mixed with a dozen different conversations drifted across the hillside. Angi sucked in a noodle, slurping loudly. "God, I love these."

"Mmmmm. Yeah, not bad." Sam smacked her lips. For an outdoor festival, the food was quite impressive.

"So, babe, when's Lynn's band playing?" Cheryl leaned against Angi's shoulder as she ate.

Angi glanced at her watch. "They're supposed to be on at three—about another twenty minutes."

"We certainly can't miss that." Cheryl wiped her mouth and stuffed the napkin in her empty bowl. "Lynn would never forgive us."

"Who's Lynn?" Sam squirmed, a sharp pain digging into her. She'd probably be a whole lot more interested if she could only get comfortable. No matter what she tried, something kept biting into her butt. She again shifted her weight to no avail. Finally about to scream, she rocked over on her left side and swept several broken nutshells out from under her. No wonder she couldn't get comfortable.

Angi stretched out her legs, smiling as she watched Sam fidget. "Oh, she's a friend of mine from college. She's in the band Blind Pariah with her partner, Kat. Lynn sings and Kat is the drummer."

"Wow, really? I've never seen them." Sam gulped down the last of her Pad Thai, wincing as it seared her throat.

Cheryl let out a loud snort. "Well, that's what you get for never getting away from your computers. They've been touring the last couple of years throughout Michigan and northern Indiana, playing most of the women's festivals and hitting the clubs."

"Yeah, yeah." Cheryl had her there. She really hadn't been into the club scene since Jennifer. Jennifer hadn't liked clubs. Then, after they broke up, she just didn't feel like going out. "So, where on earth did they get the name, 'Blind Pariah'? That's pretty esoteric."

"That would be Jodi." Angi gave her head a firm nod. "She put the band together and came up with the name. Something about needing to be blind to nasty people who are blinded themselves by their own hatred. How being an all lesbian band makes them outcasts, pariahs of music, so they might as well embrace it—hence 'Blind Pariah.'"

"Okay, I get it but it just seems a bit odd."

Angi laughed with Cheryl. "Yeah, well, that's Jodi. You'd have to know her. She's a bit…different. If you stay with us, we're going out with the band later and you can meet them."

Fed up with the hard ground and the nutshells still poking into her butt, Sam finally stood. "I'll probably head home before then."

"Jesus, Sam. Live a little." Cheryl jumped up and offered her hand to Angi.

"Yeah, we'll see." Sam rolled her eyes. What she'd really like to do is to start working on that new website. That sounded a lot more fun than sitting around and talking with strangers.

With her hand in Cheryl's, Angi gathered up their trash and threw it in the barrel. She then grabbed Sam by the arm and pulled her closer. "At least you can listen to them. They're actually really good."

Together, they meandered through the crowd, making their way to the stage. A band had just finished up and now the emcee dashed out on stage, starting her monologue and working the crowd.

"Hey, over there." Cheryl marched off toward the sound control booth where it cast a shadow across the grass.

Her legs burning as if she had in a moment of true stupidity decided to enter the Pride 5K—she just wasn't used to all this walking, not when she spent the better part of her life in front of a computer—Sam flopped down on the ground and settled back on the cushy grass, immediately welcoming the shade. Sweat again trickled off her forehead and into her eyes. Even as cool as her new black cap was, it wasn't any help.

Cheryl threw a leg around each side of Angi and pulled her back against her chest. Angi then craned her neck, brushing Cheryl's lips with hers. "This is a great spot, babe."

"Nothing less for my baby." Cheryl nuzzled against Angi's neck.

Sam let out a sigh as she watched her two best friends. She couldn't help but feel a tinge of envy. What they had seemed effortless. Why couldn't she find that? She had to work at everything in a relationship, and even then, it always seemed to fall apart. Cheryl and Angi were so lucky. She had never been with anyone who looked at her as Cheryl and Angi looked at each other, as if no one else at that moment existed. Then again, she had never found anyone herself who she looked at like that either.

The warm breeze, a combination of freshly mowed grass and automotive exhaust, swept across her face as she leaned back on her elbows and closed her eyes. Although she wouldn't mind sitting in front of her computers in air-conditioned bliss, she couldn't deny the heat against her skin felt great. And she had to admit, she could use the break, especially after the long hours she had been keeping lately. But just as she was about to nod off, a squeal of feedback pierced the air and the emcee screamed into the microphone. "Now, put your hands together and give a big welcome to Blind Pariah."

Sam jerked fully awake, the emcee's voice still echoing in her head. She then glanced up at the stage and nearly fell flat as her elbows gave out under her. Nothing could have prepared her for the sight in front of her—a tall, slender woman clad in jeans, a tight black tank top, and clunky black boots bounced across the stage, wailing on a bright blue electric guitar. "Holy shit, who is *that*?"

"*That* would be Jodi." Angi jumped to her feet, pulling Cheryl up with her, keeping her arms wrapped around her waist.

With her mouth still gaping, Sam scrambled to her feet, her eyes glued to the lithe young woman hammering out a screaming heavy metal solo, playing her guitar with both hands on the neck Eddie Van Halen style while she danced around the stage. She had never seen anything like it before—both girl and guitar a mere blur. "Oh my God, she's amazing."

Cheryl nudged her shoulder. "You haven't seen anything yet. Just wait."

Sam couldn't imagine how Jodi could possibly be any better. She seemed to play effortlessly, her fingers flying over the neck of the guitar. Although three other women shared the stage, Sam hardly noticed them.

"So what do you think?" Angi leaned close, her lips only inches from Sam's ear.

"Wow. She's…she's…she's just amazing."

Cheryl burst out laughing. "Yeah, I think you already said that."

"What?" Sam barely shot a glance at Cheryl. The band had now slowed down for their next song, a slow rock ballad. She could almost feel the emotion emanating from Jodi's guitar as it cried out each lonely note. Jodi then threw her head back as she drew out one piercing soulful note, her long thin arms wrapped around her guitar as if she were embracing the instrument as she played it.

Sam rocked up on her tiptoes, peeking over the crowd. She didn't want to miss a thing. Not only was Jodi unbelievable on the guitar, she had to be one of the most gorgeous women she had ever seen. She always had a thing for women with clipped spikes and Jodi certainly didn't disappoint with her extremely short black hair framing her narrow face.

Now Jodi hopped over to the side of the stage, kicking up her clunky black boots, and slowly began to spin around in place, her guitar cable following her like a long, thin tail. While the rest of the band, even the drummer, worked to engage the crowd, Jodi merely focused on her guitar, as if there were no one else around. With her eyes still on Jodi, Sam leaned over to Angi as she clapped with her hands above her head to the beat of the music. "Hey, what's up with Jodi? She never looks at anyone while she's playing."

Angi cupped a hand to her mouth, raising her voice over the loud music. "That's just Jodi. You'd have to know her. She really doesn't like being around people much."

"What? How can she not like people? She's a professional guitar player." Sam could understand someone like herself not liking people. That's why she preferred being around computers most of the time. But for someone who played guitar in a band, made a career out of performing in front of an audience, not liking being around people—that made no sense at all.

Angi stopped clapping and pulled Sam close, their cheeks brushing, and nodded up at the stage. "See that big scar on her neck?"

"I don't see what—" Then she noticed it, the deep angry gash running down the side of Jodi's throat, disappearing under her black tank top. She sucked in a quick breath. "Whoa, what happened there?"

"From what Lynn told me, Jodi was in a really bad car accident a couple of years ago—almost died. She won't even talk about it, not that she talks all that much about anything."

"Oh, God. That's really sad, Angi."

"Yeah, I know." Angi slowly shook her head as she watched Jodi up on stage. "What's worse is she used to frontline her own band, even had a couple of albums. I have them at home and let me tell you, she was good. Not only did she play guitar, she sang. I saw her a couple of times when Kat filled in on drums. Then the accident left her with that scar and really messed up her voice. If you ask me, that's why Jodi doesn't like being around people much. After that, Jodi gave up her solo act and formed Blind Pariah with Kat on drums. That's how Lynn got involved. They needed a lead singer and Lynn was a natural fit."

Sam turned back to the stage, a sour lump settling in her stomach. Jodi slowly twirled with her guitar again, her eyes closed, wrapped up in her own little world. At the sight, Sam swallowed. She couldn't even begin to imagine what it must be like for Jodi. All because of a car crash. No wonder Jodi didn't like being around people. To lose all that with only a jagged scar to show for it. It wasn't fair.

* * *

Jodi slipped the strap of her guitar over her head. She nodded toward the table where fans were beginning to line up. "Why don't you go and sign albums while I tear down." Her voice was low and raspy, not much more than a whisper.

"You know, the crowd always asks to see you." Lynn stretched, showing off her lean, muscular body compliments from years of dance. Although not quite as tall as Jodi, she still made a striking presence on stage with her blond faux hawk and wildly personable nature.

Without answering, Jodi continued to pack up her equipment. The absolute last thing she was going to do was sit in front of everyone and watch their expressions when she spoke. Or worse yet, the questions. *What happened to your voice?*

Hey, are you going to ever sing again? I saw you once and you had a great voice—what a shame. Yeah, what a shame. No, she didn't need that.

She watched out of the corner of her eye as Lynn shuffled away, her shoulders slumped. Lynn and Terra could deal with the crowd. She was better off back here, out of sight, without having to worry what anyone might think or say. All she needed were her guitars and she'd be happy, especially her bright blue electric guitar. She plucked it from the stand and wiped down the neck with a soft cloth before gently lowering it into the case. That guitar was her life. Her mom and dad had bought that guitar for her after her accident. She had always wanted a Paul Reed Smith Custom 24 with the abalone bird neck inlays in the deep Blue Matteo finish. The day of her accident, she had been at Guitar Center. They had just had one delivered and she played it for three hours straight in the store before reluctantly giving it up. It had almost come home with her that day but she couldn't quite afford it. Maybe if it were still there in a month or so, she would definitely get it. Then, the accident. That had changed everything.

"Hey, Jodi. Can you give me a hand?" Kat was struggling with her Roland V-Pro electronic drum kit. She had already removed the cymbals, foot pedals and hi-hat. At only five-foot-two to Jodi's five-foot-ten, she was the shortest in the band.

Jodi grabbed the end of Kat's drum rack and lifted. "Damn, and I thought my amp was heavy."

"Be thankful this is an electronic set. My old set weighed about the same as a Volkswagen."

With Jodi in the lead and Kat taking up the rear, they grunted, heaved, shuffled and swore their way to the trailer. The only thing that could have made it more miserable was if it were snowing or raining. Finally, as the last of the drum set slid into the trailer, Jodi nearly collapsed, her heart pounding in protest. "Like I said, and I thought my amp was heavy."

Kat wiped the sweat from her forehead. "The worst thing about playing drums has to be moving them. Electronic or not, it sucks."

"Yeah, I'll stick to my guitars, thank you."

Without so much as a moment to catch their breath, they bustled back to the stage and up the ramp. Jodi still had to finish packing up her gear. She peeked over to the table where Lynn and Terra were signing albums. A long line of people was still queued up. That was a good sign. The more albums they sold, the more money they made. She then turned back and picked up her Ovation acoustic. Besides her Paul Reed Smith, the Ovation was her next favorite. It probably helped that it was a Melissa Etheridge signature model. She smiled to herself as she wiped it down and placed it in the case. No self-respecting lesbian rocker should be without one.

With a case in each hand, she slogged off again to her Escape and slid them in the back, which was much better than them bouncing all over the inside of the trailer. She'd probably curl up in a ball if she opened up the trailer only to find her guitars scattered hell and gone amongst the other equipment.

"Hey, Jodi. What's left?"

"Just the amps, thank God." Jodi hooked a thumb over her shoulder at the stage. Sweat now streaming off her forehead, she trudged back up the ramp with Kat. "Why don't you see if you can get those guys to help you with Terra's amp. They need something better to do, anyway." She pointed to the two guys who were supposed to be helping out but were doing a better job of lounging around the stage and flirting with the cute guys in the crowd.

Jodi unplugged her Fender 100-watt Twin Amp and rolled up the cables while Kat worked with the burly guys to carry Terra's amp. She wheeled her amp behind them, letting gravity carry it down the ramp, but when it hit the bottom, the wheels bit into the grass and the amp stopped cold. "Shit." This was just what she needed. Well, she wasn't going to wait and she certainly wasn't going to ask for help, not from those guys, not from strangers, so she bent down and—one, two, three—heaved, her long wiry arms flexing as she lugged her amp, bouncing against her thigh with every step.

Kat turned around as the guys loaded Terra's amp into the trailer. "Good God, Jodi. We could have helped."

Jodi merely shook her head and gritted her teeth, jostling her amp into the trailer. She kept her head down until the guys were out of earshot. "I had it no problem. Besides, I didn't want to…" She waved her hand absently toward the back of the two men. "You know."

"Ah, yeah." Kat watched the men walk away. "I know you've heard me say it a thousand times but just don't let it bother you, Jodi. Who gives a damn what they think?"

"It's just hard, Kat."

"I know. Believe, me. I know." Kat squeezed her shoulder.

Jodi glanced up at the stage as the next band began to set up. What Kat didn't know—what no one knew—was how hard it was sometimes for her to be up on stage. It was a constant reminder of what she had lost. Whenever she picked up a guitar and strummed even a few chords, she felt like singing, an almost overpowering urge. At best, she could sing maybe a note or two. Then she'd hear herself, how she sounded now, and her stomach knotted and she had to fight back the all too familiar tears. Even thinking about it now, she could feel the stinging at the corner of her eyes.

"Well, I'm going up to sign some albums. You sure—"

"I'm sure. There's no way I'm going up there."

"Okay, sweetie. You know I have to ask." Kat gave a quick wave over her shoulder and then bounded up to Lynn and Terra.

Jodi stood with her hands in her pockets as she watched her bandmates signing albums and laughing with the fans. She missed that. That had always been the highlight of any show, as was talking, if only for a few moments, with each person who wanted a CD. That way she could personalize the message. She had fans ask her to address it to their partners, their parents, their bosses, their ministers—nothing surprised her. One young teenage girl once had even asked her to address one to her great-grandma. Yeah, that had been a lot of fun. Jodi reached up and absently brushed her fingers over the deep scar on her throat, something did a dozen times a day. Finally with a long sigh, she turned away and slowly trudged back to her car. That had been a different life.

* * *

"Oh my God, it's Angi." Lynn sprang from her chair nearly tipping the table over before throwing her arms around Angi's neck and planting a loud, smacking kiss on her cheek. "I'm so glad you guys could make it."

"Of course." Angi returned Lynn's exuberant hug. "Wouldn't miss it."

The crowd had finally thinned out around the table where Lynn and Terra were signing albums. Sam couldn't believe that so many people would be interested in purchasing a CD at Pride. There must have been over fifty people in line. One woman even bought five albums. Still, she wouldn't have minded meeting Jodi but she was nowhere in sight.

Lynn plopped down on the corner of the table. "So, tell me. What did you think of the show?"

"We loved it, didn't we, Sam?" Angi leaned over and nudged Sam in the ribs with her elbow.

"What? Of course I liked the show." Why Angi and Cheryl had to make such a big deal was beyond her. Sometimes it seemed as if they had nothing better to do than pick on her. And now with her cheeks turning a nice rosy red, that would probably encourage them all the more. Maybe if she were lucky, she could blame it on a wicked sunburn.

"I bet you did." Angi turned back to Lynn. "Sam here couldn't tear her eyes away."

"More like she couldn't tear her eyes off Jodi. Right, Sam?" Cheryl grabbed her by the shoulders from behind, rocking her on her feet. She then flashed a devilish wink at Lynn. "You'll have to forgive us. This is Sam, my best friend clear back from college. We're just giving her a hard time." She leaned in, cupped her hand to her mouth, and whispered loud enough for everyone within ten feet to hear. "She likes Jodi."

"Hey, all I said was I thought she's amazing. You know, playing guitar."

Terra popped her head up from the album she was signing for the last woman in line, sending her white dreads flying. With all the tattoos covering her arms and upper chest, she looked like a walking art gallery. "Well, you've got that right. The one thing you can say about Jodi is she's amazing with the guitar." She handed back the CD, kicked her feet up on the table, and leaned her chair back on two legs just as Kat walked up. "Oh, maybe you can meet her, Sam. Hey, Kat. Is Jodi coming?"

"Yeah, right. You know Jodi. She's back there hiding as usual." Kat yanked out a chair and slumped against the back.

"Bah." Lynn craned her neck over the crowd, glancing back at the stage. "Tell you what. You guys are coming over later, right?"

"Yeah, we were planning on it." Angi hooked her arm through Sam's. "What do you say, Sam? Think you can bring yourself to actually socialize with real people."

"Well…"

Angi whipped her head back to Lynn. "Yeah, we're coming."

"Great. And Jodi will be there as her normal cheery self."

Cheryl slid the large box of albums over and hopped up on the table opposite Lynn. She then started pawing through the remaining CDs. "Sure looks like things are going great here."

"Oh yeah. We've sold a ton of albums today." Lynn turned and grabbed two CDs from the stack on the table. "Here, you guys want one?"

"Wow, that would be great. We haven't got your new one yet have we Cheryl?"

"How about you, Sam?"

"What? Yeah, I'd love one." She hadn't even considered buying an album. She had been too busy still peeking back at the stage hoping for a glimpse of Jodi. But when she looked down at the CD cover, there she was staring back at her along with the rest of the band. Yet even in the picture, Jodi seemed to be hiding behind everyone, as if trying her best to disappear. "So, how much do I owe you?"

"Oh, please, don't worry about it. Consider it a gift."

"No really, I'm willing to pay."

Terra burst out laughing, nearly tipping over backward in her chair. "I like this girl."

Kat slapped the tabletop. "Amen to that. We need more people like you, Sam."

Before she could even reply, Lynn ripped the album back out of her hands. "Here. Let's sign that for you." She quickly stripped off the cellophane wrapping. "You can at least get the three of us to sign it." She then opened the front cover where she scrawled out a brief message before tossing the album to Kat.

"Yeah, Jodi doesn't sign albums. Well, at least not since…" Kat trailed off as she quickly scratched a short message across the inside flap then slid the CD to Terra.

Terra dropped her chair back on four legs and grabbed a pen. "Forget about signing an album. Jodi won't even talk to a fan. She just disappears after a show. Sad." She then tossed the CD to Sam.

"Geez, Sam. Sounds like she's perfect for you then. What was it you said you wanted to do instead of coming here today— sit in a dark room and play with your computers?" Cheryl then lowered her voice as if letting the others in on a secret. "Sam's a website designer so she never socializes with actual people."

"Hey, I'm being picked on most unfairly. Besides, computers are a lot easier to deal with than people." Sam held her hand to her chest, doing her best to pull off innocent but Cheryl was right—she hardly ever socialized. Not these days.

Kat stood and tucked the box of CDs under her arm. "Wow. You're right, Cheryl. She would be perfect for Jodi. She can't deal with people either."

Sam threw her hands up in the air. It was probably best to just concede defeat. Besides, she couldn't really argue the point. When it came to people, she was totally inept. Her ex hadn't helped matters at all either. How many months had she been cheating right under her nose? How many stupid excuses did she accept for the strange text messages and late-night meetings? After catching her in their bed with someone else and the blowup after that, she didn't feel she could really trust anyone. It was no wonder she didn't deal well with people.

* * *

Jodi kicked out her long legs and leaned her head back against the side of the trailer, her eyes slammed shut. With the sun warming her face, she listened to the music from the next band and the cheer of the crowd. The best part about sitting back there was no one bothered her—no crowd, no fans, no one. She could almost—*almost*—forget how different she was.

"Hey, there you are, Jodi." Kat dropped the box of CDs on the ground beside her feet and perched herself on the fender. "You really should have been out there. We sold a ton of CDs. Some woman bought like five at once."

Jodi rolled her head to the side and opened her eyes, blinking against the bright sunlight. "Five at once, huh? Now that's pretty cool. We can certainly do with it." Every show they seemed to be selling more and more albums, a sure sign that they were gaining recognition as a band.

"You know, a lot of the fans were asking about you again." Kat bit her lower lip.

With a long drawn-out sigh, Jodi rolled her head back straight and closed her eyes again. Her chest constricted as if steel bands were tightening around it until each breath burned.

"Jodi, I know it bothers you, but really, it wouldn't be that bad. Just sign a few CDs and smile. When you were doing your solo act before…" Kat swallowed. "…well, I remember the times when I filled in on drums, you couldn't wait to get off stage and talk to the fans. You said it was always the best part of the show."

She didn't need Kat to remind her of that. Of course she used to love talking to the fans. That was almost as much fun as performing. But how would they look at her now, some big scar gouged down the side of her body? But that wasn't nearly as bad as her voice. She sounded like a freak. Talking to the fans? All that would be is a constant reminder—a reminder of what she had lost. A tear spilled over her eyelid and she quickly brushed it away.

"Oh, hon." Kat sprang to her feet and pulled Jodi into a hug, her chin resting on her shoulder. "Please, don't cry. I'm sorry."

Tears now ran freely down the sides of her face, etching lines in the dust on her skin. "Kat, I can't…I can't face them. There's just no way." She sobbed harder, her voice breaking with each gasp. "I'm…I'm…sorry. I can't."

"Shhhh." Kat patted the back of Jodi's head as she leaned against her shoulder. "It'll be okay. I'm just an asshole. Forget I said anything."

"It's not you. Believe me, it's not. It's *all* me. *I'm* the asshole. Every time I see a smiling fan, I feel sick, like I'm going to puke. Then it's like I'm back in the hospital after the accident and I can hear the doctor telling me I'll never sing again. I…I just can't take that."

"Oh, sweetie, I guess I wasn't really thinking. I know it's been really hard for you. I certainly didn't mean to make you cry." Kat brushed away a tear on Jodi's cheek with the back of her finger.

Through clenched teeth, Jodi let out a raspy, bitter laugh. "You know, I really hate crying. Seems like all I do anymore."

"Yeah, I know. You're always trying to put on that tough baby butch act." Kat pulled her close again. "But I know better. You're a real softy."

"Hey, now don't be telling anyone." Jodi finally managed a small smile. Kat was good for that—she could always make her smile. If it weren't for her, she'd probably never even leave her house. She didn't know what she'd do without a friend like her. Probably just drink beer, eat delivery pizza and play guitar all by herself.

"Well, don't worry. Your secret's safe with me." Kat brushed away a clump of mascara from beside Jodi's eye.

Her sides still hurting, Jodi stooped down and grabbed the box of CDs from beside the trailer. She'd tuck them in the back of her car while waiting—anything to forget her little breakdown. "So, we still getting together at your place tonight?"

"Oh, I forgot to tell you. Angi and Cheryl were here today. I invited them to come also." Kat stood behind her as she slipped the box into her car.

"That's cool. I wish I had seen them." Although it had taken her quite a while to warm to Angi and Cheryl, she could now talk to them as freely as she did with Lynn, Kat or Terra.

"Now, just to give you a heads-up, they're bringing a friend of Cheryl's so don't totally freak out."

Jodi dropped her head forward, thumping it hard against the doorframe of her car. The last thing she wanted was to meet someone new, especially after losing it in front of Kat. Since her accident, she had let very few people into her life and not a single person romantically, not that she really missed that. She had always been too focused on her music for much in the way of romance anyway. "I don't know. Maybe I'll go home instead."

"Oh, come on, Jodi. We all want you there. Trust me, it won't be that bad. Besides…" Kat danced from one foot to the other, a manic grin on her lips. "I have a Guinness with your name on it."

"You know, that's bribery." Kat always knew just what to say to make her giggle. And how could she turn down a Guinness or two or three?

"So, you'll come?" Kat nudged her with her elbow.

Jodi let out a long sigh. "Yes, I'll come."

"Good. You don't have anything to worry about. Angi and Cheryl's friend seems really nice. Besides, she wanted to meet you."

"Oh, great. That's all I need." Jodi dragged her feet as she walked beside Kat. Guinness or not, heading straight home instead was becoming a better idea all the time. If it weren't tradition after a show, she'd do just that.

Kat bounced along beside her. "Trust me, Jodi. You'll really like her. Just be nice, okay. Oh, and in case you do decide to talk, her name is Sam."

CHAPTER TWO

Sam sat in the backseat of Angi's car, kicking herself. Why, oh why hadn't she driven herself? Now, she was at the mercy of Cheryl and Angi. Although the idea of meeting Jodi was intriguing, she would just as soon go home, curl up with a glass of wine, maybe even a nice long soak in the tub, and look through the latest issue of *PC World*. What could be more fun than that? Instead, she was being dragged to who knew where for who knew how long. Finally, with a hand on the back of Cheryl's seat, she leaned forward, poking her head between the front seats. "So, where are we going anyway?"

Angi turned the radio down and glanced up in the rearview mirror. "Well, the band's getting together at Lynn and Kat's for a few drinks."

Cheryl then spun around in her seat. "Yeah, they actually don't live too far away from you up in Ada."

At least that was a plus. She wouldn't be too far from home and if things got too bad, she could always whine, beg and plead for either Cheryl or Angi to run her home. Maybe there was hope for that glass of wine and her magazine after all.

Angi leaned back, her eyes still on the road. "Just lighten up, Sam. Trust me, it's going to be fun."

Sam slid back in her seat and stared out the window, watching the trees whiz by. She still couldn't get the image of Jodi out of her head—the way she played guitar in her own little world. That alone was perhaps what appealed to her the most. A lot of people wouldn't notice it but she knew that look well. It was the same for her when she was working. Nothing else mattered. After several more miles of freeway—not to mention rerunning every cool move Jodi had during the concert through her head at least twice—she tore her eyes from the window and again leaned forward. "So, who all's going to be there?"

Cheryl raised an eyebrow, a wicked smirk curling her lips. "You mean is Jodi going to be there. I saw how you were looking at her, don't deny it."

"You know, that's not the only reason I'm going."

"Well, maybe not the *only* reason."

"I just think she's an interesting person, that's all. What's wrong with that?" Sam stomped her foot on the floorboard.

"Okay, okay. I'm just having fun with you. How often do we get to tease you like this? This is a big deal. Sam's actually interested in something besides a computer."

Angi threw up her arm. "Well, I for one think it's great. You've been moping around for way too long. It's time you started getting out and socializing again."

"Oh, God." The absolute last thing she needed was to start socializing again. Certainly not after Jennifer had made such an idiot out of her. How could she have been so blind? Just thinking of jumping back into any sort of relationship turned her stomach. "Before you two start planning intimate weekend getaways and shopping for wedding dresses, I've had enough of that already if you don't mind. All I would like is to make some friends and talk."

"Well, there's certainly nothing wrong with that, Sam. Just to warn you though, don't expect too much in the form of conversation from Jodi. It was over two months before she would say more than a word at a time to me."

Cheryl let out a long low whistle. "I bet you it was more than six months for me. For the longest time, she wouldn't even speak, just nod her head to say hi."

"What? You guys are pulling my leg, right?" It wouldn't be the first time Cheryl and Angi had her going. Ever since college, Cheryl seemed to make it her personal mission in life to give her a hard time. "Maybe she's just quiet."

"Oh, believe me, quiet's not the word for it. Quiet would actually be a step up for Jodi. From what Lynn says, ever since her accident, she's been this way. Trust me, you'll see."

"Well, maybe I should have brought my computer then— you know, debug a few lines of code if it gets too boring."

Her water bottle to her lips, Angi started choking. "I swear, Sam, you're hopeless." She gasped out the words.

Cheryl quickly leaned over and clapped Angi hard on the back as she continued to cough. "What did I tell you? Before the day was out, she'd figure out some way she could have brought a computer."

What could she say? Most of the time she preferred the company of computers to people. At least she understood them. But when it came to people, they didn't make a bit of sense. Perhaps that was her biggest problem—people just didn't make sense. "Well, we could always swing past my house and grab my laptop."

"No." Both Angi and Cheryl bellowed in unison from the front of the car. Angi then waggled her finger at Sam in the rearview mirror. "For the hundredth time, Sam, no computers today."

"Bummer." Sam slumped back against the seat and once again took to staring out the window.

Cheryl turned completely around in her seat. "Oh, you'll survive. And besides, tomorrow you can tinker with them to your heart's content."

That wouldn't be a bad idea except tomorrow she had promised to have lunch with her mom. It had been over a month since they had seen each other and she was feeling a bit guilty. Not that she minded spending time with her mom. Quite the opposite. She just didn't want to have to field all the embarrassing questions. *So, is there anyone special in your life? Are you seeing someone? Anyone? Sweetie, are you even leaving your house?*

One last time, Sam crossed her fingers. "Just a quick stop—"

"No!"

* * *

Jodi rolled up in front of Lynn and Kat's house with Terra riding shotgun beside her. Terra was perhaps the one in the band most like Jodi. Although most people mistook the wild white dreadlocks and tattoos for a loud, brash, outgoing personality, Terra was actually very quiet most of the time, almost a complete introvert. Probably why Terra didn't date much either, something Jodi could definitely relate to. In all the time Jodi had known her, she could count on one hand the times Terra had gone out with someone, which compared to her made Terra look like a social butterfly.

The idea was to get everything unloaded from the trailer before Cheryl and Angi showed up with their friend so they could wind down and relax, not that she'd find it all that relaxing, not with some new person there. She could pretty much picture how the evening would go too. It was always the same. The first time she said anything, she got *The Look*. It didn't take a mind reader to figure out what was going through their heads either. *Oh shit, what happened to her? Why does she sound that way? What should I do now? If I just run away, will that seem rude?* She didn't know what was worse—the endless questions, as if she enjoyed reliving the agonizing events, or the ever-fun silence that filled the room in lieu of normal conversation. No, she wasn't looking forward to another night of that.

Terra threw off her seat belt and reached for the door handle. "You want me to jump out and help you back in?"

"Oh, please. No self-respecting dyke needs help backing up a trailer." Jodi whipped her Escape in reverse and spun the steering wheel under the palm of her hand while she peered out the passenger window at the side mirror. The trailer swung around perfectly as if on rails and zipped up Lynn and Kat's driveway arrow-straight. A bright wide grin curled her lips. "There, check that out—oh, damn it." She stomped down hard on the brakes. The trailer had suddenly veered wildly off to the right and into the hedge.

"You sure you don't need any help?"

"Not a word." She shot up a finger, not even looking over at Terra, then pulled back forward before throwing her SUV again in reverse, this time backing the rest of the way much more slowly. As she passed the crumpled hedge, now sadly drooping into the neighbor's yard, she shook her head. Today just wasn't her day.

She took one last glance at the hedge and climbed out, meeting Terra at the back of the trailer.

"Got a little too cocky there, huh?"

"I swear, it's that damn pothole in the middle of Lynn and Kat's driveway."

"Yeah, right. I still think you got a little too cocky going all Betty Badass, 'I don't need no stinkin' help backing no trailer.'" Terra bobbed her head as she mocked Jodi.

"Oh hush. Any other time I wouldn't have had a problem. I think you jinxed me."

"Yeah, that must have been it." Terra rolled her eyes. "I won't tell if you don't."

Just then, Lynn and Kat stepped around the back corner of their house. Lynn raised her eyebrows. "Won't tell what?"

"Jodi got all smart backing up the trailer and ran over your bushes."

"Geez, thanks a lot, Terra. What happened to 'I won't tell if you don't'?"

"Sorry, she beat it out of me."

"Oh, I'll beat it out of you." Jodi jumped over and tackled Terra, tickling her in the ribs. Lynn and Kat burst out laughing as Terra squirmed in her arms. When she finally let her up, tears rolled down Terra's cheeks. Her own ribs aching, she also dabbed at the corners of her eyes. It was great having friends she could joke with, laugh with. There were very few that she felt any sense of comfort around. Here she was just one of them, not the chick with the messed up voice and mutilated body.

Finally, Jodi stood up straight, blotted her eyes one last time, and then pounded her fist twice against the side of the trailer. "Well, we'd better get all this unloaded." She wrenched open the back door and everyone began grabbing whatever they could. As always, Kat's drums proved to be the most awkward. Her sides that were aching from laughter now cried out—please dear God, no more—as she heaved a corner of the drum set. The only thing worse would be a grand piano. Or maybe a small car.

"Hey, Jodi. You want to leave your amp here?" Lynn trailed behind, the heavy amp bashing against her leg with each step.

"Might as well. I'll just use my small amp at home. Besides, the big one pisses off the neighbors. Some people have no sense of humor."

"You know, Jodi, I don't think I'd have a sense of humor either at three in the morning." Kat pinched her arm as she walked past.

"It was only one in the morning, thank you very much." She now had to take it easy since her neighbors had called the police on her. Playing helped take her mind off things, especially after a particularly rough day. And the louder the better. But apparently, the sound carried quite a bit farther than she had thought. So until she installed some sound deadener, she was resigned to her small amp.

Terra threw an arm around Jodi's neck. "Oh, like that makes a big difference. Maybe if you weren't nocturnal."

"What can I say? I like it at night." She had always been a night person, but after her accident, she became even more so. Mostly, it was easier to avoid others. She even did her grocery shopping at one in the morning. It was quiet, no one was around. What could be better than that? God bless the inventor of the U-scan.

With everything unloaded, Kat closed up the back of the trailer. "Well, that should do it."

"Good, Cheryl and Angi should be here with their friend in a bit." Lynn slipped her hand in Kat's back pocket and pulled her tight.

Jodi dropped her head and closed her eyes, working hard not to grind her teeth as she leaned down to unhitch the trailer. For a moment, one precious moment, she had almost forgotten about Cheryl and Angi's friend. It might be tradition to kick back after a show and have a few beers but maybe if she could come up with an excuse, any excuse, she could take off. But where would she go—home to an empty house? Would that be any better? Well, as long as she didn't have to talk, maybe it wouldn't be so bad.

* * *

Forty minutes later, Angi edged up in front of Lynn and Kat's house. "There, I told you it wasn't too far."

"You were right about that." She only lived about fifteen minutes away in Cascade, just a hop, skip and a jump and she'd be home with her computers. At this point, she wasn't above begging. "You know, we really could have stopped quick and got my laptop or even my iPad."

"Oh good God, Sam." Cheryl spun around and pointed directly at her.

"Look, I'm not here for a date. I'm here to have a couple of drinks and have a good time. So, try not to embarrass me. No matchmaking or anything." Cheryl and Angi may have the best of intentions but she wasn't ready to be fixed up with anyone, no matter how interesting she may be. And she had to admit, Jodi *was* interesting.

"Oh, okay." Cheryl made a big show of slumping her shoulders and looking dejected. "I'll try to behave."

Angi threw open her door. "Okay, enough talk about computers and dating and all that crap. Let's just go have a few drinks and have fun."

"Amen to that."

Angi led the way across the lawn and up the driveway, past the enclosed trailer with Jodi's Escape parked in front of it, and around to the back of the house where a large deck provided a welcoming air to the spacious landscaped yard. Lynn and Kat sat together on a covered porch swing, swaying gently back and forth. At the sound of their arrival, Lynn sprang from the swing and skipped across the deck. "Hey, you guys made it." She threw her arms around each of them in turn, planting a huge kiss on first one cheek then the other, as they stepped up the stairs.

While Cheryl and Angi made their rounds with the others, Sam angled her way to the corner of the deck, the most inconspicuous spot she could find except for over by the house, but Jodi had already claimed that. She turned and took in the full view of the backyard where a Japanese rock garden under a large pergola took up the center while a series of steps led to an attached gazebo off to the right. She hadn't realized Lynn was standing beside her when she let out a soft whistle. "Wow, this is gorgeous."

"Why thank you, Sam. Make yourself at home. All that is ours is yours. There's beer in the cooler and wine in the house. You know Terra and Kat." Lynn then hooked a thumb over her shoulder. "And that's Jodi skulking over in the corner as usual."

This was the moment she had been waiting for—or was it dreading? She wasn't really sure. "Well, Jodi, it's really nice to meet you."

One leg propped up on the railing, Jodi nodded, if it could even be called that. More of a slight incline of the head, a movement barely even perceptible. She then tilted her beer to her lips, wincing as she swallowed a large gulp, all the time watching Sam from under her hooded eyes.

"Bah." Lynn waved off Jodi without even looking at her. "Don't mind her. For Jodi, that's being downright friendly."

Jodi scowled at Lynn, a look of total defiance, before slipping farther back into the heavy shade cast by the eaves of the house, still not saying a word.

Sam had never met someone so intent on being invisible. It was as if Jodi wanted to melt into the side of the house. Cheryl and Angi had warned her that Jodi would be quiet but this was more like she actively despised being there.

Lynn plopped back down beside Kat on the porch swing while the newcomers grabbed drinks. Sam fished out a bottle of Killian's Irish Red from the cooler and then retreated to the empty lounge chair between Terra and Cheryl where she busied herself as best she could with spinning the bottle around and around in her hands. Right about now, she'd settle for even a tablet PC, a smartphone, a calculator, anything. What was she thinking letting Cheryl drag her here? She didn't know these people. They were Angi and Cheryl's friends, not hers. And then there was Jodi, not exactly the life of the party that girl, not that she could talk. She was still trying not to look as if she were about to bolt for the car when Terra reached out and patted her on the shoulder.

"Hey, it's great you could make it."

She had been so completely lost in her own thoughts, or more precisely, her own escape plans, that she nearly dropped her bottle. "Um…thanks. I'm glad to be here."

Lynn leaned forward on the porch swing. "So, Sam, Cheryl tells me you're into computers."

"Yeah, I guess you could say that."

Terra scooted closer. "So, Sam, what do you do with computers anyway?"

Maybe Cheryl was right. Maybe she *had* been spending too much time with her computers. She certainly wasn't used to all the attention. Granted, the conversation was about her favorite topic so at least that was a plus. "Well, I have a website design business—designing and maintaining commercial websites." While she spoke, Jodi slid off the railing and sidled over beside Lynn and Kat, leaning back against the house with her Guinness bottle resting on her hip. "Um, I also do a fair share of sites for places like churches, organizations, smaller business info sites, stuff like that."

Her arm slung around Lynn, Kat pointed to Sam with her glass of wine. "Hey, we ought to have you do a site for the band. You know, put up some pictures and our tour dates."

"Actually, that wouldn't be hard at all."

Lynn jerked up, slopping wine on the deck in front of her. "No shit? That would be great."

Laughter echoed off the side of the house and filled the warm evening. Even Jodi cracked a slight smile, the first one Sam had seen since they had arrived. However, she quickly turned back to her usual ice-cold, half-scowling I'm-not-going-to-have-fun-no-matter-what expression when she noticed Sam watching her. Sam had never met anyone so adamant on being miserable. It was as if Jodi were fighting any possibility of joy.

Lynn stood and poured herself another glass of wine. On her way past, she laid her hand on Jodi's shoulder. "Want to join the rest of us and have a seat?"

Without a word, Jodi shrugged her off, never once taking her eyes from Sam. Lynn rolled her eyes before sitting back down beside Kat. "So, Sam, did you have a good time at Pride today?"

"Yeah, I'm actually glad Angi and Cheryl dragged me out. I wasn't planning on coming." She stumbled over her words as she watched Jodi from the corner of her eye. Every move she made, every word she said, the girl just wouldn't take her eyes off her. Defending her Master's thesis had been less unnerving.

"So, what did you like the most?" Terra now sat on the edge of her seat, her beer bottle between her knees.

Jodi edged even closer. This was quickly becoming absurd. Why Jodi wouldn't just sit down and join them was beyond her. Was it simply because she was there? Had she somehow pissed her off? In a moment of either utter brilliance, sheer frustration or some combination of the two, she spun around, fixing Jodi's eyes with hers, matching her intense stare, a wild smirk on her lips. "Well, I think that would have to be Jodi's boots."

Everyone froze, tension suddenly filling the hot, humid air.

Jodi kicked off the house, her arms tightly crossed, a finger in the neck of her beer bottle. She tapped the bottle against her side—once, twice, three times—eyeing her up and down.

She could feel those eyes piercing right through her as Jodi continued to stare. Maybe it had been a bad idea to mention Jodi—or in this case even her boots—but she just wanted to find some way to break the ice. At least something so Jodi would stop glaring at her from her dark little corner of the deck.

The moment drew out, then Jodi's voice rang out in the dead silence. "You have *got* to be shitting me. Of everything there, you pick my *boots*?"

Whatever she had been expecting when Jodi finally spoke, it certainly wasn't what she heard. From everything Angi and Cheryl had told her, she had been expecting a voice harsh and grating like a smoker who had to have her larynx removed because of cancer, but instead, Jodi's voice was low and breathy, almost ethereal.

Lynn whirled around so fast she nearly fell out of the swing. "Holy shit—she speaks." The tension seemed to break and a collective laugh rolled over the deck.

A wide smile slowly curled Jodi's lips, transforming her entire face as if a dark veil had been lifted. Sam wouldn't have thought it possible but the difference was nothing short of astounding. Here was a completely different woman now staring back at her.

Jodi stepped across the deck and dragged out the lounge chair beside her where she flopped down in it backward, her long thin arms draped over the back. "So, Ms. Funny, what besides my boots did you enjoy?"

"Well, the Pad Thai wasn't too bad."

"Pad Thai? Bah, forget that. I'm a pizza and beer girl, speaking of which…" She reached over to the cooler and retrieved a fresh bottle.

"Well, they had that too. Although I doubt they had Guinness."

"Now that's a damn shame." Froth bubbled from the neck of the fresh bottle as she popped the cap with the opener. She took a long sip then turned directly to Sam, again fixing her eyes on her with the same intensity, only this time with that soft smile still on her lips. "So, you're into computers."

"You could definitely say that. It's pretty much my entire life."

Sam lost all track of time as they continued to talk—everything from computers, to music, to fine food and wine. Even after they had ordered pizza, they kept on talking, rapid bursts of conversation between mouthfuls, never once running out of something to say. And Jodi seemed genuinely interested in what she did with web design. Even as she outlined the advantages of CSS versus HTML, Jodi didn't appear bored. Before she even realized it, the sun had fallen well below the line of trees and deep shadows crawled across the backyard. "Oh, wow. I can't believe it's so late."

Lynn lifted her head from Kat's shoulder. "Geez, it's no wonder. You two have been chatting it up all night."

"Yeah, I hate to say it, but we really should get going." Angi stifled a yawn as she stood and stretched. Cheryl joined her, wrapping her arm around Angi's waist.

Kat leaned forward, balancing her now empty wineglass on her knee. "You know, Sam, you could always stay longer and we could run you home."

She was seriously torn by the idea. Part of her, a large part she had to admit, wanted to stay and talk. If she weren't careful, she could probably talk all night, not that she was averse to that idea but it had been a long day. That and she didn't want to wear out her welcome with Jodi. "I'd love to but I have lunch with my mom tomorrow. I've been promising her for a month."

The next few minutes passed in a flurry of hugs and kisses, claps on the backs, thanks for comings, and all manner of goodbyes. Sam stepped back against the railing to avoid most of the commotion. Jodi seemed to have the same idea. Finally, Cheryl flashed her a completely shameless wink. "Just take your time, Sam." Before she could even respond, Cheryl disappeared down the steps with Angi at her side.

"It's sure been great having you here, Sam." Lynn threw her arms around Sam's neck before grabbing Kat by the hand, nearly ripping her off her feet as she tugged her quite unceremoniously toward the house.

"Yeah, catch you later, Sam." Terra hopped up and pulled Sam into a one-armed hug. She smiled at Jodi then hustled after Lynn and Kat into the house.

Now completely alone with Jodi, she let out a nervous laugh that caught in her throat and became more of a cough. "You know, if I'm not mistaken, I think everyone's trying to give us some alone time."

"Yeah, something like that. I did have a great time talking with you though."

"I did too."

They continued to stare at each other. A soft humid breeze rustled the ornamental grass alongside the deck and somewhere far off a dog barked. For the briefest of moments, Sam could have sworn Jodi had leaned forward. Something seemed to pass between them but as quickly as it was there, it was gone.

Jodi stepped back. "Um…"

"Yeah, I should probably get going. Cheryl and Angi are no doubt busy gossiping." She hooked a thumb over her shoulder, still facing Jodi as she shuffled backward. Her foot then slipped off the top of the deck and she nearly fell down the steps, only catching herself against the railing at the last second. She quickly recovered. This was like the end of a date in high school, if she had ever gone on a date in high school that is. Fortunately, it was dark enough so Jodi couldn't see her face turning red.

At corner of the house, she glanced back. Jodi again leaned with one foot against the railing, those piercing eyes watching as she walked away. Even though most of the sunlight had faded, a subtle smile on her lips was still obvious. It was all she could do not to run right back up the stairs. Forget Angi and Cheryl. They could leave without her for all she cared. Hell, she'd even walk home. But as much as she liked the idea, she really did have to leave, so with a small wave, for which she got a tilt of a beer bottle in return, she disappeared down the driveway.

When she slipped quietly into the backseat of the car, trying her best to hide the sappy grin plastered on her face, Angi and Cheryl whirled around, simply gawking, their mouths working hard but no sound coming out. Angi found her words first. "Holy shit, Sam. I just can't believe it. You two certainly hit it off."

"Yeah, Sam, I can't believe it either. Jodi's never talked to me like that. She must really like you."

It may have been a bit rough in the beginning, but once Jodi opened up—wow. Never before had she met someone with whom she could lose all track of time. And to think, she hadn't wanted to come. Although the last thing she needed was any sort of relationship, she had to admit, she liked Jodi too.

CHAPTER THREE

With her Ovation acoustic guitar in her lap, Jodi sat in her studio in the dark, the only light from two large candles. Shadows danced across the walls as she closed her eyes and leaned back in her favorite chair. It had been quite a day. They had put on a good show. There was the get-together afterward. And then there was Sam. Yes, Sam. She certainly wasn't like anyone she had been expecting. The first thing that usually popped out of most people's mouths was, "Hey, what happened to you?" Or better yet, "What's messed up with your voice?" Then there was her personal favorite, "You know you sound like a dude." No wonder she didn't like to meet new people or talk much to even those she did meet. But Sam had been different. She hadn't asked her anything about her voice or the accident, or anything even remotely pertaining to it. She hadn't even stared at her scars. Talk about refreshing, not having to explain her past. She could simply be herself and talk to someone without it dragging up the whole painful experience.

Still, she couldn't believe they had talked all evening. It could easily have been all night. And not once did she feel self-conscious. Even around Kat and the others, she still felt uncomfortable much of the time. Somehow, it was different with Sam. She had been waiting for the look from her, that *what the hell?* look, when she first spoke. She had readied herself for it, waited for it, must be anytime soon now, but it never came. Here she had all her defenses ready, had all her excuses, all her explanations but Sam had simply smiled and talked to her as if she were anyone else. That just never happened. She *always* had to give excuses. She *always* had to give explanations. What was she to make of that?

In the flickering shadows, she slammed her pick against the strings, a discordant explosion of sound resonating through the quiet darkness. What exactly *was* she to make of that? Snippets of their conversation kept popping into her mind. HTML this and CSS that. Not that she had a blasted clue what Sam was talking about but it was fun listening to her talk about it with such passion and excitement. One thing was for sure, Sam loved her computers. God, by the end of the conversation, she found herself loving computers too. She was excited to hear about the finer points of Foxfire, whatever the hell that was. Somehow, Sam's enthusiasm was infectious. Even now, she could still feel it.

She closed her eyes and started playing a classical piece she wrote in college, the notes ringing throughout the room. The sound danced in her head, a sort of musical ballet, one note flowing smoothly into the next, as her fingers flew over the neck, playing faster and faster. She hadn't felt like this since before the accident. And she really had Sam to thank for that. For once, she was able to be herself and not that chick with the freaky scar on her neck.

With a high-pitched squeak of her fingers against the strings, she suddenly stopped playing, the sound dying in the quiet, dark room. What the hell was she thinking? Here she was acting like some silly little high school girl with her first crush. Come on. She had merely shared a conversation with someone. Nothing more. People did it every day. Besides, Sam couldn't possibly be as excited about their evening as she was.

She sucked in a long, deep breath through her mouth and held it as she lazily strummed a chord. Her fingers floated over the strings as she picked out a rhythm, her tendons working through her arm—tensing, releasing, tensing, releasing—a perfect melody of movement. This was her teddy bear, her comfy blanket, her favorite pair of jeans. This was comfort incarnate. Whenever she needed to relax, to shut out the past, she could always pick up one of her guitars and get lost in the music. That was the only thing, the *only* thing that she could count on after the accident. She could still play.

* * *

"Wow, you seem to be in a good mood today." Sam's mom, Sharon, eyeballed her over the rim of her glass of pinot grigio, a lazy, lopsided smile fixed upon her face as they sat across from each other in the breakfast nook off Sharon's kitchen. Even though it was the weekend, Sharon was impeccably dressed in crisp khakis and a tailored white blouse. With her short layered sideswept brunette hair and penchant for cooking, she looked more like the host of a trendy show on Food Network than the dean of a college.

"I'm just glad to be having lunch with you, Mom." Sam tipped her glass to her lips—a very nice cabernet sauvignon—trying her best at nonchalance even as every muscle in her body begged to jump up and dance around the room.

"Huh. Nice try but you can't fool me. You've been moping around for months and now you're barely able to hold back a goofy grin. What's up?"

Now she was in trouble. Her mom had tasted blood and was going in for the kill. Maybe, if she was lucky—really lucky that is—she could head her off. "Oh, I was meaning to tell you. I've got a new client. A big corporate account out in Hudsonville. They want a new flashy website. You should have seen their old one. It was still plain HTML. Pathetic." It wasn't that she didn't want to share with her mom. She simply didn't know what there was to share. She had spent the evening talking to a woman. So what? It really wasn't a big deal. But then again, if that were the case, why couldn't she seem to lose the stupid grin?

"That's great sweetheart. I can't think of anyone better for the job."

"Yeah, I know. I've already got some great ideas and the client is really excited. It should be a lot of fun. Not to mention, it's going to be really profitable."

"That's wonderful." Sharon watched her from across the table, the crease in her forehead deepening with each second that passed.

"Yes, I'm really excited." She absently twirled her fork in her spaghetti then hoisted a huge bite to her mouth, slurping in the pasta. From her mom's expression, she wasn't going to let it rest. She would want details, details and more details. Maybe if she weren't so transparent. Even when Sam was a teenager, all her mom had to do was look at her and she knew everything.

"Hmmm." Her eyes still glued on Sam, Sharon set her wineglass to the side and leaned forward, her fingers steepled in front of her mouth. "So, why don't you tell your mother what else is up?"

"Nothing really, Mom. I'm just in a good mood. Is that so unusual?"

"Actually, yes it is. Ever since you broke up with what's-her-name, you've been distant and depressed. I just want to know what's made such a change in my baby." She slowly tapped her nose with one finger, her eyes now boring into Sam. "Have you met someone?"

Sam choked, nearly spraying spaghetti across the table. Leave it to her mom to nail it right out of the box. She couldn't be that obvious, could she? Or maybe her mom was part psychic. That would explain a lot. Now, she had no choice but to come clean. "Well, as a matter of fact, yes, I have met someone—but trust me, Mom, it's not like that." She knew what her mom was thinking. "She's only a friend."

"Only a friend, huh? Well, tell me about her. She must be someone special to make such a difference in my baby."

What was there to say? So, she had met someone. They had talked all night. And now, she couldn't seem to get her out of her mind no matter what. But other than that. "Really, it's nothing, Mom. I just met someone at Pride in Lansing yesterday. She's a friend of Cheryl and Angi's and she's a guitar player in a band. You should have seen her. She was unbelievable. And she had these really cool black boots. She's really tall and thin. We got together later with the band and ended up talking all evening." When she finally stopped for a breath, her heart skipped. So much for not blurting out everything at once.

"Wow. You can say whatever you want to, sweetheart, but it certainly isn't nothing. This girl really must be something."

"Oh, Mom, she really is. I've never heard anyone play guitar like her before. And she's really cool and funny too but it takes a lot to get to know her. She doesn't talk to very many people."

"I see." Sharon sat back and crossed her arms, her expression hardening. "She doesn't think she's above everyone else, does she—not like that what's-her-name of yours?"

"No, no, no. It's nothing like that, Mom." She didn't want her mom to get the wrong impression. Jodi was nothing like Jennifer. If anything, she seemed very humble, almost excessively so. "She doesn't speak because she was in an accident and it messed up her voice. She's really self-conscious about it."

With each of Sam's words, Sharon's eyes grew wider. "Oh, my God, Sam. I'm really sorry to hear that. That must be terrible for her. If I may, what happened?"

"Well, I'm not really sure. Angi just said she was in a car accident and it somehow messed up her voice. She doesn't sing anymore. She has a big scar on her neck. I guess she used to frontline her own band as the singer and guitar player. From what Angi said, she even had several CDs."

"Oh, Sam, that's so sad. I can understand why she wouldn't speak much."

"Yeah, I know, Mom. It took quite a while before she would even talk. But then when she finally did, I was completely surprised. I don't know what she sounded like before, but now she has this low, airy voice. Oh my God, it's beautiful, unique. I swear I could listen to her all night."

"My, oh my, Sam. So, what did you two talk about all evening?"

"That's just it—we talked about all sorts of things, Mom. Everything from computers and websites to music. You name it." Even now as she thought of Jodi, her heart began to beat faster. Never had she met anyone she could talk to so easily. It hadn't even been a day and already she sorely missed the conversation.

Sharon let out a soft whistle as she stared across the table at Sam, a Cheshire grin curling her lips. "Oh baby, you've got it bad."

"Ah…ah…ah…" What was her mom talking about? She couldn't have it bad. No, that simply couldn't be the case. She had just met Jodi. They had just talked. One evening. That was all.

The wide smile still plastered across her face, Sharon reached over the table and gently squeezed Sam's hand. "Well, tell me. What's the name of this girl that's got my baby more excited than I've seen her in months?"

Sam lowered her eyes to the glass of cabernet sauvignon still in her hands, her cheeks now the same shade as the wine. Slowly she swirled the wine around in her glass. Her mom was probably right. She had something—she just wasn't sure what yet—good or bad. Finally without looking up, she opened her mouth, her voice but a whisper. "Her name is Jodi."

* * *

"Hey, there she is—the girl of the hour." Lynn whipped around as Jodi walked in, a guitar case in each hand.

Kat leaped up from the makeshift stage. "Yeah, Jodi, we were taking bets to see if you showed at all. Lynn thought you'd be out somewhere with Sam."

"You got that right. I wouldn't have been surprised if the two of you got together again after leaving here last night. Wow." Lynn then made a big production of fanning herself. "Talk about hitting it off."

Her back to everyone, Jodi dropped her cases beside her amp and snapped open the latches. She had been dreading this. Her friends seemed to have nothing better to do than tease her about Sam, as if she needed that too. She was having a hard enough time trying to clear her head without their overabundance of enthusiasm. "Hey, if no one minds, let's just practice. That's what we're here for, isn't it?"

"Practice? That's all you've got to say, let's practice? What's up with that? I thought you'd be bouncing in here today if you showed up at all."

Her back still to Lynn, she threw the strap of her electric guitar over her neck. "I didn't get much sleep last night."

"Oh, really." Lynn nudged her with her elbow. "Not much sleep, huh?"

"It's not what you think. I just didn't get much sleep last night. Now, can we leave it at that?"

"Oh, come on. You can't leave it at that. We need details."

Kat jumped off the stage and laid a firm hand on Lynn's shoulder. "Okay, that's enough, Lynn. If Jodi doesn't want to talk about it, she doesn't want to talk about it."

And she most definitely didn't want to talk about it. She didn't need to play twenty questions about Sam when she didn't even know what was going on herself. They talked. Big deal. Leave it at that. In the end, all she could count on anyway was her music. That's what she needed to concentrate on. So she flipped the power switch on her amp and cranked the volume, bending a note high up on the neck, the pitch screaming, followed by a long series of blazing scales, ending in a progression of thundering power cords. When she finished, the sound continued to echo around the building. Lynn, Kat and Terra simply stared, their mouths hanging open. "There. Now, if you don't mind, can we please get to practicing?"

An hour and a half later, Jodi brushed the sweat from her forehead with the back of her hand and slipped the strap of her electric guitar over her head, her black tank top clinging to her body. While she normally played aggressively—that was her style, her signature—today she took it to a whole new level, attacking each note with an almost manic vehemence. It had been years since it hurt to play, with calluses upon calluses covering her fingertips, but the pressure biting into her flesh was a welcome distraction from the whirlwind of crap flying around in her head. She could easily handle another couple hours of practice if only it meant she didn't have to think about Sam. Anything but Sam.

Lynn fanned herself with a stack of sheet music. "Good God, I need something to drink before I drop. Anyone else?"

Kat waddled out from behind her drums, tugging her sweaty shorts away from her legs. "Oh, you read my mind, babe. Something cold and wet."

Terra dropped her bass in the stand. "Yeah, Lynn, wait up and I'll join you."

"Hey, what about you, Jodi?"

"Yeah, I guess maybe a beer." She didn't look up as Lynn and Terra bustled out the door. When they were safely out of sight, she lifted her Ovation acoustic guitar from its case and perched up on the tall stool she liked to use when playing slower songs.

Kat plopped down beside her on top of her amp, her brow deeply creased. "You sure you're okay, Jodi?"

Jodi stared down at her guitar, slowly tuning each string, anything so she wouldn't have to look at Kat. How could she put into words what was whipping around in her head? It didn't make any sense to her. How could anyone else make sense of it? Finally, she let out a long, agonized breath. "Honestly, Kat, I don't know."

"Hey, what's up, hon? You've been off all afternoon. Did something happen with Sam?"

"Well, yes…no…I don't know." She barked out a harsh laugh. "It's hard to say."

"I'm sorry, Jodi, but I'm really not following you. I thought you had a great time with Sam. Did she do something?"

"That's just it. Not really. She looked at me like I was a normal person."

"That's a good thing, isn't it?"

"Well, yes. But for how long? How long until everything becomes an issue? How long before she looks at me and thinks I'm a freak. Tell me, Kat, how long?"

"Whoa, whoa. Who's to say that will even happen? Besides, I don't see you like that. Lynn and Terra certainly don't see you like that. I'm sure that Cheryl and Angi don't either. You're not a freak."

"Yeah, but Kat, it took you all quite some time to see beyond my scars and my voice. Don't lie to me."

Kat let out a long sigh, twisting her fingers through her short hair. "Okay, Jodi, I admit it. It did take me a bit to get used to everything but not because I thought you were a freak. God, I never wanted you to feel like that because that wasn't it at all. It was all me. I don't know why but I found myself staring at your scars when I first saw you after the accident. I know it's not right. And your voice is a bit different now, but honestly, I don't even notice it anymore."

"I know. I know. But seriously, Sam never once batted an eye at my voice or my scars. She didn't ask me a ton of questions or stare at my throat. She didn't look at me differently at all."

"Jodi, that should be a good thing then."

"Geez, I don't know. Maybe, I guess. I'm half afraid if I do let my guard down, somehow it will come back to bite me in the ass."

"Hon, that's a risk we take with everyone, every day. Sometimes you have to take a chance. Sometimes it bites us in the ass…but sometimes…sometimes it doesn't and believe me, it's worth the risk."

"I just don't know what to do, Kat. It was so great talking to Sam. We talked and talked all evening and never once ran out of things to say. I've never had that before—certainly not since the accident."

"Just take it slow, hon."

"Yeah, well Lynn's ready to rent a U-Haul and load up all my stuff."

"Don't worry about Lynn. Trust me, she can be a real pain in the ass sometimes. I should know."

Jodi finally smiled. "You've got that right, but don't tell her."

"Oh, she knows. I tell her that all the time. It's my job to point out when she's being a pain in the ass just like it's her job to point out when I'm being an ass."

Kat always knew just what to say to cheer her up. Still, she couldn't get Sam out of her head—the conversation, the ease, the comfort. What was she to make of all that? And could she ever take the risk? And if she did, what then? Finally, she began fingerpicking a delicate chord progression, each note ringing out in the hot late-afternoon air.

"Hey, that's from one of your old albums, isn't it?"

"Yeah, the first one." She stared down at her guitar, her eyes half-closed, her fingers gliding over the strings. "It's the first song I ever wrote."

"You know, Jodi. You really should play some of your old stuff. It's really good."

"I don't know, Kat, that was a different life."

"Maybe so, but still, that song is so beautiful. It's always been one of my favorites."

"Mine too. I wrote it when I was coming out. You know, all the fear, the confusion, the anxiety, the excitement, half-sick to my stomach, not knowing what to do. All that wrapped up together and more."

"Oh, I know what you mean. I felt like that too. I think everyone who's gay has gone through that."

"Thing is, Kat, that's how I feel now."

* * *

"Argh." Sam rolled over in bed and ripped back the covers. She had been tossing and turning for well over two hours now and she was seriously about to lose it. She'd tried reading a magazine—no luck. She'd sipped a glass of wine—nada. She had even tried debugging a few lines of computer code. Nothing helped. No matter what, she couldn't get Jodi off her mind.

Even at her mom's, she had felt as if she were back in high school, giggling about the crush she had on the cute girl in class. What was wrong with her? She didn't giggle, not even in high school. But she couldn't deny it, she had been floating around all day. Even now, just the thought of Jodi and her breath caught in her throat. "Her name is Jodi." She liked how the words felt on her lips. "Jodi."

She wouldn't mind more than just the sound of Jodi's name on her lips. Maybe feeling her full, soft lips against hers, the warmth, the firmness, the urgency—

"Whoa, whoa, whoa." She sprang bolt upright in bed, her pillows spilling to the floor. Where the hell had *that* come from? She didn't want to be fantasizing about any sort of romance, no matter how gorgeous Jodi had been. And she couldn't deny it— Jodi had been gorgeous. Drop-dead gorgeous. With her long, lean legs, and strong fingers—

Slap!

Her cheek now stinging, she kicked the rest of the sheets off her legs and piled out of bed. "Come on, Sam. Pull it together." Up and down her bedroom she began pacing, the light from outside throwing her shadow on the wall, looking like some crazed woman. What was with all these thoughts of lips and long legs? After Jennifer, she had learned her lesson. Romance and love were not for her. She had her computers. She had her business. What more did she need? This was all in her head, anyway. They had talked, nothing more. Maybe Cheryl and Angi were right. She had spent way too much time with computers. She didn't even know how to act around another woman— granted a very beautiful and extremely intriguing woman.

CHAPTER FOUR

Jodi twiddled Sam's business card, the edges now frayed and tattered. She had been looking at it all week, trying to find the courage to call. But was it a good idea? She smacked her phone against her forehead. This was ridiculous. She was going to give someone a call and see what they were doing, maybe get together. What was so hard about that? No big deal, right?

It was now or never so she grabbed her phone from the counter and punched in the home number Sam had scribbled on the back of her card, leaning hard against the doorway to the kitchen to steady herself. Besides, what did she have to worry about? Sam probably wouldn't be home anyway. One ring, two rings, three—her heart hammered. After four, she was about to concede defeat when the line picked up.

"Hello."

She froze, her mouth suddenly dry. Shit, Sam answered—she actually answered. Her breath caught in her throat. "Uhhh."

"Hello?"

"Uhhh." She was going to have to do something, and quickly. She couldn't just sit there and mumble into the phone.

She needed to say something—anything. But nothing came to mind—not a thing. Now what? She shouldn't have called. Seriously, what was she thinking?

"Jodi? Is that you?"

Busted. Now she was going to have to say something or Sam would think she were an even bigger freak than she already must. "Um. Sorry about that. Yeah, it's me. How'd you know?"

"Caller ID, silly. You must be one of the last persons on earth to still have a landline."

"Oh, yeah." She thumped the back of her head against the doorjamb. Damn caller ID. She should have thought of that. "So…um…I was maybe wondering what you were like…well, up to?" Good God, what was wrong with her? Now she seemed to have lost the ability to form complete sentences. Calling Sam was turning out to be a worse and worse idea all the time.

"Nothing." Sam drew the word out. "How about you?"

"Um. Nothing here too." She leaned her head back and closed her eyes. Why on earth was she so nervous talking to Sam on the phone? In person, they had never stopped talking. But the phone was different. She couldn't see Sam's face. She couldn't see if her voice freaked her out.

"So…want to do nothing together?" Sam giggled.

That little giggle—that more than anything set her at ease. Even now, miles apart, she could picture the soft smile on Sam's lips. "Sure. What would you like to do?"

"Hmmm. Let's see. You up for dinner?"

"Actually, that sounds like a great idea." At the mention of food, her stomach let out a loud growl. It wasn't uncommon for her to forget to eat all day and today was no exception. She hadn't eaten anything since she had a piece of cold pizza and coffee for breakfast.

"In that case, how about we go for Thai?"

"Ah…" Thai? That wasn't quite what she had in mind.

Sam then laughed. "I'm just teasing. How about steak and beer?"

"Now you're talking—a girl after my heart. I can definitely handle steak and beer."

"Have you ever been to Judson's Steakhouse at the B.O.B. downtown on Monroe?"

"Not really, but I've heard of it."

"Oh, you'll love it. I haven't been there in forever. It's one of my favorites when I'm in the mood for steak."

"Okay, sounds good, but you'll have to give me a little bit to get ready. I've got to find something to wear." It had been a long time since she'd been out somewhere fancy to eat so Judson's would be a nice treat.

"Just wear something comfortable like that black top you had on the other day and your boots. You looked really hot in that."

Jodi nearly fell out of the doorway, catching herself at the last minute with a painful crack to the elbow. She looked hot? What did that mean? Was Sam flirting with her or was that just a friendly compliment? It had to be only a friendly compliment. Sam couldn't possibly see her as anything else, not with her scarred up body.

"Hey, you still there?"

"Yeah, I'm here." She swallowed hard. "So, you want to meet there or do you want to ride together?"

"Parking sucks downtown so if you don't mind, we should probably ride together."

"Okay, since you chose the restaurant, I can drive."

"In that case, you can just MapQuest me."

"Um…" She didn't want to sound like a complete technological idiot but she had no idea what Sam was talking about.

"You need directions, don't you?" Sam giggled.

"Please."

Another giggle. "Someday, Jodi, we'll have to bring you into the twenty-first century."

A quick set of directions later—only a twenty-minute drive across town—and Jodi hung up, tearing down the hallway to her bedroom and ripping her black fitted tee over her head as she went. She burst through the doorway and skidded to a halt in front of her dresser where she snatched a black spaghetti strap tank from the seemingly never-ending pile teetering on the top. Kat always teased her that the reason she wore black shirts all the time was that it matched her mood. Kat was probably right, but not tonight. She was going to see Sam. Three tries and she finally yanked the black tank over her head. Then a quick glance in the mirror, just long enough to tousle her short hair with her fingers and she bolted out the door.

* * *

Sam gawked at the phone in her hands. All week she had been waiting for a call, ever since she had handed her business card to Jodi. She would have called Jodi herself but she didn't have her number and she wasn't yet ready to call Cheryl to see if she did. She'd never live that down. *So, you want Jodi's number, do you? Thinking about coming out of your antisocial black hole of despair, huh?* No, she could do without that.

She dashed down the hallway to her bedroom. So much for lounging around for the evening in her comfy shorts and favorite baggy T-shirt, her laptop firmly planted in front of her. Now she had less than twenty minutes to get ready for her date. She froze midstride. Dinner, she'd meant to say *dinner.* What was up with her anyway? No matter what she tried, she couldn't get Jodi out of her mind. She had even screwed up a website update, which took her nearly five hours to track down the problem, all because she had been daydreaming about Jodi. God, could she be that pathetic? Had she become so socially isolated that just meeting someone new and talking was such a big deal that she couldn't seem to get it out of her mind?

Quickly, Sam yanked her T-shirt off and flung her shorts on the floor. Now in only a pair of green string bikini panties, she darted back and forth, scrounging through her clothes. She didn't want to dress up too nicely or Jodi might get the idea that this was indeed a date. But she didn't want to look like a slob either. Then a smile curled her lips. She'd take a page out of Jodi's book—jeans and tank top. She whipped around and pawed through her pile of jeans, finally tugging out a pair just snug enough to show off her backside. Next, she slipped a white tank over her head, pulling it over her small breasts. Then, a quick check in the mirror—she pulled an errant curl of red bangs back over her ear—and she skipped out into her living room.

With nothing better to do, she paced from one end of her house to the other, stopping each pass to check out the window. After what must have been the tenth time in as many minutes, she ripped back the blinds once again. Still no Jodi. God, what would happen if she didn't show up? Jennifer had been good at that. How many times had she sat home all night waiting for her to show up only to get a call the next day saying something had come up, usually another woman as it had turned out? It was no wonder she had sworn off romance.

Once again, she peeked out the window and her breath seized in her throat, every muscle in her body suddenly rigid. Jodi was there. She was actually there. Up until this point, only part of her believed Jodi would actually show. But there she was. Her hands now shaking, she stepped back and ran her fingers through her hair, forcing herself to take long slow breaths. She could do this. Just good food, good conversation. That was it. Besides, it wasn't as if it were a date. One last breath and she reached for the door.

* * *

Jodi sat behind the wheel in front of Sam's house with her eyes closed, trying her best to bring her heart rate back down into the sixties instead of what felt like well over a hundred. But why was she so nervous? She hadn't felt that way when they chatted it up after the concert. Not once had she felt uncomfortable. So, why now? They were only going out to dinner. Seriously, it was no big deal. Finally, before she could completely psyche herself out, she took a deep breath, kicked open the door and hopped out.

She let out a small whistle as she tromped up the cobblestone path in her heavy black boots. Sam's house was a rustic Cape Cod set back from the road. Mounds of tall ornamental grass filled the front yard along with several hickory trees that shaded most of the house. Behind, a series of retaining wall blocks created a terrace up the sloping hill. Apparently, website design paid well.

Jodi took the cobblestone steps two at a time. She steadied herself, smoothing down her tank top, and then reached out to knock. Before her knuckles even touched wood, the door flew open.

"Hey, you made it."

"Ah…yeah, I made it. Your directions were great." She shoved her hands in her pockets.

"Wonderful, wonderful. Shall we get going then? I've got us reservations for eight thirty." Sam hopped out onto her porch, threading her arm through Jodi's.

Sam's eagerness allayed her fears. So much for sweating it out all week. "Wow, Sam, you're certainly in a good mood."

"Well, of course. I've been hoping you'd call. Besides, you've saved me from an evening of junk food and boredom."

Together, they walked down the path and climbed into Jodi's Escape. Jodi fumbled with her keys, dropping them on the floorboards once for good measure, before she was finally able to feed the correct one into the ignition. Her hand still shaking, she gave the key a twist only to be met with an instantaneous explosion of sound. "Holy shit." Her heart nearly jumped up her throat as she frantically slapped at the radio, once, twice, trying her damnedest to lower the volume. Finally, blessed silence replaced the deafening roar.

Sam shook her head, tapping her ear with the palm of her hand. "Good God, Jodi. I'm surprised you're not deaf."

"Yeah, sorry about that." She cringed. Talk about making an impression.

"No biggie. I like my music loud too. Maybe not *that* loud." Sam chuckled, still shaking her head. "So, whatever made you get into music?"

"Now that's a long story." Jodi let out a nervous laugh and rubbed the back of her neck as they set off. "I guess it all started when I was about eight. My parents had me taking piano lessons."

"Oh, wow. I didn't know you could play the piano also."

"Yeah. I was pretty good but to my parents' horror, I wanted to play guitar instead. They weren't really for that, so my mom made a deal with me. If I learned everything my piano teacher could teach, I could get a guitar. So I practiced and practiced and boy were they surprised when less than six months later, my piano teacher told them there wasn't anything more she could teach me."

"You've got to be kidding. Six months?"

"Yeah, but you know, I think I got more lucky than anything." She leaned in and lowered her voice. "She wasn't a very good teacher."

Sam burst out laughing. "So, they had to buy you a guitar then?"

"Yep. They didn't have a choice at that point. So, I got a classical guitar and learned classical music."

"Classical? I would have thought you'd have bought a bright blue electric guitar or something."

"Nope. That came later. I first learned classical guitar. I had this great teacher and took lessons two, sometimes three times a week. I was obsessed."

"Holy crap, I guess. And I thought I was bad."

"Yeah, I couldn't get enough. By the time I was thirteen, I was playing constantly—classical, blues, jazz, you name it. Then I auditioned and got into Interlochen Arts Academy."

"No way." Sam stared at her wide-eyed. "Isn't that where Jewel went?"

"Yeah, but I was after her. I won a scholarship for guitar." She could feel the heat beginning to rise in her cheeks.

"Geez, Jodi. That's really cool, a scholarship and everything."

"Yeah, it was pretty cool. And while I was there, I also learned voice—" Suddenly her chest tightened. Without even thinking about it, she reached up and traced her fingers along the deep jagged crevasse carved down her neck. That one scar just wouldn't heal.

Sam gently laid her hand over Jodi's arm, not saying a word as they drove along in silence, the moment drawing out. Finally, she went on as if nothing had happened. "So, after Interlochen, what then?"

What a refreshing change. No questions, not from Sam. Maybe she really was different. "Well, you're probably not going to believe this, but after Interlochen, I went on to Juilliard."

"Jesus, Jodi. I didn't realize I was in the presence of such greatness."

Jodi let out a loud laugh. "I wouldn't say greatness. More like dumb luck. I won another scholarship."

"Well, that's still pretty impressive. I can't even imagine. That must have been so much fun."

Fun wasn't what she'd call it—not in the least. Living hell was more appropriate. "Actually, my time at Juilliard was pretty rough. That's when I came out."

"Oh…I'm sorry. Weren't the others very accepting?"

"No, it wasn't that. They were all very accepting. Pretty much what you'd expect from the artistic elite." She let out a bitter laugh. "*I* was the one who wasn't. I kept thinking I'd lose my parents and they'd completely cut me off. I was so stressed out, sick all the time. It was terrible. I couldn't sleep, couldn't eat. Finally, I lost so much weight I ended up in the hospital. I couldn't take it anymore, so when I was lying there, I just blurted out, 'Hey Mom and Dad, I'm gay.'"

Sam bit her lip. "I'm almost afraid to ask. Did you end up losing them?"

"That was the shits. They already knew. Here I was all worried since I was a teenager and they already knew. Doesn't that just figure?"

"Oh, that's like my mom. I was something like thirteen and had this major crush on this girl in my class, Mary Hansen, not that I realized that was what was going on. We used to talk all the time but then she started dating this guy who was a real jerk. I got really depressed for a couple of months, spent most of my time in my room, either sleeping or playing on my computer. It must have been pretty obvious because finally my mom sat me down at the kitchen table and began saying that there was nothing wrong with being a lesbian." Sam laughed. "At first, I thought she was going to tell me that *she* was gay but then she told me that it didn't matter if I was gay or not, she would always love me no matter what. Apparently, she had known from the time I was ten."

"What about your dad? Was he okay?"

"Oh, you mean specimen four seventy-five?"

"Specimen—*what*?" Jodi nearly plowed into a parked car.

Sam laughed. "Yeah, that's usually the reaction I get. Sounds better than 'unknown sample.'"

"So, your mom like went…"

"To a sperm bank? Yep. Picked me out from a book and all. High aptitude in the math and sciences. Probably where I get my computer skills. Anyway, Mom was always pretty career driven, didn't have time for dating, romance and such. But that didn't stop her from being a great mom. She always had time for me. That's why we're so close, and probably also why she had picked up that I was gay even before *I* did."

"It's crazy how parents sometimes just *know*." Jodi pulled around the corner onto Monroe Avenue. Cars lined both sides of the street. "Oh, this doesn't look good."

"No big deal. Just pull around the corner, there's usually a spot." Sam pointed out the window to the left.

Sure enough, she turned and there about half a block down was an open parking space. "Wow, Sam, you were right."

"Before you get too impressed, my office is only a few blocks away so I'm downtown all the time. After a while, you get pretty good at it."

Jodi slipped her car into the empty spot and threw open her door. Instantly, hot humid air blasted her in the face, seemingly boiling right off the pavement. She gasped, taking in another quick breath of the thick damp air. "Boy, it's pretty stuffy down here, isn't it?"

"Oh yeah, in the summer it gets like this later in the evening. Wait till August." Sam fanned herself with her hand. "I tell you, it can get downright stifling."

"I bet. It can get really bad playing during the Festival of the Arts with the sun beating…" Jodi trailed off, her attention following the crowd of young people walking by. One guy, a tall man with a short goatee, turned and gawked at her as he passed. He started snickering and then thumped his buddy on the arm, jerking his head back at her. His buddy whipped around, ogling her as they continued up the street. This was just what she needed—two people getting a good look at the freak show. Why did it always have to be like that—people staring and talking? Why couldn't they mind their own damn business? It's not as if she didn't wish every second of every day that she was whole again. Like always, she should have just stayed home.

* * *

What the heck just happened? Sam glanced over at Jodi and then up the block at the passing crowd. Did she miss something? Jodi had been chatting it up but now she only stared at her shuffling feet, her shoulders slumped and her head hanging. All since passing that crowd. Maybe she shouldn't have suggested coming downtown for dinner, not if it meant Jodi would feel uncomfortable. Finally, she threw her arm out and wrapped it around Jodi's waist, pulling her closer. "You know, I'm really glad you called."

"Huh?" Jodi caught her toe on the sidewalk and stumbled sideways into her.

"Wow, Jodi. You okay?" She bumped her back with her hip. "You were like a million miles away."

"Sorry. Must be the humidity." Jodi slowly lifted her eyes from the ground in front of her feet and flashed a shy, apologetic smile.

"Oh, isn't it great? You just can't get a better night." The smell of grilled steak wafted through the thick air and she inhaled deeply, savoring the intoxicating aroma. It would be fine by her to keep walking around all night together, but her stomach let out a long, low growl, so she dropped her arm from Jodi's waist and taking her by the hand, pulled her up to the front of Judson's. "Well, we're here."

Jodi closed her eyes and drew in a deep breath. "Mmmm, that smells so good."

"Oh, wait until you taste it." Hand in hand, Sam led the way through the doors and up to the short, pudgy host sporting a pencil-thin mustache. She hadn't seen a mustache like that since the last time Cheryl and Angi had literally dragged her out to drag king night at the gay club. Fighting back a giggle, she gave Jodi's hand a soft squeeze. "Two for Werstler."

The host thumbed through the book. "Werstler, Werstler. Oh yes, here you are." With a firm nod of his head, he picked up two menus. "Right this way."

Still holding hands, they followed their mustachioed host through the restaurant. The evening rush had pretty much thinned out and the noise had settled to a low din. Their host then stepped up to a small table for two and fanned out a pair of menus before pulling out a chair on each side. "Your server tonight will be Dwayne. Have a good meal." With a quick nod, he turned and left.

Jodi glanced around the room, taking in the artwork hanging from the walls and the linen tablecloths. "Wow, this is a lot fancier than I'm used to."

"Yeah, that's why I like it. It's quite classy and sometimes I'm just in the mood for something other than sports blaring on the TV and people cheering while I eat. I like a good steak but I don't want a hoedown to get it."

Jodi snorted, covering her mouth. "I can see your point. Most steakhouses lack a bit in sophistication. At least here, we won't have to worry about some big guy in bibs belching loudly at the next table."

"Well, you never know." Sam held her gaze, the moment drawing out, before she finally picked up the menu.

Jodi flipped from one page to the next, the entire time biting her lower lip. Finally, she leaned forward. "Geez, Sam, I don't know. What are you having?"

Sam set her menu aside. "Hmmm, I was thinking about the porterhouse with a green herb butter sauce. That and a glass of pinot noir. How about you?"

"It was hard to decide but the roasted garlic crusted New York strip with forest mushroom sauce sounds good with a beer."

"Oh, let me guess—Guinness?"

A wide grin lit up Jodi's face. "Now, you know me too well."

"I like someone who's predictable." Again, she held Jodi's gaze.

Just then, a tall muscular man stepped up to their table and cleared his throat. "Hello, I'm Dwayne and I'll be your waiter tonight. Can I start you off with any appetizers?"

"Nope. I think we're ready to order." With a sigh, Sam tore her eyes from Jodi. She quickly pointed out her selections on the menu.

Dwayne then turned to Jodi. "And you, miss?"

Jodi leaned forward. "I'll go with…"

Dwayne jerked back slightly, giving Jodi a subtle double take. He recovered quickly but not before Jodi had noticed.

Jodi gulped and lowered her head.

At first, Sam simply stared, her mind stuck in neutral as the scene unfolded in front of her. Across the table, Jodi seemed to crumble before her eyes. Where only a moment ago a bright, smiling, beautiful, young woman sat, now the Jodi she had first met—sad, depressed, silent, shutting the entire world out—cowered with her eyes lowered and unfocused. Then it hit her, a sort of protective anger seething up. Maybe Dwayne's response had only been a reflex, but it was not appropriate and certainly not fair to Jodi. No, correct that—this was bullshit, plain and simple. Why couldn't people give her a bit of a break and treat her with some damn respect?

Her head hung, Jodi now merely pointed at the items on the menu, not making eye contact with either Dwayne or her.

Dwayne scratched down Jodi's order. "And…and…um…to drink?"

Sam gritted her teeth. Jodi must deal with this all the time, people treating her differently because of her damaged voice or her scars. There was no other way to put it—this was absolute bullshit. But before she totally lost it, she quickly cut in with as cheerful a voice as she could muster. "Good grief, man. What kind of question is that? Can't you see she'll have a Guinness?"

Dwayne jumped, a deer in the headlights look as he took in the full glare from Sam. "Ah, yes, very well. Yes, I'll get this right in." He scurried away so fast he nearly plowed over another waiter delivering a round of drinks.

Jodi stared down at the table, twisting the edge of the tablecloth in her fingers, her voice barely above a whisper. "Thanks."

Sam wasn't sure she had ever heard more sadness than in that whispered little thanks and she swallowed the hard lump in her throat. No wonder Jodi didn't talk much or want to be around people. Had it been her, she wouldn't feel like talking either. It had to be hard enough for Jodi without her making a big deal about it so she went on as if nothing happened. "For what?"

Jodi slowly lifted her head. "You know, for that with the waiter."

She met Jodi's tentative glance and her heart nearly broke at the pain in those gorgeous deep blue eyes. So wretched. So dejected. She certainly didn't want to cause her any more pain. So with the brightest smile she could manage, she leaned forward, gently covering Jodi's hand with hers. "Oh, that? You know, I think our waiter must be off his meds."

* * *

Jodi couldn't help but smile. If not for Sam, she'd have been out the door by now. Since her accident, she had come to expect the stares, the whispers, the awkwardness. But Sam had taken it all in her stride. One quick quip and everything was better. No one had ever done that before. "So, Ms. Funny, besides comedy, been working on any new stuff this week?"

"Oh, I'm always working on new stuff. This week, I've been putting together a new website for a small law firm. You wouldn't believe what their old one looked like. It was so late nineties." Sam wrinkled her nose.

"Wow. Is that like really bad?" When it came to the Internet, she seriously didn't have a clue. Yahoo and eBay were about the extent of her experience. That and a couple of music sites.

"I'll tell you, Jodi, bad is an understatement. It was horrible. I don't think it had been updated since then. And on top of that, they were being ripped off big-time. I'm going to save them a ton of cash."

"Well, if I ever need any computer stuff, I'm definitely coming to you."

Just then, a short, blond woman with an eyebrow ring stepped up to their table, a large steaming plate in each hand. "So, who had the roasted garlic crusted New York?"

Without a word, Jodi simply lifted her hand. Their waiter, Dwayne, was nowhere in sight. Perhaps he didn't want to risk another go with Sam. At that thought, Jodi actually smiled. She wouldn't want to face the wrath of Sam again either.

The young blonde then turned to Sam. "And you must have had the porterhouse."

"Yep. That's me."

The waitress slid Sam's plate in front of her and straightened up. "Is there anything else you need?"

Sam pointed down at the table. "Um, how about our drinks? A pinot noir for me and a Guinness for my gorgeous friend." She met Jodi's eyes and gave her a wink.

"What? No one's brought your drinks yet? I'm so sorry. I'll run and get them right now."

When their surrogate server disappeared back into the kitchen, Sam leaned forward, cupping her hand to her mouth. "You know, I'm beginning to think there's a serious lack of competence here tonight. They all seem to be suffering from some sort of cognitive difficulty. Maybe they should check the kitchen for carbon monoxide poisoning."

"Good one, Sam. I think you're right—definitely some sort of cognitive difficulty." Again, Sam's humor completely set her at ease. This evening would have been a total disaster by now if not for her.

A minute later, their drinks arrived without a word—not surprising either. Nothing like being treated as if she had the plague. But that couldn't ruin the evening, nothing could, not with Sam here. She took a long swallow of her Guinness, savoring the frothy bitterness, and then leaned over, deeply breathing in the intoxicating aroma rising from her steaming plate. This was definitely better than the discount steak houses and a world better than her typical meal of delivery pizza and beer. Next, she attacked her steak with her knife, cutting it completely into bite-sized pieces before tasting it, a trait she had acquired as a teenager much to her parents' dismay. Finally, she stabbed a large juicy piece with her fork and ran it around in the sauce. Lifting it to her mouth upside down on her fork, she paused before taking her first bite. "So, Sam. Tell me, how did you get into IT?"

Sam held a finger to her lips as she swallowed. She then took a sip of wine before answering. "Well, that all goes back to my coming out. I think all comings out suck." She forcibly stabbed at her steak.

"Yeah, I think you may be right."

Sam leaned in closer. "Well, you remember how I told you that I spent a couple of months locked in my room either sleeping or on the computer before my mom sat me down and asked me if I was gay?"

"That was after that girl started dating that jerk, right?"

"Oh, yeah." Sam rolled her eyes. "Well, I thought after coming out to my mom, things would be fine then. Boy, was I wrong."

"I thought your mom was okay with everything."

"Mom was great. The kids at school were horrible. Well, not all of them but enough. They used to call me dyke and lesbo as I walked down the hall."

Jodi winced. "Geez, Sam. I'm sorry."

"Yeah, it pretty much sucked. So I got on my computer and started making this little website." She giggled. "Oh, it wasn't much of anything—only a couple of pages, all HTML, but I loved it. It gave me a chance to voice my thoughts, share some stories and post a few pictures. Every day I would work on it, change it here and there. Mom thought it was pretty cool, so she bought me all sorts of books on programming and web design. By high school, I knew more than the teachers."

"Wow, Sam. You were like a total computer nerd."

"That's putting it mildly. It really helped me get through the rough times with the other kids. My computer teacher, Miss

Sherd, encouraged me a lot. She said not enough girls were in IT. You know, the more I think about it, she may have been gay too."

"You never know. Maybe that's why she encouraged you. She knew how difficult it was to be gay."

"You might be right. Anyhow, she found all sorts of extracurricular things I could go to—computer camp, programming seminars, night classes. I couldn't get enough. Then I graduated and went to Tech. The students there could care less if I was gay."

"Well, I'm glad you found something you loved to get you through all that. I don't know what I would have done without my music."

Across the table, Sam met her eyes and held her gaze. "You know, Jodi, it's the things we love that make it all worthwhile."

* * *

"So, Jodi, what would you like to do now?" Sam wrapped her arm around Jodi's waist, the humid summer night air again caressing her face. Up and down the street, groups hustled along, venturing between restaurants and clubs.

Jodi entwined her fingers in Sam's. "I don't know. You want to go to one of the clubs?"

Clubbing wasn't exactly what Sam had in mind. And after the near disaster at the restaurant, the idea of another crowded place where someone might say something stupid to Jodi didn't appeal. "Too noisy. I was thinking something a bit more intimate."

Jodi stared at her a long moment before blowing out a deep breath. "I'm sorry, Sam. I don't have a clue."

She didn't have any better idea what to do either. The only thing she did know was that she didn't want the evening to end, not yet. "Hmm, how about we just walk and talk then?" She squeezed Jodi's fingers and turned right onto Division, traffic buzzing in both directions.

"Now that sounds good to me." Jodi swayed as they walked, a much different picture than her earlier slumped, shuffling stance.

At the corner of Fulton Street, they met a group of seven or eight obvious lesbians, if the rainbow shirt on one of them was any indication. They were in their early twenties, out for a night on the town and bouncing between the gay clubs.

"Woo hoo." One of the young women, wearing baggy jeans with a chain wallet and mirrored sunglasses, pumped her fist in the air and hollered out when she spotted them with their arms casually around each other. "You go girls."

Sam glanced over at Jodi and they both began to laugh. She waved back at the vociferous young woman. "Well, that's a lot better response then we normally get."

"Oh, tell me about it. Last summer, I had this nut come up to the stage at a show and start screaming something about vile sin against nature. Then he chucked an entire fast-food drink at me."

"What? No way. You've got to be kidding."

"I wish. It was even supersized."

She nearly doubled over. "Didn't scrimp on the drink then, huh?"

"Nope. Thankfully his aim sucked. It flew right over my head."

"That's just nuts."

The temperature dropped ten degrees as they passed over the Fulton Street bridge, a cool mist rising up from the water and sending a shiver through Sam. This was definitely better than hitting the clubs. Plus Jodi didn't seem nearly as self-conscious either. When she let down the walls, there was only one word that came to mind—wow. Granted, who was she to talk? She had some pretty tall walls herself. At the end of the bridge, she took Jodi by the hand and pulled her across the lawn in front of the Eberhard Center. "Hey, let's have a seat over here."

Jodi dragged her feet. "But won't we get in trouble?"

"What will they do? Tell us to get off the grass?" Sam plopped down in the middle of the lawn and stretched out, propping up her head with her arm.

"I guess you're right." Jodi slowly sat beside her, wrapping her arms around her long legs and drawing them to her chest.

"Besides, I think it's worth it." Sam pointed out across the river. As the grass sloped down to the water's edge, thick mist hung in the air. The lights from the buildings glistened over the surface of the water. Farther up the river, lights outlined the bridges, illuminating the architecture against the night.

Jodi sucked in a quick breath. "Wow."

"You can say that again. I sometimes walk down here when I work late. I just sit here and clear my head."

Jodi leaned back on her elbows. "I can see why. This is gorgeous."

Sam turned and fixed Jodi with her eyes. "Yes, the view *is* gorgeous."

* * *

Jodi peered out at the river, the cool breeze brushing against the rising heat in her cheeks. Was Sam blind or something? Her? Gorgeous? How could she possibly find her gorgeous? How? Couldn't she see the huge scars? Couldn't she hear her voice? How could Sam not be repulsed? Yet, she looked at her as if she were like anyone else, as if she were normal.

Sam leaned closer, her voice soft. "What are you thinking?"

Jodi barked out a hollow laugh and immediately regretted it. She hadn't meant for it to sound so bitter. But that was the story of her life—at least since the accident. More scars that refused to fade away. "Oh, it's nothing." She turned to Sam, meeting her eyes. "I was just thinking how great it is to be here with you."

"I'm glad to be here with you too, Jodi. I've had a great time."

"I have too, but…"

"But what?" Sam reached over and traced her fingers up her arm, a lazy smile on her lips.

A shiver ran up her spine at Sam's touch. And that smile—oh my God—she could get lost in that smile. "I'm sorry, Sam. I'm not really good at this."

"What? You're not good at sitting and talking? I think you've been doing fine."

A huge part of her screamed to jump up and run away. Just get the hell out of there. But another part—the part that was getting louder with every second that passed—wanted to believe, needed to believe. She rolled onto her side, leaning on her arm, and gazed into Sam's eyes as they reflected pinpoints of light from the buildings, the passing cars, the river.

"You know the best part?" Sam closed her hand over hers and squeezed. "I'm so glad I found someone who likes my goofy sense of humor."

Jodi couldn't help but laugh. Again, Sam knew just what to say at just the right time to completely set her at ease.

Finally, the traffic died down and all talk faded into the heavy humid night as they lay on the grass staring into each other's eyes. The moment drew out, silent, comfortable. Inch by inch, they leaned forward, eyes still locked. Jodi swallowed, her breath caught in her throat. Was she ready for this? Was it even a good idea? She could feel Sam's hot breath growing ragged against her chin and she closed her eyes. Just then, the sprinklers popped up, dousing them in icy jets of water. Jodi gasped at the sudden shock and leaped to her feet. "Holy shit. That's freezing."

"Come on." Sam grabbed her by the hand. They ran through the sprinklers, arms wrapped around each other, dodging frigid streams of water and laughing so much they could barely stand. By the time they reached the sidewalk, they were both dripping wet, clinging to each other and laughing between gasps.

"I don't think I've ever had a better evening with someone, Jodi."

"Me either, Sam. Me either."

CHAPTER FIVE

"Shit. Shit. Shit. Noooo." Sam stared at her computer screen, digging her fingers into her hair. This couldn't be happening. One of her servers had just crashed. "You have *got* to be fucking kidding me. Shit." She drew out the last word. It was turning out to be a bad day. So much for an easy update. She should have known better. With a long moan, she dropped her head down on her workstation, thumping it against the tabletop. Could it possibly get any worse? At the knock, she slowly looked up, her hair ruffled every which way.

"Sorry, boss." Her sole employee, Sandy Johnson, tentatively stepped into the room, her hands in the pockets of one of the numerous tailored vests she favored. That and a bowler hat. Somehow, Sandy made the look work for her. "But there's a woman here who wants to see you."

"Oh wonderful, now what?" The way her day was going, it was probably a customer here to complain. Could anything more go wrong? She really should have stayed in bed. Taking a deep breath, she pushed back in her chair. "Fine, I'm coming."

She followed Sandy down the hall to the lobby, expecting the worst, but as she walked in, her breath caught in her throat as Jodi sprang up from the couch. This was certainly a surprise and the way her day had been going, quite a welcome one at that. "Hey, it's you!"

"Hey, it's me. I thought maybe I could interest you in lunch—" Jodi then stepped back, the smile quickly disappeared from her lips. "Sam, you okay?"

"Actually, Jodi, you're a sight for sore eyes."

"Why? What's wrong?"

"Oh, it's just one of those days. One of my servers crashed." But as she told Jodi, it didn't seem like quite as big a deal. In fact, every server she had could crash and it wouldn't seem that bad now that Jodi had stopped by.

"Oh, that doesn't sound good. Um, sorry, I should have called." Jodi spun on her heel to leave.

"No, it's cool. I'm glad you're here." Actually, Jodi showing up was the first thing that had gone right all day.

"I hope you don't mind that I just stopped in." Jodi still looked unsure.

"No really. I could definitely use a break."

Jodi finally relaxed. "So, what happened?"

"Oh, same old story." She rolled her eyes. "Here I was installing an update on one of our servers—you know, supposed to be a fifteen minute job—and the entire thing crashed."

Jodi winced. "Hmmm, I haven't got a clue what any of that means but it sounds bad."

"It could be a lot worse. I have everything backed up on another server but still, it's a pain in the ass."

"Tell you what—let me treat you to lunch then."

"Now, I'll take you up on that." Sam then whirled back around, patting her hand on top of the reception desk. "Hey, Sandy, I'm taking off for lunch. If anyone calls to complain about their site being down, tell them we're doing a scheduled update and their site will be back up in a couple of hours."

"Okay, boss. No problem." Sandy peeked up from her computer, giving her a sly wink. "Have fun."

Since it was past the major lunchtime rush, the streets were mostly free of the normal stampede of business foot traffic. Jodi leaned over and wrapped her arm around Sam's shoulders. "So, where would you like to go?"

"Hmmm. Now that could be a loaded question, Jodi. After a morning like this, maybe somewhere like Cancun."

Jodi chuckled. "No, I meant for lunch."

"Bummer." She certainly wouldn't mind a long vacation somewhere warm and sunny—beaches, cold drinks, Jodi in a hot bikini. She grabbed Jodi loosely by the hand, swinging their arms back and forth as they walked. If not for Jodi, she'd still be hammering her head against her workstation. "Well, in that case then, what were you thinking?"

Jodi turned onto Monroe Center and her eyes suddenly lit up. "Hey, you up for sushi?"

"Oh, that's a great idea. I'm always up for sushi." Sam then stopped and spun around to face Jodi, her free hand on her hip. "Now, wait a minute. I thought you didn't care for that type of food."

Jodi gave her a sly grin. "No, I said I didn't care for Thai food. I love sushi."

Sam cocked her head to the side. "Huh. I'll be damned. I never would have guessed you as a sushi type of girl. Steak, fries, beer, yes, but not sushi. This is definitely a plus."

"Just because my typical diet is pizza and beer doesn't mean I don't appreciate different types of food. I do have a little bit of culture, you know."

"Uh…uh…" Talk about putting your foot in your mouth. She hadn't meant to offend Jodi. She was only joking. Then she noticed the devilish grin on Jodi's face and she elbowed her in the side. "Oh, you're bad. You're just giving me crap."

Jodi covered her mouth, stifling her giggles. "I got you pretty good, though."

"Yes, you did."

"Actually, I'll eat almost anything—just not Thai. My parents were big on experiencing a lot of different cultures and their cuisines."

Still holding hands, they slowly crossed the street, rocking their arms back and forth as they walked. Quickly moving clouds cast shadows between the buildings. The aromas of various restaurants and bistros intermixed with auto exhaust and motor oil filled the block. Turning into Marado Sushi, they were greeted by a young Japanese woman. "Welcome."

"Hi." Sam bowed slightly. Jodi nodded her head toward the young woman.

"Table for two?"

"Yep." With her arm wrapped around Jodi's, she turned, meeting Jodi's bright blue eyes. "Just the two of us."

She slid in across from Jodi, quickly scanning the menu. They could probably split a couple of rolls, depending on how hungry Jodi was. But when she looked up, Jodi sat hunched over, following the waitress out of the corner of her eye as she walked away. Jodi was worried about her voice, but what could she say to convince her that her voice wasn't that bad? Different, yes. Bad, no. Finally, she leaned forward. "So, Jodi, you want to split a couple of rolls or something?"

Jodi shot one last glance over her shoulder and then flashed a bright smile. "Oh, I don't think so. You're on your own, girl. I'm starving."

"Oh really?" She threw her shoulders side-to-side and bobbed her head. "In that case, I'll order *just for me*." She emphasized the last part, unable to keep from laughing. It was refreshing to be with someone who would joke and give her a hard time, something Jennifer had never done. That was one thing she swore she'd never do without again. If someone couldn't joke and have a good time, then what was the point? Being in a relationship should be fun.

When they finally set their menus down, their waitress immediately appeared as if she had been lying in wait. "Ready to order?"

Sam started off. "I'll have a California roll and a Philly roll with a green tea."

A single nod and the waitress turned to Jodi.

"Ah…" Jodi slumped in her seat, her voice not much more than a whisper. "I'll have…" She then pointed out the salmon roll and veggie roll on the menu.

"Anything to drink, miss?"

Staring at her hands in her lap, she took a deep, labored breath. "Green tea."

After the waitress scurried off with their order, Jodi slowly peeked across the table, the pain in her eyes apparent, and Sam felt her heart drop. If only Jodi wasn't so self-conscious about her voice. Sure, it was low and breathy, but she really liked it. It was unique. But the struggle she must go through every day. It tore at her heart. She reached across the table and patted her hand on top of Jodi's. "So, I need to hear that someone's been having a good day. What have you been up to?"

The tension seemed to lift from Jodi's shoulders. "Not much. Just the usual. I practiced guitar for three hours this morning."

"Wow, three hours. Do you practice that much every day?"

"Yeah, most of the time. I used to practice a minimum of six but that caught up with me."

"Caught up with you? What do you mean?" Sam leaned forward, her elbows on the table, propping her chin in her hands.

"Apparently, too much practice can be a bad thing. I had to have surgery for carpal tunnel syndrome after my freshman year at Julliard." Jodi turned over her hands, pointing at the deep scars at the base. "See? It looks like I tried to slit my wrists and missed."

Sam snorted, quickly covering her mouth. "Tried to slit your wrists and missed? Oh, that's bad, Jodi. You're just terrible."

"Well, I thought it was pretty funny. I do have to be careful though. I've known other musicians who had their careers end due to wrist injuries."

"You know the weird thing—I've had problems with carpal tunnel too. Who would think a guitar player and a computer geek would have that in common?"

"Makes sense, though. You type a lot. Typing and guitar playing are both repetitive motions. You'd better be careful or you'll have to have surgery and everyone will think you tried to slit your wrists and missed too."

"Jodi Price, you are just horrible." She dabbed the corner of her eye with a napkin. When Jodi wasn't worried about people around her, she truly was hilarious. But as their food arrived, the walls flew back up and Jodi sat silent. Again, if only Jodi wasn't so self-conscious. She really didn't need to be. But anything she could do or say would only draw more attention, so she poured soy sauce into a small dish and swirled a dollop of wasabi around in it with her chopsticks. Then a quick taste test and she smacked her lips. "Perfect."

Now that their waitress had moved out of earshot, Jodi prepared her own sauce dishes to her liking and then snagged a fat section of her veggie roll. She dipped it lightly in her sauce, flipped it over dipping the other side, and then plopped it in her mouth. "This was a good idea if I do say so myself."

"I agree." Sam worked on her Philly roll. "So, besides practicing your guitar, what else have you been up to today?"

"Not much really." Jodi now attacked her salmon roll—dip, flip, dip. "I visited my dad at work and helped him inventory a new shipment of cars."

"Oh, so your dad works at a car dealership? I didn't know that. Which one?"

"Have you heard of J.P. Motors?"

"Of course. Who hasn't? It's like the biggest dealership in Grand Rapids. So, what does he do there?"

Jodi lowered her eyes, a sheepish grin now on her face. "Well, he pretty much runs the place. You know, J.P. Motors—as in Jim Price Motors."

Something just didn't click at first. *J.P. Motors—as in Jim Price Motors.* Jim Price. Jodi Price. Then it hit her. "Holy shit. Your dad owns J.P. Motors?"

"Yep." Jodi laughed, seeing the shocked expression on Sam's face. "It's pretty much a family business. I help out there from time to time when I'm not playing guitar. Actually, all I do is walk around and help Dad with some paperwork once in a while. They're hoping I take it over someday."

"Good grief, Jodi. I had no idea. Why didn't you tell me?"

Jodi shrugged. "I don't usually want a lot of people to know. I found that out when I was in middle school and all the other kids would pick on me because of it. You know how kids are—lots of jealousy and cliquishness. It's easier sometimes if people don't know your dad owns a huge car dealership. Besides, I've never really been into cars—not like Dad. He loves cars as much as I love guitars."

Her chopsticks now forgotten in midair, she simply gawked at Jodi. "Wow. I knew your family had to be pretty well off for you to go to Interlochen and Julliard but I had no idea."

Jodi began to blush and lowered her eyes. "Everyone always thinks we're rich, we own a car dealership, but if it weren't for me winning scholarships, I wouldn't have been able to go to either school."

Damn, what was she thinking? She hadn't meant to make Jodi feel uncomfortable. She could see how a lot of people would think her family was rich. Even she got that when she was growing up. Just because her mom was the Dean of Student Services at Grand Valley State University, people thought they must have a lot of money. Some people wanted to be friends because they thought she came from money. But still, she didn't want Jodi to think she was like that. She put her chopsticks back onto her plate and reached across the table, covering Jodi's hand with hers. "Hey, I just want you to know that it doesn't matter to me one way or the other. But what I'm really worried about is will they hate me because I drive a Volkswagen?"

Jodi nearly choked on her green tea, slapping her hand to her mouth. "Geez, I don't know, Sam. I'm sure it will be difficult at first but they realize no one's perfect."

After lunch, they walked slowly up the nearly empty street, most pedestrians safely tucked back at their jobs. That's where she should be but she'd much rather stroll around downtown Grand Rapids with Jodi than attend to what awaited her back at her office. Finally, she turned, dragging her feet as she went. Inside the door, she turned to face Jodi. "I wish I didn't have to get back to work but I've got to fix my crashed server."

Jodi stepped forward, taking both of her hands. "I wish I could help."

"That's okay." She peered deep into Jodi's eyes. Damn, she could lose herself in those pools of deep blue, flecked with bits of gold. Of any day, why did her server have to crash today? Talk about crappy luck.

Jodi leaned in closer and closer, now only inches away, her hot breath searing against her forehead. Despite the heat, a shiver ran up her spine. Then, she blinked and Jodi hopped back, blowing a deep breath out through her lips. "Well, I should go."

"Yeah, me too."

Before she even realized what was happening, Jodi ducked down and brushed her lips against her cheek. One small kiss and she was gone, the door slowly swinging shut behind her. She stood there frozen, her fingers covering the spot where Jodi had kissed her. It was all she could do not to rip open the door and yell out, "Hey, Jodi, wait up." Any other day. Finally, she turned and dragged herself away from the door.

Sandy popped her head up from her workstation. "So, boss, was that *the* Jodi you've been floating around the office and talking about?"

Leave it to Sandy to make her blush like a teenager with her first major crush. "Yeah, that was Jodi."

"I thought so. No wonder you've been in such a good mood. She's hot." Sandy waved her hand as if fanning herself. "You lucky girl. I'm jealous."

Shaking her head, she sat down on the corner of her computer desk. "Tell me about it. Jodi's great. I know that we're just getting to know each other but I already feel such a connection."

"It certainly must be. I'm surprised you haven't been dancing around the office."

"Hey, I'm not that bad. Well, maybe not *quite* that bad."

"Pretty close, though." Sandy leaned closer. "It's probably none of my business but I was just curious. Is there something up with her voice?"

Her chest nearly seized and she leapt up from the computer table, scattering paperwork across the floor. "Oh, my God. You didn't say anything to her, did you? Jesus, Sandy, tell me you didn't."

"No, no. Why on earth would I do that? I wouldn't, believe me. Why?"

She really needed to give Sandy credit. It could have gone really badly, even if she had only said something offhand. "Well, please don't say anything to Jodi about it. It really bothers her and she's very self-conscious about it. She won't even talk to new people she meets for a long time until she feels comfortable."

"Geez, boss. I'm really sorry. I feel like a real jerk now. What happened?"

"Don't worry about it, Sandy. Jodi was in a really bad car accident. That's why she has those huge scars." She traced along her neck. "I'm not really sure what happened, but I guess it damaged her voice somehow. It's not something she talks about."

"God, that's horrible." Sandy clapped her hands over her mouth.

"I know it's been really hard for her. The worst part of it is that she used to be a professional singer."

"Oh, man. That has to be so hard."

Hard didn't really even come close to what she saw Jodi experience. To lose such a fundamental part of yourself had to be devastating. That was her identity. She was a *singer*. And to have that taken away. "Well, I really should get that server back up and running."

"Okay, boss. Good luck." Sandy scooted back to her computer.

In front of her workstation, Sam leaned back in her chair with her hands locked behind her head. Jodi turning up had been just the break she had needed. And thank God Sandy hadn't said anything to her either. Everywhere Jodi went, the first impression people had of her was her unusual voice and the scars on her neck. Well, the first impression she had of Jodi was that she was tall and gorgeous. So what if her voice was different—different was nice.

* * *

Jodi drove across town, tapping her hand against the steering wheel to the song blaring from the radio. The lunch with Sam had turned out well, much better than she had hoped. At first, she wasn't sure if it would be a good idea, showing up spontaneously without an invitation and wanting to go to lunch. But Sam had seemed genuinely delighted. She only wished that they could have been together longer.

Since she now had the afternoon to herself, what better way to spend it than a trip to Guitar Center? She could go around and play dozens of different guitars on dozens of different amplifiers. Besides, it had been quite a while since she had been there and she could use some new strings and picks. She was running low on both and this would be the perfect time to stock up, not that she ever needed an excuse to visit.

Ten minutes later when she walked through the front doors to the deafening maelstrom of competing guitars, drums, basses and a whole slew of clamor, she felt at home. There was no better feeling than to be around so much musical energy. Granted, she preferred the equipment to the people. While some musicians were fine to be around, willing to acknowledge others' talent and skill, some were arrogant jerks. Particularly guitarists. Or more precisely, *male* guitarists. She was better than most. She had the schooling and the training. But she still found that a lot of guys didn't really care for her. Still, it was fun to watch their mouths drop when she ripped through a blazing solo.

First things first—the wall where hundreds of guitars hung just begging to be played. She never had a specific guitar in mind but just browsed along until one caught her eye. That had been the case with her Paul Reed Smith, as if it had jumped right off the wall into her hands. Right then she knew she had to have it. Then after her accident, her mom and dad had bought it for her while she was still in the hospital. She had simply held it as she lay there, the weight of against her chest, tears running down her cheeks. It was probably her best motivation for getting better.

About halfway down the wall, a Relic series Fender Strat piqued her curiosity. Since the fun of being there was trying new and exciting guitars, she plucked it from the wall and trotted it over to a bench where she plugged into a Fender Cyber Twin Amp. She trilled through a scale up the neck, limbering up her fingers. Two guys—one with a Shit Happens T-shirt and his sidekick, I Like Boobs—gawked over at her. Like usual, their expression was a combination of incredulity and envy. A quick roll of her eyes and she continued to play, working through a few of her easier solos. Although the Strat was a fast-playing instrument, she didn't care for the low frets and slightly thin sustain. The three thousand dollar price tag didn't add to the appeal either.

She winced and unplugged the guitar. No matter which song she played, she didn't like the Strat. It certainly wasn't her Paul Reed Smith, so she hung the guitar back on the wall and continued to browse. One of the guys who had been staring at her earlier, Mr. Shit Happens, stood beside her checking out a Gibson SG. As she stepped around him to take a look at a Dark Fire Les Paul, he leaned back against a stack of amplifiers, bobbing his head.

"So, have you been playing long?" His eyes traveled up and down her as he leered.

"Ah, yeah." She went back to examining the Les Paul, her skin crawling. She didn't have time for that, even if she weren't gay.

"So, you play in a band?" Now he leaned closer and dropped his eyes, not even trying to hide that he was checking out her ass.

"Yes." She focused more on the guitar in front of her. Hopefully, he would get the message and walk away. Why she seemed to attract that type of guy, she didn't know. They couldn't just admire her for her talent. They had to ogle her body at the same time. It was sickening. Granted, she certainly wouldn't mind Sam admiring her talent while ogling her. With that thought, she smiled. Sam could ogle her all she wanted.

Finally, Mr. Shit Happens nodded and pushed off from the stack of amplifiers. "Okay. Well, see you later." One last leer before he turned and walked away.

She glanced up and down the wall again but nothing was really jumping out at her. She had played most of them before.

She was about to give up when she peered at the used guitars on the wall behind the guitar counter. She usually didn't care for them. If she were going to get a new guitar, she wanted it to be hers from the beginning. That way it would have her personality and feel to it. It would be her fingers that wore the frets and neck. It would be her that put the small dings and scuffs in it. Then, as she was about to turn away, it caught her eye—a Paul Reed Smith in Pride Purple. Her chest tightened and she froze, unable to move. Holy crap. She had never seen a Paul Reed Smith like *that* before.

Slowly, she shuffled up to the guitar counter as if on autopilot, her eyes zeroed in on that guitar. The tag hanging from the headstock said this was a two thousand and three Custom 22 Artist model in a deep purple finish. However, she couldn't make out the price on the back, not that it really mattered. There was no way she could afford this guitar, especially it being an Artist model. But God, it was beautiful.

"Hey, Jodi."

She tore her eyes from the guitar. "Hey, Mark." She was enough of a regular that she knew most of the sales staff and many of them also knew her by name.

Mark tossed his long blond dreadlocks over his shoulder and followed her gaze behind him. "Ah, checking out the Paul Reed Smith, huh? That one's a real beauty."

She found herself once again staring up at the guitar on the wall. At least she wasn't drooling—not yet anyway. "Yeah, it sure is. I've never seen one in purple before."

"It was a special color they offered for a few years then discontinued it. I don't know why either. It's really gorgeous." He paused for a moment, looking up at the guitar again then turned back around. "Don't you have one in blue?"

"Matteo Blue, yes. A Custom 24."

"I thought so. This is the 22—a little shorter." He leaned in, an arm resting on the countertop. "So, would you like to have a closer look?"

Was he kidding? Of course she wanted a closer look. What kind of silly question was that? Still, she didn't want to seem too eager even as she fought the urge to jump up and down. "Yeah, I guess so."

Mark turned around and pulled out a short stepladder. He then climbed up and reached as high as he could, teetering back and forth. Barely touching the bottom of the guitar, he stood on his toes to slip it out of the padded hanger. With every muscle in her body tense, Jodi bit down hard on her lip—anymore and she'd taste blood. She held her breath as he lowered the guitar, clenching her teeth every time it came close to another guitar. It wasn't until Mark gently set the guitar on the countertop that she finally let her breath out.

She reached out and ran her fingers lightly over the guitar. She couldn't even see a scratch, ding, dent, anything, anywhere on the body. "Wow, this is in great shape."

Mark bobbed his head in agreement. "Yeah, I don't even think the guy ever played it."

She barely even heard Mark as she continued to trace her fingers over the guitar. She already knew it was going to be too expensive. Hers had cost nearly four thousand. She couldn't justify paying that for another Paul Reed Smith, even if it did look brand-new. Finally, she worked her way up the headstock and grasped the sales tag, closing her eyes. It wouldn't hurt to look at least, so holding her breath, she flipped over the tag, and opened her eyes. "Eighteen hundred? That can't be right."

"Yep, that's right."

"You're kidding. I thought it would be a lot more than that." Her heart pounded against her chest. An Artist model Paul Reed Smith for eighteen hundred dollars. She had to be dreaming.

"Well, since it's kind of older, the manager put a lower price on it. It's a really good deal too."

She didn't need anyone to tell her that. It was a phenomenal deal—once in a lifetime.

"So, would you like to play it?"

"Oh, yeah. You don't have to ask me twice." She could barely feel her feet touch the floor as she walked back to the Fender amp she had been using earlier, grinning like a fool the entire way. Every muscle in her body tingled as she sat on the guitar bench, simply holding the guitar in her hands. Then she wrapped her fingers around the neck and fretted a couple of silent notes. Oh God, it felt good. She couldn't deny that. Now was the moment of truth. She carefully plugged in the cable, turned up the volume and closed her eyes. One deep breath, then another, and then a thundering series of chords burst from the amplifier.

When she next looked at her watch, over two hours had passed. The guitar played like a dream, not that she would expect anything less from a Paul Reed Smith. The feel was a little different from hers since the neck was a touch shorter but overall, she liked the action. It definitely needed a new set of strings. She had to retune it after every couple of songs, a clear sign that it hadn't been played in a long time. That wouldn't be a problem though. She had to get new strings anyway. What would a couple more sets be? But should she get it? She had the money. And it was a fantastic deal. But should she splurge and buy it? The deep Pride Purple would certainly be a plus at concerts, if nothing more than it would be flashy. Plus she had to admit, the Pride connection had a certain appeal for her. Maybe it was meeting Sam that had something to do with it too. She hadn't had anyone new in her life in a long time, not since the accident. It was silly but somehow the bright purple made her feel a bit taller, proud that she was a lesbian rocker.

Finally, when she couldn't think of another song, she stopped and flexed her fingers. They were beginning to sting from the old strings. That was easily fixed. Some new strings and she'd be all set. But should she buy it? That was the question. She loved the guitar, she really did. And she couldn't beat the price. So, why was she balking? It was only a guitar—buy it or not. Still, she couldn't quite bring herself to commit. What she needed was a second opinion or maybe even a swift kick in the butt, so she ripped her cell phone from her back pocket and punched in Lynn and Kat's number.

She nearly jumped up when someone answered. "Hey, Kat."

"Hey, Jodi. Where you at? It sounds like a rock concert going on in the background."

She tried to cover her phone with her hand to block out some of the noise, not that it would make that big of a difference. "I'm down here at Guitar Center."

"Aw, I wish I was there. I haven't had a chance to get down there in forever."

"Why don't you hop in your car and drive over here."

"Damn, Jodi, I wish I could but I'm waiting for Lynn to get home. We're going over to her parents' for dinner tonight."

"Bummer. I had something I wanted to show you."

"Oh, a new set of sticks. I could really use some." Kat giggled.

"No, not a new set of sticks. What would I do with those?"

"Give them to me, what else?"

"Nice try, Kat." Leave it to Kat to think of drumsticks. "I'm checking out a new guitar."

"Sweet. What is it?"

"It's a Paul Reed Smith, like mine. Well actually it's used but you wouldn't know it." As she described it to Kat, her pulse quickened. "It's a Custom 22 Artist but get this—it's Pride Purple."

"Oh wow, Jodi, that's pretty cool. That would sure get some attention at the Pride events."

"Yeah, that's what I thought." She didn't mention any of the other reasons like how she was feeling a little more pride in herself since meeting Sam. "I've been hashing around whether I should get it or not. I'm having a terrible time deciding. Help me, Kat. What should I do? Please, please, please tell me."

"Geez, Jodi. I don't know. I can't tell you what to do. For one thing, I'm a drummer and I know like zero about guitars. I bet it's pretty expensive though, isn't it?"

"Well, it's eighteen hundred." Hearing herself say the price, she bit her lip again. Even though it was a great deal, it was still a lot of money.

"Hmmm. That sounds like a pretty good deal. That's like half of what your blue one cost, right?"

"Yeah. It is. It's a hell of a deal. I guess I need a kick in the butt to get it."

"If you want it, get it. You'll just kick yourself if you don't."

"We'll see." Talking to Kat was helping a bit. And she was right—if she didn't get it, she'd just kick herself later.

"Hey, Jodi, I've got to go—Lynn's here. But if I were you, I'd get it. I'll stop by tomorrow and you can show me."

She tucked her phone back in her pocket and stared down at the guitar in her lap. Like Kat said, she should just get it—that's all there was to it. If she didn't, she would only regret it later. Still, she needed just a little longer to fully convince herself so in the meantime she might as well get strings. Maybe by then, she'd work up the courage.

With both arms, she cradled the guitar all the way back to the guitar counter. Her chest immediately tightened the moment she gently laid it down, and she traced her fingers along the neck. God, it was beautiful.

"You know, if you played it any longer, we'd have to charge you rent." Mark peeked up from the guitar he was restringing and with a flick of his dreads flashed her a bright smile.

Jodi gave him a sheepish grin. "It would be worth it too. It plays like a dream."

"So," Mark leaned forward, "the million dollar question—is it going home with you?"

Jodi stared down at the guitar, biting her lower lip. It was all she could do not to blurt out a wholehearted yes, pack it up, it's going home with me. Still, she couldn't quite bring herself to commit. "I…I…oh, crap, I don't know. Give me a little bit. I've got to get some strings so let me give it some thought and I'll be back."

"Okay, I'll keep it safe up here for you." He picked up the guitar and hung it behind him on the wall.

She continued to stare at the guitar, leaning farther and farther forward until she nearly sprawled over the entire counter. She didn't want to leave it. What would happen if someone else bought it? That would be just her luck—here she dragged her feet and dragged her feet all afternoon and someone else swoops in and snatches it up. And look what happened last time she hesitated. If only she had decided to buy *that* guitar instead of putting it off, she never would have been in that accident.

Just the time it would have taken to swipe her credit card and she would have traveled home, excited to play her new guitar, and Mr. Drunk Escalade would have been happily on his way, blowing through an intersection when she wasn't there. Well, she'd go get the strings and then she could decide for good. She managed only two steps before she quickly whipped back around. "Um, could you like hold it for me for a bit?"

Mark rolled his head back and laughed. "Don't worry. I'll hold it for you for a while."

One last glance at the guitar and she hustled over to the accessories department. Pro-packs of strings were on sale so she wanted to stock up. Even though each pro-pack had ten sets of strings, the way she went through them with her aggressive playing style, she could use a good twenty or thirty sets. But as she wandered through the store, everything around her a faded blur, the only thing on her mind was that guitar, the feel of it in her hands, the strings under her fingertips. If she did get it, she could spend the rest of the evening playing it in her studio at home. She'd love to plug it into her effects board and really put it through its paces.

Already working up a playlist she would tear through once she got it home in her studio, she rounded a stack of amplifiers only to come face-to-face again with Mr. Shit Happens. He sat beside his sidekick, I Like Boobs, playing a Jackson Flying V. She barely even noticed him as she walked past.

"Hey, that's the chick that sounds like a dude."

Everything suddenly came into sharp relief, the words crashing in her head like a broken cymbal, and she nearly stumbled into a Marshall half-stack. Slowly, she turned around. "What?"

He turned to his friend. "See what I mean." They both began snickering.

She stood there frozen on the spot, unable to move a muscle. All she could do was stare at them as they laughed, their cackling echoing through her head. The taste of bile spilled into the back of her mouth as she fought the nausea rising up her throat. Her stomach then lurched and she clapped her hand over her mouth as she gagged. She had to get out of there. She had to get out of there right then.

At a run, she staggered for the door with her arms wrapped tightly around her stomach and across the parking lot to her car. She fumbled her keys from her pocket and popped the locks as her vision faded in and out. Finally, she ripped open the door and climbed behind the wheel only to double over and retch beside her car. She clung to the doorframe, the only thing keeping her from spilling onto the asphalt, as violent shivers tore through her body. When the wave finally passed, she threw herself back against the seat, sweat pouring from her forehead, and dug her nails into the scars on her throat. Why did this have to happen to her? Why did she have to lose her voice? Why did people have to be so mean? She beat her fists against the steering wheel. Why? Why? Why? With one last slam of her fist, she collapsed against the steering wheel and wrapped her arms around it as if clinging on for life. Her chest heaved and she began to cry, starting slow at first, then building to great gasping sobs. Why?

CHAPTER SIX

"Jodi, sweetie. Wake up."

Jodi awoke with a start, kicking the throw pillows off the end of the couch. She rolled over and blinked slowly, meeting the concern on Kat's face as she stood over her peering down. Moaning, she threw her arm over her eyes, shielding them from the light. Apparently, she had slept on the couch all night and now pain shot through her back. Also, her head thundered. And if that weren't enough, she just generally felt like shit. But after yesterday, she didn't really care. "Ahhhhh, Kat. How did you…?"

"You left your door unlocked." Kat pushed aside the nearly dozen empty Guinness bottles lining the top of Jodi's coffee table and sat down. "What's up, hon. Looks like a pretty rough night."

"It's nothing." Jodi rolled onto her side, her arm draped over her head blocking out the light. What could she say to Kat—her life sucked and she just wanted to be left alone?

Kat gently rubbed her arm. "Jodi, what's wrong? Did something happen with that guitar?"

If only. That would be the least of her problems. "Believe me, it's not that."

"Well, is it to do with Sam? Did she do something?"

"No, it's nothing Sam did. It's…it's…hell, I don't know…" She then slammed her arm against the couch and whirled around, kicking her feet into the coffee table and sending empty beer bottles crashing to the floor. How could she explain it to Kat? How could she possibly understand? How could anyone understand?

Kat jumped back, an empty bottle rolling up against her foot. Calmly, she knelt down and set it back on the coffee table beside her. "Sweetie, you're not making any sense. Tell me what happened."

Jodi twisted her fingers through her short hair and cradled her head in her hands, staring at the floor. She really did feel like shit. Her head pounded, whether from the alcohol or the night of sobbing, she wasn't sure. Probably both.

Kat stood and slid in beside her on the couch, slowly rubbing her hand on Jodi's back. "Jodi, sweetie. What's wrong? You can tell me."

"It's just…just everything." She threw her hands up. "Everything's wrong." Tears then spilled down her cheeks and she quickly scrubbed them off with her balled up fists. Just wonderful. On top of it all, she was crying again. That's all she seemed to do anymore. Ever since her accident, she didn't seem to have any control over anything—not her tears, not her emotions, and certainly not her voice. She slammed her fists into her knees and began to sob, her chest heaving.

Kat pulled Jodi to her, tucking her head against her chest. "Shhh. Shhh. It's going to be okay." She slowly smoothed Jodi's hair with her fingers. "Tell me, what happened with Sam? I thought you two were hitting if off."

Jodi pulled away, drying her eyes with the back of her hand. "Well yeah, it's really not that. It's just…hell, I don't know. Sam's great, yes. But eventually, I know she won't be able to deal with my voice. She'll look at me like everyone else—like a freak."

Kat's eyebrows shot up. "Whoa—did she say that?"

"Well, no." Jodi stared at her hands folded in her lap.

"Jodi, I've seen how Sam looks at you. She doesn't see you as a freak." Kat lowered her head, trying to look Jodi in the eyes.

"I don't see you as a freak. Where's all this coming from. Last I talked to you, you were flying high, about to buy a new guitar. What happened since then?"

Jodi took a deep breath. "That's just it, Kat—everything *was* going fine. I had just put the guitar back for a bit—they were going to hold it for me—and I went to buy some strings. Then, I walked past these two asshole guys." She went on to tell Kat what they said and how they sat there and laughed at her.

"Oh, my God. I can't believe someone would say that. Oh, Jodi. I'm so sorry." Kat leaned over and rested her head against Jodi's.

"They thought it was really funny. Hey, that's the chick that sounds like a dude."

"Sweetie, trust me, you don't sound like a man."

"Yeah, well, they sure thought so. I just stood there like a dipshit as they had a good laugh. Then I was so sick, I just left."

"So, you didn't get the guitar then?"

"No. I just wanted out of there."

"Well, I can understand that." Kat stared over at Jodi and her shoulders fell. "Hon, I know that was really horrible what happened—I'm sick just hearing about it—but what does that have to do with Sam?"

Jodi let out a long sigh. How could she explain it to Kat? "Sam has been wonderful. She hasn't said a word about my voice. Actually, she's simply treated me as if I were anyone else. But what happens if someday that changes? What happens if one morning Sam wakes up and can't stand to hear my voice anymore? What if she looks at the scars on my body and can't stand to look at me anymore? What then? It may not be a big deal now, but someday it might."

"Jodi, what makes you think that will happen? I've seen the look in Sam's eyes when you two are talking. Trust me, it doesn't bother her at all."

"Yeah, but..."

"Yeah, but what? Listen, I know losing your voice was really difficult—more difficult than I can possibly ever imagine. I can't begin to say how much my heart aches for you. But I don't see you as any less because of it. I certainly don't see you as a freak and believe me, Sam doesn't either. And fuck those guys yesterday. Don't let them ruin your life."

At Kat's brashness, she couldn't help but crack a smile. "Fuck guys? What kind of lesbian would I be?"

"See what I mean? Don't let them get to you. Now, what about this guitar you were going to buy?"

A smile now slowly lifted her lips. That guitar had been spectacular, that was for sure. And it had been such a great deal. She should have just bought it. Now, it was probably gone. If it hadn't been for those guys. Her smile slowly drained away. "I don't know if they even still have it, Kat."

"Well, why don't you give them a call, have them hold it."

Kat was right. She should call and see if they still had it. If they did, she could run down and pick it up. Maybe that would take her mind off from everything. If she put all of her energy into playing, maybe she could forget about the people who stare at her and whisper comments, sometimes not even quietly, as she walked by.

It took several minutes before she was connected to someone who could tell her whether the purple guitar was still there. The entire time, she chewed on her bottom lip. If she had to be connected to one more person, she was sure she would have drawn blood. Finally, Mark picked up on the other end.

"Yep, we still have it here. I thought you were going to take it yesterday so it's all set up with a new set of strings and everything."

"I would have but I started feeling unwell." She didn't want to get into why she left in such a hurry. "But if you can hold it, I'll be down in an hour or so."

"No problem. It'll be here waiting for you." Mark barked out a deep, rolling laugh. "And don't worry, I'll keep it safe."

She felt better. Maybe she was just being silly. She shouldn't have let those assholes get to her. They were probably just jealous of her talent anyway. Like Kat said, fuck 'em.

"So, they've still got it?" Kat appeared to be holding her breath.

"Yep, it's still there." She resisted the urge to jump up and down, maybe even dance a jig. The more she thought about yesterday, the sillier she felt. She was going to buy a new guitar. That's all that mattered. "You want to go with me and pick it up?"

"I'd love to, Jodi. It's been forever since I've been there, but I've got to get back home." Kat's face lit up. "Hey, tell you what. I've got a great idea. Why don't you take Sam with you?"

Kat's idea was perfect. She could show the guitar to her and see what she thought too. But then again, would it be too presumptuous to give her a call? She had dropped by her work yesterday unannounced. Would she seem too clingy calling her today also? Again, she bit her lip. "I don't know, Kat. You don't think it would be too much. I mean, I just saw her yesterday."

"Psst. Call her. Trust me, she'll love it." Kat made as if she were dialing an imaginary phone. "I've got to go, hon. Are you going to be okay?"

"Yeah, I'll be fine." Jodi lowered her eyes. "And hey, Kat, thanks for everything."

"Don't worry about it. That's why I'm here. I know it's hard sometimes, but just don't let it get you down." Kat pulled her into a firm embrace. "Just remember, we're all here for you." Then holding Jodi by the shoulders, she gave her a gentle shake. "Now, call Sam, get into the shower and go get that guitar."

Jodi jumped into the shower. She was supposed to call Sam first but with the low level pounding in her head, she figured a long soak under the warm water might be best. By the time she finally climbed out, her skin beginning to prune, her head felt much better. She quickly toweled off and threw on her trademark jeans and black shirt. Now, she had no excuse to put it off any longer, so before she could completely psyche herself out, she grabbed the phone and stabbed in Sam's number, crossing her fingers as it began to ring.

"Hey you, what's up?"

Obviously, Sam had checked her caller ID. "Hey back at you. I'm heading downtown to Guitar Center to check out a new guitar and wondered if you'd care to come with me?" She held her breath.

"Wow. I'd love to." Sam nearly shouted out the words. "You want me to meet you there or at your place?"

Jodi flopped down on her couch. So much for worrying that Sam wouldn't be interested. "Well, if you'd like, you could come here first. I could show you my place." She clenched her teeth as she waited for Sam's response.

"I'd love to see your place, Jodi. You've seen mine, at least from the outside."

"Sounds like something we need to remedy." Seeing the inside of Sam's house, maybe even on a very regular basis, had a distinct appeal.

"Yes, we definitely have to…soon."

"I agree. So, I guess I'll see you in a bit then."

Sam's voice became serious. "Well, Jodi, I have a big problem though."

She snapped bolt upright, her chest tightening. Sam had a big problem? Had she done something wrong? "Geez, Sam, I…I didn't mean—"

Sam then burst out laughing. "No, silly. I need your address."

She slapped her forehead and collapsed against her couch. "I guess that would help, wouldn't it? You need directions too?"

"This is the twenty-first century, Jodi. All I need is your address and my iPhone."

"Too fancy for me."

"Jodi, Jodi, Jodi, one of these days…" Sam giggled.

All Jodi could do was shrug. Then with a quick goodbye, Sam was on her way.

*　*　*

"Well, I'll be." Sam couldn't stop that silly smile. Jodi calling was certainly a pleasant surprise. All she was planning today was sipping some wine and working at home. Not that she'd admit it to anyone, but she had planned to spend the afternoon playing computer games, her one guilty pleasure. She didn't have a clue about anything musical but sharing Jodi's company would be fun. But the last thing she needed was another relationship. And who was to say that Jodi was even interested in her that way. For all she knew, Jodi saw her as nothing more than a friend at best, someone free to tag along to the store on a Saturday afternoon.

But five minutes later when she climbed behind the wheel of her car, her hand was shaking so badly she couldn't feed the key into the ignition. "Come on, girl. You need to get a hold of yourself. This is just a friendly trip together. Stop overanalyzing everything." She then laughed. "And stop talking to yourself."

* * *

Jodi slumped back against the couch with her eyes closed. Sam was coming to her house. She then shot to her feet, nearly falling over. *Sam* was coming to her house. Shit. She glanced around at her living room. Oh, dear God. She was screwed.

Now in full panic mode, she tore through the house. First she grabbed all her clothes and tossed them into her room, closing the door behind her. Then she gathered up the empty beer bottles and stowed them away with the rest of her empties. Next, she stared at the kitchen sink. She was in serious trouble. She was supposed to do the dishes yesterday. She stuffed them all into the dishwasher. She would worry about rinsing them later. Just as she dropped the last glass on the top rack, she heard a knock on her front door. Without turning it on—she'd have to pull everything back out later anyway—she closed the dishwasher and hustled through the house to the front door, glancing around one last time for embarrassing clutter. A bra hanging from a chair or something. She then took a deep breath, smoothed out her tank top, and opened the door.

Sam stood there with her hands behind her back. "Well, I made it."

"You made it." Jodi leaned one-handed against the doorjamb. Her heart hammered, whether from her marathon cleaning or Sam standing on her doorstep, she wasn't sure.

With her hands still behind her back, Sam shifted her feet, slowly peering around at the outside of Jodi's house. "Well, I love your place. Very peaceful here."

Jodi chuckled. "My neighbors probably wouldn't agree with you when I'm practicing at three in the morning."

"Oh, that would be bad. I'm not sure I'd be happy about it at three in the morning."

She gave her shoulders a dramatic shrug, trying her best to look innocent. "Well, you know—when the muse takes you. What can you do?"

Sam stood up on her toes and peeked around her, glancing inside her house. "So, would you like to show me around a bit maybe?"

"Oh, yeah. Duh." She slapped herself on the forehead. What was up with her anyway, gawking at Sam as if she had never seen a woman on her doorstep before? "Yes. Please, come in."

"Why thank you, ma'am." From the middle of the living room, Sam slowly spun around, taking in the eclectic decor, most with a music theme. "Wow, Jodi. I like what you've done with the place."

"Gee thanks, Sam. It's sort of my sanctuary." A bit of an understatement. More like her impregnable refuge. She couldn't count the times she had come home and locked out the world after something had happened like it had yesterday. She could close her door and feel safe, and if she tried, she could almost forget about everything—almost. Finally, she cleared her throat and hooked a thumb back at the door. "So, would you like to get going to the guitar store?"

Sam quickly whipped around. "I thought you'd never ask. I can't wait."

"All righty then. Since I invited you, I can drive if you don't mind." Jodi grabbed her keys from beside the door.

"Works for me." But as she turned toward the door, Sam grabbed her hand, staring directly into her eyes. "And Jodi... thanks for inviting me."

"Thanks for coming." She returned Sam's hard gaze. Sam seemed nearly as excited as she was, almost infectiously so.

As they pulled away from the curb, Sam dragged out the large leather case from beside her seat and started pawing through Jodi's CD collection as they drove across town. "Damn, girl. You've got almost every type of music imaginable here. The only thing I don't see is opera."

Jodi popped up the center console and pulled out a Pavarotti album, waving it in the air.

Sam slapped her leg. "Wow. I stand corrected."

"I like all types of music."

"I guess." Sam held up a Metallica album. "Pavarotti and Metallica. Now, that's quite a contrast."

"Actually, Sam, not as much as you might think. A lot of metal bands like Metallica use classical elements in their music. Most of my stuff is classically-based."

"Wow, I would have never guessed that. See, I'm learning a lot here." Sam reached over and intertwined her fingers with Jodi's, giving her free hand a squeeze.

Twenty minutes later, Jodi pulled into Guitar Center. For what seemed like a long time, they sat holding hands. Although she was about to buy a new guitar—and what could be more exciting to a guitar player? Still, she didn't want the moment to end. Not yet.

Sam finally broke the silence. "So, what's this new guitar you're checking out?"

Jodi let out a soft sigh. The moment couldn't last forever. "Well, you know my blue guitar? It's a Paul Reed Smith like that but a little different. You'll have to see."

"Cool. I can't wait."

Jodi took a deep breath. "Well, let's get going." She hopped out of her car and waited at the back as Sam walked around to meet her. Overhead, clouds floated across the sky while a refreshing cool breeze competed with the heat boiling from the pavement. Or maybe it was being with Sam that made her feel so warm. Whatever it was, the breeze felt good against her face.

When they walked through the front door, the concussive force of the discordant music hit them like a strong summer wind. Jodi laughed as Sam froze, her eyes flying wide. She leaned in close. "It's pretty loud at first but you get used to it."

"Holy crap, you ain't kidding, Jodi." With her eyes agog, Sam peered around the store. "Wow. It's huge in here."

"Yeah, it's a guitar player's heaven." She led Sam through the store to the guitar counter but as she walked up, the purple Paul

Reed Smith was nowhere in sight. Her stomach began to churn. Maybe they had sold it after all. That would just be her luck—here she had Sam with her and the guitar was gone.

Mark stood behind the counter, stringing a Fender Strat. Seeing Jodi, he looked up. "Hey, there you are."

With her shoulders falling, she stepped forward. "Um…" She glanced around, still not seeing it anywhere. "You still got that Paul Reed Smith?" She bit her bottom lip, waiting.

Mark let out a laugh. "Yep, don't worry. I put it back here for you, nice and safe." He reached behind the counter and pulled out the guitar, carefully handing it to Jodi.

She cradled it in her arms, and turned to Sam with a wide grin. "Well, this is it."

"Oh wow, Jodi. It's absolutely gorgeous. Purple is one of my favorite colors." She then lowered her voice and leaned in. "Wouldn't have anything to do with being gay either."

"That's why I like it too. It's bright Pride Purple. What better for a lesbian band?"

"Oh, I agree. Can you play it for me?"

"Sure. I'd be glad to. Follow me." She led Sam over to the amplifiers where she sat down on a stool and plugged in. Sam pulled up another practice bench to face her. Although Sam had seen her with the band at Pride, now it was just the two of them, one-on-one. But what should she play? She had a ton of different songs but which would be best, especially now that she had Sam all to herself? Then it came to her—one of her favorite slow ballads. With a little light distortion, she turned up the volume and swept the pick across the strings.

She worked each note, each chord, pouring feeling and emotion into the song. This ballad was from her first album. It talked about finding that one person who had complete understanding, complete acceptance. Normally, she didn't play anything from before her accident, but with Sam, somehow it felt right. When she finished, she slowly peeked up. Sam stared back, her eyes bright. "So, you like?" She held her breath.

Sam gaped, searching for the words. "It…it…oh Jodi, it was gorgeous. Your playing is so beautiful…just like you."

She nearly fell off the guitar stool. Beautiful, just like her? How could Sam think that? Yes, maybe her playing was beautiful—she could accept that, but her? Even with her scars? Even with her voice? She never thought anyone could ever look at her like that again. Her eyes began to mist and she quickly blinked. If only they were anywhere but Guitar Center, anywhere there was no one else around. Maybe then, she could see if Sam was truly being sincere or just being nice. Finally, when she opened her mouth, all she could do was stammer. "Um…um…so are you."

Sam stared into Jodi's eyes, holding her gaze. "Mmmm. You're really sweet."

After a minute, Jodi blinked and nearly leaped up from the stool. "Hey, how would you like to try?"

Sam gasped, waving her hands in front of her. "Oh, no, no, no. I'd probably break it."

"You won't break it, trust me." Jodi flipped the guitar around and sat it in her lap.

"Seriously, Jodi, I don't know anything about music except how to put a CD in my player. This is a really bad idea."

"Don't worry." Jodi knelt in front of her. "I'll help you." Jodi reached out, taking her left hand in hers, and wrapped her fingers around the neck. "Here, do what I do." She formed a D chord then pulled away.

Sam tried to duplicate Jodi's example, twisting her fingers this way and that but they just wouldn't cooperate. How Jodi could do that with such ease was beyond her. Finally, with her fingers beginning to cramp and stabs of pain shooting up her arm, she glanced up. "Like this?"

"Close." Jodi giggled and gently moved Sam's ring finger over a string. She held it for a long moment as she peered into Sam's eyes. "There."

Instead of glancing at her fingers, Sam continued to gaze at Jodi. She could still feel Jodi's touch as she guided her fingers, the warmth of her breath against her bare neck. She swallowed. "Now what?" Her words were low and breathy.

Jodi then took Sam's right hand in hers and lowered it over the bridge of the guitar, lightly running her fingers over the back of her hand and up her forearm. She leaned closer, staring deep into Sam's green eyes. She then whispered into her ear. "Now, gently strum across the strings."

Sam had to swallow again. What was Jodi doing to her? Damn, any more and she wouldn't be able to take it. She shifted her weight and ran her fingers slowly over the strings as Jodi had showed her. An unmistakable D chord poured out of the amplifier. Her mouth dropped open. "Holy shit, I did it."

Jodi threw her arm around her and pulled her in tight. "Yep, you did it." She quickly leaned in and brushed Sam's cheek with her lips. "We'll turn you into a guitar player yet."

Sam froze, her heart suddenly racing, and she absently covered the spot with her hand where Jodi's warm, soft lips had pressed if but for a second. Their eyes locked and slowly, she began to lean forward, more and more, her lips beginning to part.

But then Jodi blinked and the moment was gone. "Um… maybe we should get going, huh?" She let out a soft laugh.

"Yeah, maybe we should." With both arms, she cradled the guitar and handed it back to Jodi. For a moment, she had forgotten it was even in her lap. All she needed was to drop the guitar in front of Jodi, all because she couldn't concentrate after an innocent kiss.

Jodi hoisted up the guitar by the neck. "So, you think I should get it?"

"What?" She didn't know what to tell Jodi. Maybe if it were a computer, she could give some sound advice. But a guitar? "Oh geez, Jodi. I don't know what to tell you. Isn't it really expensive?"

"Actually, it's used and a lot cheaper than my blue Paul Reed Smith."

"Oh, it's secondhand?" She leaned in to examine it closer. She couldn't find a mark on it. "Good God, Jodi, it looks brand-new."

"Yeah, I know. It's an awesome deal." Jodi bit her lip.

It was obvious Jodi loved the guitar. She looked like a kid at Christmas. But what should she say? She knew zilch about guitars. "Awesome deal, huh?"

Jodi nodded, bobbing up and down with excitement.

Finally, she gave an exaggerated shrug. "Well, in that case, I'd say get it."

"Great." Jodi nearly sprinted up to the guitar counter. She gently sat the guitar down and smiled at Mark. "I'll definitely take it."

"Somehow I knew you would. I'll get the case and write up everything for you then." He set the guitar against the wall behind the counter. "I'll be right back."

"That's okay. I've got to get some strings too." Jodi continued to stare at her new guitar before finally tearing her eyes away and turning to Sam. "Come on, I can use your help." She led the way to the accessory department.

Sam ran her finger over a metal box with various switches, dials and blinking lights. For all she knew, it could be a waffle maker. "So, you have to get some new strings?"

"Yep—these right here." Jodi held up three pro-packs.

"Holy crap, Jodi. What's that like a year's supply or something?"

"Hardly. I go through a lot."

"Good God, I guess. How many sets is that?"

"Oh, thirty. I put on a new set at least before every show and sometimes I'll have to replace them in between too." Jodi laughed and gave a one-shouldered shrug. "With my style of playing, I'm a tad hard on strings."

"See, I know like zilch about any of this."

"Well, I think it's great that you're taking an interest."

"What's not to be interested in?" And that went for Jodi too. Everything about her was interesting—her music, her personality, even her past.

Jodi flopped the strings down in front of Mark, who began ringing everything up. "So, you all set?"

"I think so." Jodi dug her credit card out of her wallet. With a swipe and a signature, the guitar was hers. With an almost manically wide smile, she closed the case of her new guitar and slid it from the counter.

For a moment, Sam thought she might actually jump up and down. She leaned in close. "Not excited at all, are you, Jodi?"

"Geez, Sam, talk about excited—you look almost as excited as I am."

"Well, I guess I'm just excited to see you so excited." They both began to laugh as Sam plucked up the bag with the strings and Jodi's new strap. "That and I'm tickled you asked me to come along."

"And I'm tickled you agreed."

Together, they walked out to Jodi's Escape. With her free hand, Jodi popped the back hatch and slid the guitar case in. Sam then plopped the bag down beside the guitar and stepped back with her hands locked behind her. Now what? Jodi had her new guitar. She was probably going to want to play it. If it were her and a new computer, she'd want nothing more than to fuss with it the rest of the day. That she could understand. But still, she didn't want the afternoon to come to an end—not yet.

Jodi closed the hatch and turned slowly around. She took a deep breath. "So, what would you like to do now?"

That seemed to be the question. What indeed? Then it popped into her head, the perfect end to the day and she gave Jodi a sly grin. "Hmmmm. How about we go back to your place? Then you could give me a private concert."

* * *

Jodi wasn't sure which she was more excited about—getting her new guitar or having Sam over for what she called a private concert. Playing for Sam at Guitar Center had been nice but there were other people walking around and a ton of noise. This would be more intimate, just her and Sam in her music studio. So by the time she pulled into her driveway, she could barely sit still. She kicked open her door and quickly grabbed her new guitar from the back while Sam snatched the bag with strings. She bustled up the sidewalk and through the front door to her dimly lit living room with Sam right at her heels. "Please make yourself at home."

"Now Jodi, that's a dangerous proposition. I might not want to leave." Sam tilted her face up, giving her a devious little wink as she walked past.

"Oh, I see." Jodi drew out the words. "Am I going to have to rent a U-Haul then?"

"Hmmmm." Sam seemed to be giving the idea a lot of deep thought. "Well, maybe that would be going a little too fast. I'll settle for my private concert."

"That I can definitely do." Actually, as far as she was concerned, Sam could stay as long as she liked—granted a U-Haul might be a bit much. Still, there was a part of her that cried out to take it slowly or at least as slowly as she could. "Come on. I'll show you my music studio."

At the end of the hall, she opened the door and flipped on the light. Along the far wall sat her guitar stool with her practice amp beside it. In front of that, her massive effects pedalboard lined the floor. To the left was a long multiple guitar rack with her Ovation and her other Paul Reed Smith electric guitar. A baby grand piano took up the center of the room with several other instruments, including a twelve-string guitar, a mandolin, a banjo and a five-string bass, lining the walls.

Sam's mouth gaped in awe. "Holy crap, Jodi. You can play all these?"

"Well, yeah, to varying degrees." Her cheeks now flushed a bright brick red.

"And a piano." Sam slowly drifted over to the black Steinway in the center of the room and lightly ran her fingers along the top. "So you still play."

"Somewhat. I took piano as a second instrument at Juilliard. My mom was thrilled, finally taking it up again." She leaned up against her piano, watching Sam as she continued to trace her fingers along the keys. A shiver shot through her body. If only those fingers were lightly brushing over her bare skin instead of her piano. "But I'm…I'm not sure how good I am."

"I'd still love to hear you. Do you mind?"

"Well, I'll see what I can do." Jodi held Sam's gaze, the moment drawing out, before she swallowed hard, pulled out the piano bench and sat down. Sam stood leaning against the side of the piano, watching. Jodi closed her eyes, taking a long deep breath. She reached forward and began to play. The notes rolled out of the piano, deep bass notes and crystal clear high notes, reverberating off the walls and filling the entire room with music that seemed to wrap around them as she played. She started out slow and soft, but like her guitar playing, it soon picked up with fast intricate melodies. She worked the notes, her shoulders flexing and her body swaying. Her hands floating over the keyboard, the sound increasing and increasing until it culminated in a flurry of quick, heavy chords, ending with a single thundering low note that seemed to resound not only throughout the room but also from deep inside her chest. As the note faded, she slowly lifted her eyes to Sam and held her breath.

Sam stared back, her mouth gaping. "Um…um…"

Her heart sank. "I know I'm not quite as good on the piano."

"What are you talking about? Jodi, you're…you're…Jesus, Jodi, I can't even find the words to describe it." Sam breathed out the words.

Jodi now relaxed, a wide smile lifting her lips. "Well, I'm really glad. I didn't want to let you down."

"Like that would happen. I can't say it enough, Jodi—you simply amaze me."

"Thanks, Sam. I think you're pretty special too."

"Okay, now how about playing that fancy new guitar for me?"

"That I can do." She certainly didn't need asking twice so she hopped up and flung open the case. She then sat down on her guitar stool, plugged in the cable and flipped on the amp. But as Sam sidled up beside her, she nodded over at her baby grand. "Why don't you pull up the piano bench, Sam? That way you don't have to stand."

Sam quickly dragged the piano bench over so she could sit facing her and plopped down, hardly able to sit still. "Okay, I'm ready."

"All righty." Jodi began with a slow wailing guitar solo. As she picked the notes, it sounded as if she were crying through her guitar, each note choked and drawn out. She played everything from classical to heavy metal to blues. Over an hour passed before she finally flipped off the amp and carefully set her new purple guitar in the stand beside the others. "So, how's that for a private concert?"

"Oh my God, Jodi. I could listen to you play forever. Thank you." Sam leaned forward on the piano bench, her hands beside her.

"My pleasure." Jodi stood up and held out her hand to Sam. "Now, how about we get something to drink?"

Taking her hand, Sam jumped up beside her. "Sounds great to me."

Together, they walked out to Jodi's living room. "Why don't you have a seat and I'll get you something." Jodi took two steps toward the kitchen and then spun back around. "I guess I should ask what you want first, huh?"

Sam flopped down on the couch. "I'll take a beer if you've got one."

Jodi scurried out of the kitchen with two bottles of Guinness and slipped in beside Sam. "Here you go."

Sam stared down at the bottle. "So, tell me Jodi, do you ever drink any beer other than Guinness?"

Jodi let out a loud gasp and violently shook her head. "Oh, heavens no." She then leaned over and bumped her arm against Sam. "There is but *one* beer."

Sam laughed and threw her leg over Jodi's, twisting sideways on the couch. She then peered directly into Jodi's eyes and lowered her voice. "You know, Jodi, I really did have a wonderful time today."

Jodi reached over and pulled Sam in closer, their bodies pressing together. She stared straight into Sam's deep green eyes, eyes she could easily get lost in, and slowly leaned forward, closer and closer. This was it. This was what she had been waiting for before Sam had even stepped into her life. She hadn't even dared to hope until now. But here she was, Sam tight in her arms, her mouth opening more and more. Sam then rolled back her head and with a soft whimper, their lips met. When Jodi finally pulled up, she could barely whisper. "So did I, Sam. So did I."

CHAPTER SEVEN

"Hey, Sandy, let me know when Jodi gets here." Sam draped her arms over the side of Sandy's reception desk with a can of Diet Coke in her hand, her third for the day.

Sandy peeked up from her computer screen. "This wouldn't have anything to do with the surprise you've been working on all week?"

"Yep. I finally finished it late last night." Sam had put in nearly every waking moment on it, ever since Jodi had given her a private concert in her studio. Now if only Jodi liked it.

"Believe me, boss, from what you've shown me, she's going to love it."

"I sure hope so. I don't want to freak her out or anything. I mean, she didn't ask me to do it."

"I wouldn't worry about it. From everything you've told me, it sounds like she'll really be touched."

"That would be great." Sam started up the hallway then quickly spun back around. "Just let me know when she gets here."

"Okay, boss."

She then held a finger to her lips. "And remember, hush, hush."

"You got it." Sandy gave her an exaggerated wink before spinning her chair back around to face her computer.

Back in her office, Sam kicked her feet up on the corner of her workstation and popped open her drink. She probably should have asked if it was okay but that would have ruined the surprise. Still, she was nervous. She certainly didn't want to mess things up with Jodi, especially since everything seemed to be going so well. She still couldn't help smiling when she thought of last weekend. A private concert in Jodi's studio had led to a night together at Jodi's house, even if they had only kissed and held each other.

The intercom on her desk cackled. "Boss, there's someone here to see you." She could hear the giggle in Sandy's voice.

Her heart somersaulted. Finally, the moment of truth, so with a quick breath, she kicked her feet off her desk and fumbled with the intercom button. "Okay, Sandy. I'll be right out."

She counted each step up the hallway, forcing herself to slow down. How'd it look if she came busting into the lobby as if she'd just run the hundred meter hurdles? This was supposed to be a casual visit, no big deal. But try telling that to her heart. It had graduated from somersaults to an all-out gymnastics routine by the time she reached the end of the hall. She sucked in a deep breath and popped around the corner. "Hey you."

"Hey you." Jodi spoke at the same time.

They both laughed and Sam threw her arms around Jodi's waist, pulling her in tight. "I'm glad you could come down here." Just as she was about to release Jodi, she pulled her in again. "I've missed you."

With her arms also wrapped around Sam, Jodi smiled. "I've missed you too even though it's only been five days."

"It's only been five days? Huh, seems a lot longer than that." Couldn't possibly have anything to do with her marathon software writing session either. She slowly released Jodi from her arms and stepped back.

Jodi slipped her hands into her back pockets. "So, what have you been up to?"

She tried not to smile. She didn't want to give away her surprise—not yet. "Oh, not too much. Just been working on a few projects. Actually, I wouldn't mind getting your opinion on one if you've got a minute."

"Sure." Jodi then giggled. "But I've got to warn you, I'm totally inept with computers so all I'll be able to do is mostly nod and pretend I know what you're talking about."

"Don't worry about it. I wondered if you'd take a peek at a website I designed—tell me if you like it."

"Okay. I can do that." Jodi gave two thumbs-up.

"In that case, follow me." Her stomach now completely twisted in a knot, she led Jodi down the hallway. God, she hoped this was a good idea. Jodi was such a private person, she didn't want to invade that privacy. "I figured since you're a musician, you might get a kick out of this. It's a music site I did for someone—nothing big." She gave a dismissive wave beside her head as she turned into her office.

Jodi followed her into her office, glancing around the room at the multiple computers. "Wow, so this is where you spend most of your time?"

"I think I spend more time here than anywhere."

"Yeah, that's like my studio. I spend most of my time in there."

Sam grabbed the back of her chair and pulled it out for Jodi. "Here, why don't you take my chair?"

Jodi flopped down and cocked her head back, her eyes locking with Sam's. "Why thank you, miss."

Sam couldn't help but smile and brushed her lips lightly against Jodi's cheek. "Why, you're welcome, miss." She then pulled a second chair up to her desk and slid the keyboard over in front of her. "Now, remember—this is only a draft. So, let me know if there's something you'd change."

"Okay, but like I said, I'm not sure I'll be any help."

A couple mouse clicks later and the website popped up on the screen. "Well, here you go." She scooted to the side and bit down hard on her lip, watching Jodi as she scanned over the content.

Jodi sat up straight and leaned forward, both elbows on the desk and a deeply puzzled look creasing her forehead. Her mouth dropped open and she tilted her head first one way then the other. Finally, she clapped her hand to her mouth and pointed to the screen. "Holy shit. That's me." She then rounded on Sam, still pointing at the screen. "That's me."

"Yep, that's you." At the total look of shock on Jodi's face, Sam began to laugh. "So…do you like it?"

Jodi clapped her hands on Sam's shoulders and squeezed, emphasizing each word. "It's…it's…holy shit, Sam. I don't even know what to say. When did you do all this?"

Sam slumped back in her chair and wiped her damp forehead. She couldn't have asked for a better response. "Well, I'm so glad you like it. I've been working on it ever since you gave me the private concert. Kat helped me out with a lot of it."

"Kat helped with all this?" Jodi once again pointed to the computer screen. "She didn't say anything about it."

"I asked her not to say anything. I wanted it to be a surprise. She's been helping me with the pictures and information and I put it all together." Sam then let out a soft chuckle. "I don't know anything about music so I really couldn't have done it without her."

Jodi spun back around in her chair, leaning even closer to the screen as she took it all in. "This must have taken you forever."

"Actually, it didn't take as much as it might seem. Once I had the layout, it was simply a matter of adding information." Sam pointed to the homepage. "I even used a picture of the band playing onstage as the background."

"Wow, Sam. That's just too cool." Jodi breathed out the words, her mouth gaping wide open.

A huge smile now firmly plastered across her face, Sam scooted in so close that their chairs touched. She leaned over, her arm brushing against Jodi's, sending a shiver through her body, and continued pointing out features of the website. "And you see here, we have your upcoming tour dates. Over here is the link to all the lyrics. And this is the link to the history of the band—"

Jodi immediately snapped bolt upright, her voice now cold and every muscle in her body rigid. "I want to see that—now."

Sam froze, her chest seizing tight at the chilling tone of Jodi's words. *I want to see that—now.* From the sound of it, Jodi was about a second from storming out. Could this have been a mistake after all? Did she go too far? She'd give about anything to go back ten seconds and not mention the link to the band's history. Or better yet, leave it out altogether. But it was too late for that. So she bit down hard on her lip again and with a shaking hand, clicked the link.

Jodi stared at the page as it loaded, her brows deeply furrowed and her jaw set. Slowly, very slowly, she began to relax, no longer grinding her teeth as she read. "Wow, Sam, that was really good. Made me even want to read it to hear how the band got together."

"Oh, thank God." It had been a bit of a gamble putting a history section. She knew Jodi was very sensitive about her past, never talking about her music career before she lost her voice. But she had talked it over with Kat to only include everything since the band formed, nothing from Jodi's solo days.

"So, what else is there on here?" Jodi traced her finger over the screen.

"Well, there's some bio pages about you and the others. You know, pictures and a little info, instruments you play, stuff like that." She clicked on the link. Unlike the band history page, she didn't figure she had anything to worry about. Kat had helped her write everything and they had been deliberately vague.

As soon as the picture popped up of her playing guitar upside down, Jodi burst out laughing. "That's such a cool picture. I forgot I did that."

"Yeah, I love that picture too." Sam ran the cursor around the screen. "I noticed that you don't have your last name on the inside of your CDs so I only put your first name here too."

"Oh, good." Jodi continued to scan over the page, reading through the small bit of information Sam had included, mostly about her education and musical background.

"Well, if there's anything you don't want on here or that you would like included, let me know."

Jodi whirled around, a smile nearly ear to ear. "Geez, Sam. I can't think of anything I'd change. Everything looks perfect to me."

"I'm so glad you like it."

"What's not to like? You did a great job, Sam." Jodi spun around and leaned forward with her elbows on her knees. "Actually, I'm absolutely blown away with everything you've done here. So, how much do I owe you for all this?"

"*What?* Oh, please, you don't owe me anything. I didn't do it to get paid." As far as she was concerned, Jodi being happy with it was payment enough.

"Really? Sam, you didn't have to do that." Jodi slowly shook her head.

"Really, it was my pleasure. I had a great time putting it together. Like I said, this is what I do for fun." Sam then quickly snapped her fingers. "Oh, I almost forgot. I had an idea of something we could add if you like. I ran it by Kat and she was all for it but you'll have to tell me if it's even something you'd be interested in. You guys sell quite a few CDs at your performances, right?"

"On a good day, yeah. Why?" Jodi rolled her eyes.

Sam now slid to the edge of her seat. "Well, if you're interested, I can set up a merchant account and an online store where you merchandise right through your website."

Jodi stared at her, her mouth gaping open and closed. "You mean people could buy our CDs online?" She drew out each word.

"Definitely. And not only that, you could sell individual songs as downloadable MP3s, T-shirts, mugs, travel kits, lunch boxes—"

Jodi began to laugh. "Seriously, Sam, you could do that?"

"Oh, yeah. It wouldn't be a problem at all. I'd just have to set up a cart and checkout, which wouldn't be very hard. Believe me, there's just so much that can be done online." She might not understand what Jodi did with her guitar, but that didn't mean she couldn't appreciate her talent. And this website seemed like a natural way to embrace Jodi's love of music with her love of computers.

With her mouth still hanging open, Jodi slowly shook her head. "Sam, I…I…" She quickly glanced from the computer back to Sam, still trying to form words. "I…holy shit…I simply don't know what to say."

"I'm really glad you like it." Again, she couldn't have asked for a better response. Now she could relax. No more antacid and Pepto.

"*Like* it?" Jodi leaped from her chair and grabbed Sam by the hands, yanking her to her feet. She then wrapped her arms tight around her and planted a firm, full kiss on her lips. "Sam, I *love* it!"

* * *

Forty minutes later, Jodi bounced into her dad's office at the dealership. "Hi Dad." Since she had been downtown, she figured she'd drop in and see what he was doing. Besides, it had been a while since she stopped by.

Jim Price lifted his eyes from the paperwork littering his desk and immediately smiled. With his shirtsleeves rolled up and his hair silver around his temples, he was the picture of the quintessential businessman. Even to the slight paunch around his midsection. But it was his eyes that really got people's attention—piercing intense blue, just like Jodi's. "Well, hi sweetie. To what do I owe the pleasure?"

Jodi slid into the chair across from her dad. "I just wanted to stop in and see how everything's going. How are you doing? How's Mom?"

"We're doing pretty good. Although your mom would like to see you more often. She's beginning to think you've disappeared or something." He raised an eyebrow.

"Yeah, I know. I've been really busy lately. Sorry, Dad."

"No need to be sorry. We know you're busy. I keep telling your mom we need to get you working more at the dealership and then we'd both get to see you more. You know, you're welcome here any time. Your old man won't be able to do this forever and you'd be perfect for the job."

Oh God, not again. She slumped back against her chair, a deep groan rising up her throat. It had always been her dad's dream for her to take over the dealership someday. Even with her music career, it had always been assumed that she would take the reins when he stepped down. After all, she couldn't play guitar and tour around doing weekend gigs at clubs and women's festivals forever. But that would mean that she would have to actually talk to people and she didn't want to deal with their response to her voice. No, she would rather stay in her studio and play music. "I don't know, Dad. I…I don't think I'd be good at that."

"What are you talking about? You'd be great, a real natural just like me." Jim puffed himself up and gave her his best salesman's smile.

"Maybe someday, Dad…maybe someday. But for now, I have my music. That's what I love."

"I know, baby. Can't blame your old man for trying." He let out a dramatic sigh as he peered at her from across his desk. "Now tell me, what brings you downtown and don't tell me it was just to see your dear old dad."

Leave it to him to read her like a book. Nothing escaped him. "Well, Dad, you remember that girl, Sam, I told you about—the one I met after Pride a few weeks back. She wanted me to stop by her business."

"I see." Jim propped his elbows on his desk and leaned forward with his fingers steepled in front of him. "Hmmm… seems like you've spent quite a bit of time with this Sam lately. Is she treating you okay?"

She nearly laughed out loud at the stern look on her dad's face. Whether she was gay or straight, he'd always be her protective daddy. "Well actually, Dad, things are going really good. Trust me, you don't have to worry, not with Sam."

"I wouldn't worry so much if we actually got to meet her."

"I know. I know."

"You need to invite her up to Rose Cottage for grilled steaks."

"Dad, you'll use any excuse to grill."

"Maybe so, but you'd better ask this Sam or you know your mom—she'll call her up and invite her for you."

"Okay, okay. I'll invite Sam. Promise." She could just picture her mom calling up Sam and laying on the old guilt trip—how they never got to see their one and only daughter—until she gave in.

"Now that that's settled, what did you do? Go out to lunch with Sam?"

"No, it wasn't that. She's put together a website for the band. She's talking about setting up online sales, instant downloads, tour dates and all sorts of things like that." Jodi found herself talking faster and faster. She finally took a breath. "You wouldn't believe it."

"Wow. Sounds like it." Jim leaned back in his chair, his chin cradled in one hand. He tapped his finger to the side of his face. "Hmmm. Maybe I should have her look at our website. I haven't been really happy with it and we're paying a damn fortune."

"You know, Dad. You really should. Sam could really do a wonderful job. Plus, from what she says, she's cheaper than a lot of her competitors." That would definitely grab her dad's interest. One reason the dealership was so successful was that he was such a good businessman.

Jim slapped the arm of his chair. "Well, I'll have to set something up. After you bring her out to the cottage for steaks, of course."

"Of course, Dad."

"Good." Jim pushed back from his desk and stood. "Why don't you come walk the lot with your old man and then we'll go for lunch." He motioned for Jodi to join him.

"Okay, Dad. That sounds great." Jodi stood up and followed him out the door. Even though she was tall with her long legs, she still had to hustle to keep up with her dad. Once out on the lot, the heat wrapped around her like a thick woolen blanket after the cold air-conditioning inside.

Halfway across the lot, Jim stopped in front of a row of top-of-the-line SUVs. "So, when are you going to let me trade in that little Escape of yours and put you into something fancier like this?" He pointed to a black Explorer Limited.

"I love my Escape, Dad." She stood back and cringed at the Explorer. "That is *way* too big."

"You sure you wouldn't feel *safer* in something bigger." With his best salesman's pitch, Jim tried to sell her on the Explorer.

"Seriously, I'm okay with my little Escape, Dad." She wrapped her arm around her Dad and gave him a hug. That's why she loved him. He was only trying to be protective. Ever since she had nearly died in the accident, he had been trying to get her into a bigger car. At least he wasn't trying to get her to drive a huge Super Duty truck anymore. "Besides, I'd feel like I was driving around a bus."

"Well, if you're sure. But anytime you want something bigger, you come down here and we'll put you in it."

"Thanks, Dad." At the mistiness in her dad's eyes, Jodi patted him on his big barrel chest. He had taken her accident especially hard. Besides family, cars were his life. And since he had put her in the car in the first place, she knew he felt guilty that she was hurt, not that it was his fault. Just some damn drunk on a beer run. That's who stole her voice and scarred her body so horrifically.

Jim reached out with one arm and pulled her in tight. "So, how about we go get something to eat now?"

Jodi leaned her head against her dad's shoulder, swallowing back the bile that threatened to rise up in her throat once again. "I'd like that, Dad."

* * *

"Hey, boss. I'm getting ready to take off." Sandy poked her head into Sam's office.

Sam glanced up from her workstation. She had been setting up a shopping cart and inventory for the band's website. "Is it that time already?"

"'Fraid so. You've been pounding away in here all afternoon." Sandy leaned up against the doorway. "So, how'd it go with Jodi? Did she like the surprise?"

"Oh, yeah. She loved it, thank God." Sam leaned back in her chair and threw her hands behind her head. "Now I can relax a bit."

"But what made you think she *wouldn't* like it?"

"Sometimes you never know with Jodi. She doesn't like to talk about her past or anything to do with her accident, which I can totally understand. But then sometimes something will pop up, something will be said or she'll see something, and she'll either get all distant or angry or both. It's hard to say." Sam took a deep breath. "Damn, Sandy, it just sucks."

"Yeah, I can imagine. Geez, boss, if you don't mind me asking, aren't you worried you'll accidently say the wrong thing someday, I mean, even something innocent and you end up hurting her feelings?"

"You have no idea." She let out a long, low whistle. "I swear, Sandy, I worry about that all the time. Will I slip up and say the wrong thing and have Jodi storm out? Will she completely shut down? I've seen it before—someone will look at her oddly or hear her voice and get all weird, and then Jodi throws up all these walls and withdraws into herself. Like the first night I met her—she didn't speak a word—not a *single* word—for half the evening, just stayed to herself in her own little world. It's so sad. I only wish I could make everything all better so she never had to feel that hurt again."

"Well, she's lucky to have you, boss. Don't work too late." With a wave, Sandy disappeared down the hall.

Long after Sandy had left, Sam continued to lean back in her chair with her fingers intertwined behind her head. Sandy had said Jodi was lucky but really, *she* was the lucky one. If it weren't for Jodi, she'd be holed up with only her computers for company. And she wasn't doing anything that anyone else wouldn't do.

* * *

All the way home, Jodi kept thinking about what her dad had said about having Sam look at the dealership's website. She had no doubt her dad would love what she would come up with.

And if she could save him some money in return also, he would be ecstatic.

She also had to call Sam to invite her to her mom and dad's for a cookout at Rose Cottage or her mom *would* end up calling Sam and inviting her herself. Hopefully, this wouldn't be too soon for Sam. Bringing her home to meet the family was a big step. Besides, her parents could be a bit intimidating at times. She didn't want to scare Sam away.

Now completely lost in thought, she didn't see the light turn green until a horn honking behind her grabbed her attention. She glanced up in the rearview mirror and with a little giggle, she gave a wave to the driver behind her and pulled through the intersection. What was up with her anyway? She had no reason to be uptight. It was only Sunday dinner, nothing more than that. They'd just go there, eat, drink, talk and have fun. Sam wouldn't mind doing that, would she? Looking down at her white knuckles, she forced herself to release her iron grip on the steering wheel.

"Arg. That's it." She ripped her cell phone out of her hip holster, flipped open the lid and quickly scrolled down her contact list to Sam's cell number. If she didn't just get it over with, she'd go nuts. Seriously, what was the worst that could happen, her parents send Sam running from the house screaming? With a deep breath, she hit the dial button and listened as it rang— four, five, six. After the eighth ring, she slowly flipped her phone shut. Damn, just her luck. Although part of her was relieved, she still would have loved to hear Sam's voice.

Just as she was about to toss her cell phone in the passenger seat, it rang. She jumped and jerked the steering wheel, a small squeal escaping from her tires. She quickly regained control of her car, her heart now racing, and fumbled to flip open her phone. "Hello."

"Hey, Jodi, you okay there?" Sam giggled on the other end.

"Yeah, yeah." She glanced up in the rearview mirror, giving herself a wry smile. She'd be okay if she kept her car out of the ditch. "I wasn't ready when the phone rang and I almost dropped it."

"So, it's been what, all of five hours since we talked?"

She could hear the playfulness in Sam's voice. "Oh, has it been that long?" She tried to act innocent. "I thought it had been a lot longer than that."

"Nope, it's only been five hours." Sam giggled again lightly. "What's up?"

Now that she had Sam on the phone, she was simply going to have to blurt it out and get it over with. Besides, worst case, Sam would say no. "Well, I was having lunch with my dad and he wanted me to invite you over to their house for a cookout next Sunday, but it's okay if you don't want to go. Dad just—"

"I'd *love* to, Jodi."

"Wh…*what*? You'd *love* to?"

"Of course, silly. I'd love to go with you to your parents'."

"Um…well…great." Sam genuinely sounded excited. She had been scared she would think she was pushing things too quickly. Hey, come and meet the family, let's pick out linens and choose paint samples. Again wrapped up in her thoughts, she nearly missed her street. As distracted as she seemed, she probably shouldn't even be behind the wheel.

"Great." Sam's voice squeaked as she replied. "So, what are you up to right now?"

"Not much. I'm just driving home. How about you?"

"Not too much either. I'm just at home, bored."

"Oh, that's not good."

"Nope, it's not." Sam paused on the other end of the phone for a moment. "Hey, since you're out and about in your car, why don't you stop here?"

"Hmmm. If I did stop over, what would we do?"

Sam lowered her voice to a husky whisper. "I'm sure we could think of something."

"I'm sure we could." Jodi's breath caught in her throat. The last weekend they had spent together popped into her mind—Sam in her arms, brushing her soft, moist lips with hers. They most certainly could find something to do.

With her voice still low, Sam breathed into the phone. "How soon could you be here?"

"Twenty minutes."

Sam chuckled softly. "I can't wait."

She quickly pulled into her driveway, her tires chirping again, and without getting out, she threw her Escape in reverse and backed into the street. She hadn't been planning on seeing Sam tonight, but she certainly wasn't going to complain. And she definitely owed one to her dad. If it hadn't been for him insisting on inviting Sam to a Sunday cookout, she'd be spending the evening by herself, eating a TV dinner, drinking a Guinness and practicing scales on her guitar.

Less than fifteen minutes later, she squealed up in front of Sam's house. It was a good thing she hadn't passed any police on the way or she'd probably be the proud recipient of a ticket. Then again, it would have been worth it. She had met Sam outside her house to go out to dinner, but she hadn't been inside. She didn't want to read too much into things but she had the feeling she was going to be spending a lot of time at Sam's from now on and vice versa.

She jogged up the cobblestone path to Sam's front door. Her entire body tingled. She couldn't remember the last time she had felt like this. Certainly not since her accident. She had spent so much time shutting herself away from everyone, afraid that if she got involved with anyone, it would be a constant reminder of what she had lost. But when she was with Sam, none of that mattered. When she was with Sam, she felt normal, safe.

Just as her knuckles were about to hit the door, Sam yanked it open and wrapped her arms around her. "This is such a pleasant surprise." She stepped back with a wide grin, holding Jodi's hands in hers. "It's great to see you again."

"Yeah, it's great seeing you again too." Even though it had only been a few hours, she had been missing Sam already. More and more she missed Sam whenever they were apart.

Sam placed a hand on her hip. "Well, it's about time you came to see my house." She giggled, spoiling the scolding.

"Well, you know—you *could* have invited me earlier, Sam." Jodi mirrored her with a hand on her own hip. She really enjoyed their banter—light and easy. That had been missing from her life.

"Hmmm." Sam paused, tapping her finger against the side of her face. "I guess you've got me there. I *should* have invited you over a long time ago. At least you're here now."

"Yep. I'm here." She shifted her weight from one foot to the other and with her hands clasped behind her back, glanced around at the flowers lining Sam's porch. "Love your porch, by the way."

Sam slapped her forehead. "What am I thinking? Please, come in." She reached out and took Jodi by the hand, pulling her through the doorway.

"I was beginning to wonder if you were ever going to let me in."

"Yeah, well, it's all your fault, you know. I couldn't take my eyes off you."

"Oh, really. My fault, huh?" She threw an arm around Sam's waist, pulling her tight. "Well, now that you have me here, are you going to show me around?"

"You bet." With Jodi's arm still firmly around her waist, Sam led her around the house, stopping by each room—from the kitchen to the living room to the large home office filled with computer equipment. She finally wrapped up the tour outside her bedroom. "And that is my bedroom." She flashed a wide grin.

Jodi peeked into the bright sunny room. With the bamboo roman shades pulled up and the windows flung open, she had to squint the room was so bright. In the center, Sam's bed was neatly made, a stark contrast to her normally messy bed. "Wow. I love your bedroom but how can you stand it so bright?"

Sam stepped through the doorway and slowly spun around with her arms held out. "I wouldn't have it any other way. I love waking up to the sunshine and jumping out of bed."

"Arg. Not me. I need it dark when I sleep."

"Maybe if you weren't a vampire, Jodi, and slept at night, it wouldn't be a big deal." Sam poked her lightly in the ribs. She couldn't argue with Sam on that one. She hadn't seen a sunrise in years. "Besides, sometimes it's not a bad thing to have light in the bedroom."

"I see."

Sam leaned in close and lifted her eyebrows. "That's the idea."

Jodi's face was beginning to burn. From the feel of it, she must be a decent shade of salmon well on her way to brick. But how should she respond to Sam's flirting? A huge part of her wanted nothing more than to take Sam into her well-lit bedroom and see what she could see. Still, she didn't want to rush things. At least Sam seemed to be having quite a bit of fun with her.

"Yeah." Sam paused for a moment with her mouth open as if she were about to say something then thought better of it. "Hey, so how did lunch go with your dad?" Together, they walked back to the couch in the living room where Sam flopped down and patted the cushion beside her.

She slipped in beside Sam on the couch, tucking her leg under her. "Pretty good. Dad tried to get me to trade in my Escape on something bigger again." She gave her head a small shake. "He's always doing that."

"What's wrong with your Escape? I think it's really cute."

"So do I, but Dad's just being overly protective. He thinks a bigger car will give me more protection. Ever since...um... well, he's been worried." There it was again. No matter what, she couldn't get away from the past. It was the nightmare that never ended.

"Oh." Sam sucked in a quick breath and her eyes flew wide. She then quickly relaxed and bobbed her head as if nothing had happened. "I think all parents are overly protective."

Jodi glanced at Sam out of the corner of her eye. "Yeah, you're probably right." Once again, Sam didn't pry. Talk about refreshing. From her experience, most people wouldn't let it rest. They wanted to know everything—every gory detail. It was bad enough that every syllable, every glance in a mirror, was a constant reminder. She didn't need to relive it by talking about it also. Another quick glance over at Sam—yes, maybe she really was different—and she pushed the thought from her head. "Oh, I was meaning to tell you—I was telling Dad about the website you did for the band and he was interested in maybe having you take a look at the dealership's."

Sam sat up, her eyes wide. "Really?"

"Yeah, I told him you did such a wonderful job, he should have you do a new one for him."

Sam blew out a soft whistle. "Wow, Jodi. I don't know what to say."

"Just say you'll take a look at it."

"Yeah, yeah. I'll take a look at it."

"Great. Now, it's nothing definite but Dad will probably talk to you about it Sunday. Oh, and don't tell him I told you. He wants to think updating the website is his idea." She leaned over and winked.

"Okay, no problem." Sam scooted closer. "Thanks, Jodi. I really appreciate it."

"Oh, don't thank me yet, Sam. You can see what the old website looks like." She cringed and patted her on the knee. "Believe me, you're going to have your work cut out for you. It's a real mess."

Sam nearly bounced in her seat. "Oh, a challenge—I can't wait."

Jodi laughed as she watched Sam. It wasn't hard to tell she was excited, as if Christmas, New Year's and her birthday all came early. She glanced back over at Sam and their eyes locked. A deep shiver shot through her entire body, from the pit of her stomach to the tips of her fingers and toes. Suddenly, she wanted nothing more than to have Sam's body against hers, feeling the warmth of her skin, the beating of her heart. Slowly, they leaned closer and closer. She had to fight to catch her breath. Damn, was she going to pass out right there in Sam's arms? Finally, their lips touched, softness on softness, arms wrapped around arms, a long, low moan filling the late evening air.

CHAPTER EIGHT

On Sunday, Jodi pulled up in front of her parents' house on the east side of Kalamazoo Lake in Saugatuck. It was a large two-story dwelling overlooking the scenic lake dotted with cabin cruisers and speedboats puttering between the marinas and Lake Michigan. A large sprawling cedar deck circled the sides of the house to the front where it terraced down three levels toward the shore.

Sam stared out the window, her mouth gaping. "Jesus, Jodi, I thought you said we were going out to your parents' cottage?"

"Actually, this is." Jodi laughed and pointed to the intricate wrought-iron sign on the side of the house. "See? It's named Rose Cottage but everyone just calls it the cottage."

"I was picturing a small cabin beside a lake—you know, wicker chairs and a hammock. Maybe even an outhouse." Sam turned back to the house. "This place…holy shit, Jodi, this place is huge."

"Yeah, I know. Mom and Dad were looking for a getaway but when they found this, they fell in love with it, so they sold their house in East Grand Rapids."

"Wow." Sam continued to stare. She clutched the bottle of cabernet sauvignon in her lap.

Jodi leaned over and gently rubbed Sam's shoulder. If the knots in her muscles were any indication, Sam was pretty nervous. The size of the house probably didn't help either. The first time she had seen it, she had been a little overwhelmed herself. But her parents were going to love Sam, especially her dad if she could update the website *and* save him money. "Don't worry. It will be okay."

Sam let out an anxious giggle. "I don't know, Jodi. I feel like I'm back in high school and about to meet my girlfriend's family for the first time."

"Wow, you had a girlfriend in high school?" Jodi nudged her in the side with her elbow. "Damn girl, I'm impressed. Took me until college."

Sam gave her a wry smile. "Yeah, right. You know what I mean. I'm afraid your parents won't like me or I'll make an ass of myself or something."

Jodi pulled her close until their foreheads touched. "Sam, don't worry. They're going to love you. And if it will help, I'll make an ass of myself also."

At last, Sam laughed. "You're the best, Jodi. I don't know what I've done to deserve you."

Jodi swallowed funny and began coughing. "Actually, Sam, it's you that's the best."

Sam raised her eyebrows. "We'll see if you still feel that way when it's your turn to meet my mom."

Jodi sucked in a quick breath. "Oh, I hadn't thought of that."

Sam giggled, still sounding nervous. "Now, see what I mean?"

"Yeah, I guess." Jodi felt her chest tighten. She definitely wasn't looking forward to meeting Sam's mom. What if she freaked when she heard her horrible voice? What if she didn't think she was good enough for her daughter? What if? But Sam truly didn't have anything to worry about. Sam was the sweetest and kindest woman she had ever met and her parents would see that too. She patted her on the knee. "Seriously, hon, it's going to be fine. They're going to love you."

"I hope so." Sam spun the bottle of wine around in her hands.

"They will." Jodi leaned in and quickly brushed Sam's cheek with her lips. She paused, savoring the smooth, soft warmth of Sam's skin, then finally with a guttural groan, she threw open the door. "Well, we'd better get going before they wonder why we're still sitting out here in the driveway."

Sam took one last deep breath before opening her door. She joined Jodi in front of the car. With the bottle of wine in one hand, she stood up straight, smoothing her shirt, and then clasped Jodi's hand in her other, giving it a firm squeeze. "Okay, I'm ready."

Together, they walked along the side of the house to the front facing the lake, their feet crunching on the crushed stone. As they rounded the corner and stepped around the forsythia bush that was getting out of control, Jodi led Sam up the stained cedar steps to the main deck. Jim Price stood before the grill with his back to them. "Hi Dad."

Dressed in a flower-print apron, Jim spun around with a long spatula in his hand. "Well, hi there, sweetheart. I'm glad you're here." He walked up and gave Jodi a big bear hug. He then lowered his voice and nodded his head sideways toward the house. "Your mom keeps threatening to put me to work in the kitchen. I told her I had to get the grill going but I don't think she's buying it." He let out a big belly laugh.

"So, what's Mom doing?"

"Oh, you know her. She's in the kitchen coming up with some sort of culinary creation." Jim shook his head. "I told her all we needed was steaks and mushrooms but try telling her that."

Jodi giggled as she patted her dad on his wide chest. "Yeah, I know, Dad."

After giving Jodi another hug, one-armed this time, Jim turned to Sam. "So, you must be the Sam I've heard all about." He stepped back and gave her a wide smile.

"Um, yes, sir."

"Bah, no sirs here. Call me Jim." He threw out his arm and pulled Sam in, giving her a one-armed hug the same as he had given Jodi.

With Jim's large arm around her shoulders, Sam chuckled. "Okay, Jim."

"Come on, Dad. You're going to scare her away." Jodi shot a quick glance at her dad. Why was he making such a fuss over Sam? He was treating her as if she were already a part of the family. He had never done that with any of the other girls she had brought home. Then again, she hadn't brought anyone home since her accident. Maybe that was why he was being extra nice.

Jim finally let go of Sam but not before his eyes became misty. "Why don't you head on in and give your mom a hand." With a wide smile, he turned back to the grill.

Jodi led Sam to the house and gave her a quick peck on the cheek. She turned and opened the glass slider, pulling Sam close until they were only inches apart. "Make yourself at home." With a wink, she took Sam's hand and led her into the large open kitchen, tiled in tan stone with matching maple hardwood cabinets. Pots and pans hung from the ceiling overhead, reminding her of an Italian bistro. Her mom, Diane, prepared the salad at the large kitchen island in the center of the room. Jodi stepped up with her hand resting on the small of Sam's back. "Hi Mom."

"Well, hello to you too. I'm glad you're finally here. I could use some help. Your dad is outside pretending to be busy with the grill." Diane peered up from the countertop, giving Jodi a warm but guarded smile.

"Well, Mom, you know Dad. He likes to disappear whenever you even mention the word kitchen."

Diane then glanced from Jodi to Sam. "So, are you going to introduce me to your friend?"

"Oh, yeah." With her hand still resting on the center of Sam's back, Jodi stepped forward. "Mom, this is Sam. Sam, this is my mom, Diane."

Sam glanced from Jodi to Diane. It was easy to see where Jodi got her looks. Diane was Jodi, tall and lanky, just older with gray streaks in her jaw-length black hair versus Jodi's short spiky jet-black hair. "It's a pleasure to meet you, Mrs. Price."

Diane tipped her head toward Sam, a thin smile on her lips. "Likewise."

With a quick glance to Jodi, Sam cringed. She then stepped up to the kitchen island and held up the bottle of cabernet sauvignon. "I brought a bottle of wine." She held the bottle out for Diane.

Unable to hide a look of surprise, Diane slowly set the knife down on the countertop and took the bottle from Sam, holding it up in front of her. "Fenn Valley Cabernet Sauvignon? That's my favorite. How were you able to get this? They've been sold out for months."

"My mom had a couple of bottles so I grabbed one from her."

"Well, thank you." Diane nodded to Sam. "This will go perfectly with dinner."

Jodi hopped up beside Sam. "I'd like a Guinness instead."

"Jodi Lynn Price, show some class." Diane eyed her with a frown. "*Wine* is for dinner. *Beer* is for after."

With a loud groan, Jodi slumped against the kitchen island with her arms crossed in front of her. She'd much rather have Guinness but she couldn't argue with her mom's sense of refinement. That was a losing battle. "Okay, Mom, I guess."

"Well, since your father took off, why don't you girls help out?" Diane slid a ripe tomato and clump of carrots across the counter.

"Okay, Mom." Jodi pulled a knife from the block then turned to Sam. She lowered her voice. "You don't have to help out."

Sam reached over, grabbed a knife of her own, and pulled the carrots to her. "Don't be ridiculous. I'd love to help."

Diane looked up from the opposite side of the island bench. "So, Sam, what do your parents do for a living?"

Without a pause, Sam continued to slice up carrots, the blade a blur. "Well, my mom is the Dean of Student Services at Grand Valley. It keeps her very busy."

Diane continued shredding lettuce. "I can imagine. That would be a very demanding position. So, what does your father do?"

Jodi jerked while cutting a tomato, nearly taking the tip of her finger off with the knife. Dear God, don't let Sam bring up the sperm sample. The mood her mom was in, she'd probably keel over.

"It's only Mom and me. I don't have a father."

"Oh, I *see*." Diane glanced up and crossed her arms. "I'm sorry to hear that."

"It's no big deal. Mom was great when I was growing up. She was both mom and dad." Sam let out a soft giggle. "I never felt like I was missing something. She made sure of that."

Jodi stared at her mom. This wasn't like her. Why was she asking so many questions, especially *these* questions? It was as if she were interrogating Sam. What was going on? "Hey, Mom, I'm sure there will be plenty of time for questions during dinner."

Diane turned to Jodi, placing her right hand to her chest. "I was only being friendly."

Now, she knew there was something up. Her mom never asked a bunch of questions only to be friendly. Something was going on and whatever it was, she hoped her mom didn't offend Sam. She quickly changed the subject. "So, how was the meeting at the Chamber of Commerce last week?"

"Oh, I was elected secretary again." Diane let out a laugh although it sounded forced. "If you ask me, it's only because no one else wants the job with all the notes and minutes."

"Someone's got to do it, right, Mom?" Apparently the interrogation was over for now but first chance she got, she was going to find out what was going on. Sam didn't need someone drilling her all afternoon.

"You know, Jodi, someday you could be involved with the Chamber."

"I'm not sure that's really for me, Mom. I don't need a bunch of people staring at me every time I open my mouth."

Diane flinched, almost as if she had been slapped. "I was just saying that I think you'd be good at it."

"You know, Mom, all I want to do for now is concentrate on my music." She had no interest in being on the Chamber of Commerce. Her mom knew that. Something was definitely up.

"I know, honey. I was just saying…" She trailed off.

At the silence, Sam chimed in. "Speaking of music, Jodi was fabulous at her last show. The crowd was absolutely blown away."

Jodi bumped her hip against Sam's and shot her a smile. Not for the first time, Sam seemed to know just the right thing to say. "It *was* a really good show." She then turned to her mom. "You should see the website Sam made for the band. You wouldn't believe what it looks like."

Diane smiled, her lips pinched. "So I've heard. That's all your father's been talking about for the last four days. He checked it out online and has been going on and on about it."

"Really? Dad checked it out?"

"Oh, yeah. He's been going on about how the dealership's website looks horrible compared to your band's." Diane rolled her eyes. "I believe his exact words were, 'looks like shit.'" She lowered her voice to imitate Jim and began to laugh, the first genuine laugh Jodi had heard since they had arrived.

Jodi and Sam both burst out laughing. "That sounds like Dad!" She blotted the corner of her eye. Maybe her mom was having an off moment earlier.

"Speak of the devil." Diane pointed to Jim as he walked into the kitchen still wearing the flower-print apron.

He froze in midstep and opened his eyes wide. "What?"

"Nothing, dear. We were just talking about you."

"Oh, okay." Jim shrugged it off as if it were nothing. "I'm ready for the steaks. Have they been marinating?"

"Yes, dear. They're over on the counter by the fridge—right where you left them." Diane pointed over her shoulder.

"Great, great, great." Jim walked up behind Jodi and Sam, wrapping an arm around each. "I'm going to need some help, so which one of you lovely young ladies would like to assist me?"

"Why don't you take your daughter? Sam can stay in here and we can chat." Diane tried to act nonchalant but the tension in her stance betrayed her.

Without a glance at Diane, Jim shook his head. "I don't think so. I'm going to have this beautiful young woman help me." He smiled at Sam. "We have a little business to discuss."

Sam followed Jim across the kitchen. While he stacked the thick slabs of deeply marbled steak on individual stoneware plates, she glanced back to Jodi with a half-smile, half-wince.

Jodi mouthed the words, "You'll be fine." Thank God her dad had plans of his own. There was no way she was going to leave Sam alone with her mom until she found out what was going on.

After Sam followed Jim out to the grill, both holding a plate in each hand, Diane cleared her throat. "Your dad sure seems to have taken a liking to your new friend." Her voice anything but warm, she busied herself with slicing mushrooms to sauté.

"Yeah, he sure has." Jodi stared at her mom, her eyes narrowed. What could she have against Sam? She had never met her before. Yet she obviously didn't like her. Finally, she walked around the island and stood beside her. "Hey, Mom, what's up?"

"I don't know what you mean." Diane continued to stare down at the pile of mushrooms as she diligently sliced them with the large kitchen knife.

"Oh, come on, Mom. You've been giving Sam the third degree. *What* do you have against her?"

"It's not that. I mean…well, how well do you even know this girl, Jodi? How do you know if you can trust her?" Diane set the knife down but didn't meet Jodi's eyes.

"Whoa, where's all this coming from, Mom? Sam's great. She's the first person I've met since my accident who has looked at me simply for who I am, not someone covered in scars with a freaky, screwed-up voice."

Diane cringed. "I don't want anyone hurting you, honey. This Sam might be trying to take advantage of you *because* of your voice. She could be preying on your vulnerability and using that to manipulate you."

Jodi dug her fingers in her hair and shook her head in frustration. She'd have thought her mom would have been happy that she had found someone. Why was she so determined to attack Sam? "Why would she want to do that? Mom, seriously, where is all this coming from? Sam hasn't done anything like that. She's been nothing but kind and understanding. She hasn't once said anything about my voice. She treats me like a normal person—a *normal* person, Mom."

Diane looked up and met Jodi's eyes. She brushed away a tear. "Baby, I just want you to be happy. I don't want you to get hurt."

"Mom, I am happy. Sam makes me happy." Jodi fought back tears. Why couldn't her mom accept that Sam made her happy? Why was it so hard for her to believe that?

"Are you sure?" Diane's voice cracked as she placed her hands on Jodi's shoulders.

"Yes, Mom. I really am." Jodi stared directly into Diane's eyes. "Sam is great, Mom. Please give her a chance and get to know her."

"Okay, baby. I'll try to get to know her." Diane sniffled, dabbed both eyes with the side of her hand, and then tried to smile. "You'll have to forgive me. I'm your mother and I don't want to see anything else bad ever happen to you." She reached out and with her thumb lightly traced the deep scars on Jodi's throat.

"I love you, Mom. Trust me, you don't have anything to worry about with Sam." Jodi threw her arms around her mom and pulled her into a big hug. Her mom meant well in her overprotective way. Her accident had not only changed her life forever, but also her mom and dad's. That's why she liked Sam so much—she looked at her as if her accident had never happened. When she was with her, she could almost forget it had happened at all—almost.

"I love you too, baby." Diane stepped back, still holding Jodi with a hand on each shoulder. "And I'll try to give this Sam a chance."

* * *

Sam quickly glanced back at Jodi as she followed Jim out to the grill with the steaks. She would have given anything to stay with her but as Jim put it, they had business to discuss. At least, she didn't have to stay in the kitchen with Diane, thank God. Even though they had just met, she had the distinct feeling Diane didn't like her at all. And what was up with all the questions? Still, she didn't want it to ruin the afternoon. This was important to Jodi so she would make the best of it no matter what.

"So, I sure hope you're hungry." Jim slipped the two plates he carried beside the grill and turned to take the two Sam carried from her. "These are prime cut Angus, marinated in my special blend." He gave a huge wink.

"They look delicious." Sam stood beside Jim and closed her eyes, inhaling the intense aroma that wafted up as each steak hit the grill. Her mouth began to water immediately.

Jim gave each steak a hefty poke with the long grilling fork, perhaps just for good measure. Then, setting his shoulders, he turned to face Sam. "Now that we're alone, I was meaning to talk to you about that website you made for Jodi. I'll be the first to tell you, I don't know a damn thing about music or what Jodi does with her band, but I do know quality when I see it and that site you made was quality work. Everything appeared professional, fresh and most importantly, interesting. The way everything was laid out made me want to continue looking. And as I'm sure you know, Sam, that's very important in business."

"Yes, sir." That was one of the first things she had learned in business—it didn't matter how things looked, without customer interest, people were unlikely to buy. In Jodi's case, it wasn't just the CDs—they were also selling the band.

"Please, call me Jim." He flashed her a warm, easy smile. "Now, I would like to talk to you businessman to well, I guess, businesswoman. I have a website for my dealership but it certainly doesn't have the pizzazz of the site you designed for Jodi. Hell, I don't know if anyone even looks at it." He leaned in close. "I want that to change."

Thank God Jodi had given her a heads-up so she was able to check out the website for J.P. Motors. She had a pretty good idea what she was dealing with. "Well, Jim, hope you don't mind but after Jodi mentioned this to me, I took a peek at what you have currently."

Jim let out a deep rolling chuckle. "Not at all. I like someone who's prepared and takes initiative."

"Good." Sam settled on her feet. "If you don't mind my bluntness, your website is way out of date. If it were a car, we're talking circa nineteen-fifty—something with tailfins and portholes."

Jim smiled. "A car girl, huh?"

"Not really. I just mean that we're talking very antiquated technology. The site isn't much more than plain HTML and frames."

"I'm afraid you've lost me. I don't understand all that techno mumbo-jumbo." Jim clapped Sam on the shoulder. "Just put it in terms this old fart can understand."

She had to fight back laughter. As much as she liked Jim already, businesswomen didn't giggle during a sales presentation. "Okay. Let's put it this way. I don't think your site's been updated in at least five years. It was probably cutting edge when it first came out but now it's clumsy and amateurish by today's standards. And you're probably paying way too much for hosting and maintenance for what you get back from it."

Jim thought for a long moment. "That's what I wanted to hear. I want someone who will tell me how it is and look out for my best interests. Now, tell me what you'd do if you were to design a site for J.P. Motors."

She was ready for this. Over the past few days, she'd given a lot of thought to what she'd do with the site. She had some great ideas. At least she thought they were great ideas. Now, all she had to do was convince Jim. "I was thinking, what is it that most people are interested in when they come to your dealership?"

"Why, that's easy. They're looking at the cars."

"That's right. So, shouldn't a website for J.P. Motors provide the same thing online?"

"That makes sense." Jim stroked his chin as he thought. "But how would we do that?"

"Simple. We can tie in the inventory so it can be browsed online. At any moment, someone can get on the computer and see exactly what cars are setting on the lot. They can email a salesperson and get quotes, hear about the options or even schedule a demo. This works with the used car sales too." Sam found herself excitedly listing off what could be done. This was what she liked most about this work. In some ways, the sky was the limit.

"I had no idea you could do all that." Jim wrinkled his brow. "Sounds very complicated and expensive."

"Not really." She took a deep breath. Now she was on a roll. "Once it's set up, it's really easy to update inventory. I'll provide a very simple user interface that anyone can use. The hardest part would be that someone would have to walk out to the lot and take a picture of the car."

Jim barked out a loud laugh, echoing off the front of the house. "I must tell you, Sam, I like what I'm hearing."

"I'm glad to hear that." She didn't want to seem too pushy but now came the sale. "I'd love to design a site for your dealership, Jim. I think we can put together something with a lot of pizzazz and also save you a bit of cash in the long run."

"I think we can do that. Stop down sometime next week and we can hammer out all the details." Jim gave a firm nod.

"That sounds great, Jim." She had to resist the urge to jump up and down. This was a big deal. It could easily lead to more high-profile business sites. And she had Jodi to thank.

Jim stabbed one of the steaks with the long grill fork and rolled up a corner, peeking underneath at the deep crisscrossing sear marks. "Good, good. Now that we have that settled, there's one more thing I would like to discuss."

"Sure, Jim. Anything."

Jim leveled a stern look at her. "My daughter."

In an instant, her chest seized, cutting off all breath, and her mouth went bone-dry. Had she read the situation wrongly? Did Jim only invite her here to talk business but wanted her to have nothing to do with Jodi? That would be pretty low. And after how Jodi's mom was acting in the kitchen, did the entire family have it out for her? "Sir, Jodi and I—"

Jim held up his hand, stopping her before she could say anything more. He then slowly flipped the steaks on the grill before turning to face her directly. "I just wanted to tell you that the difference I've seen in Jodi recently warms the heart of this old man and I think we have you to thank for that." He offered a warm, open smile.

"I...I..." What could she say? She couldn't take credit for that. She hadn't done anything special. "Sir, I don't know how much I've had to do with it."

"Well, I do. Trust this father, I know my little girl, and since she's met you, she's like the Jodi we knew before..." His voice then broke and he held up a finger while he looked away, swallowing back tears.

A hard, painful lump lodged in Sam's throat. She knew Jodi had had a rough time since her accident and that had to be hard not only on her but on everyone who loved her. But she couldn't take the credit for any changes in her. All she had been was a friend. Well, maybe a bit more than a friend, but still. "Jim, really I haven't done anything."

"Please. You've done plenty. Whatever you've done, you've made our little girl happy. Since her accident, she has been so angry, so miserable. She didn't smile. She didn't laugh. It has just about broken our hearts seeing our baby so miserable. I don't know how much she's told you about what happened to her."

"Well, I know a little bit. Her friends filled me in on a few things. But actually, Jodi and I have never talked about it."

Jim raised his eyebrows. "You mean to tell me, you've *never* talked about her accident?"

"No, sir. I figured if she ever wanted to tell me, she would, but I wasn't going to push her. If not, I understand." She shrugged. What more could she do? It wasn't her place to force Jodi to relive something so painful.

Jim stepped back as he eyed her, a slow smile lifting his lips. "Sam, you truly are an impressive young woman. No wonder Jodi likes you so much. There aren't many people who could simply let it rest without wanting to know all about something like Jodi's accident. It's only natural curiosity."

"I have to admit, I have been curious. I mean, I can't imagine what she's been through. I can see how much it bothers her, especially her voice, and I see how other people look at her sometimes. But it makes me so angry to see people treat her the way they do."

"I know what you mean. I have to fight my fatherly instinct not to pound them a good one." Jim chuckled although it sounded harsh. "It's probably not my place, but there's something I think you should know about how hard it has been on Jodi that she lost her voice. You knew she used to be a professional singer?"

"Yes, I did know that. I've heard her sing on some of her old CDs but I haven't told her that."

"That's probably a good thing." Jim sucked in a deep breath before continuing. "Her accident was pretty severe. She was cut up pretty badly. Huge blood loss, nerve damage to her vocal chords. We weren't sure she was even going to make it for over a week. Then when she woke and found that her voice was gone, at least the voice she used to have, she lost her will to live. All she wanted to do was sleep all the time. She wouldn't eat. She wouldn't drink. Whenever someone walked into her room, she turned away from them. No parent ever wants to see their child suffering like that. Nothing we did seemed to make a difference."

She hadn't heard any of this before. All she knew was that Jodi had been in a severe accident that robbed her of her voice and scarred her body, not the horrific struggles and intense suffering she endured. Even picturing that now, she had to swallow hard.

"She was in the hospital for nearly two months. When we brought her home, we thought she'd snap out of it. She would be at her house, surrounded by her guitars and everything. But she didn't seem to get any better. A week later, she overdosed on the Vicodin they gave her. I found her just in time." Jim held his fist up to his mouth and lowered his chin slightly, swallowing hard.

Sam clapped her hands to her mouth. "Oh my God. I never knew that, sir. I…I don't know what to say."

"You don't have to say anything." He looked up, his eyes moist. "I just want you to understand what Jodi's been through. And also to know why we are so thankful to you for bringing our old Jodi back to us."

"All I've done is tried to be a good a friend, sir." Why did everyone keep praising her? She hadn't done anything special. "I'm just glad she seems a lot happier."

"I'm glad too, Sam." Jim threw an arm around her and pulled her in tight as if she were his own daughter. "And please, it's Jim."

"She's a very special woman. And I promise never to do anything to hurt her." She hugged him back.

"I'm sure you won't." He gave her another firm squeeze. "One more thing though, don't be surprised if there comes a day when Jodi does everything in her power to push you away. She did that with everyone after her accident, including her mom and me. The doctors said something about the loss seeming worse for her when she's close to someone. Now, I don't pretend to understand it but I want you to know. Just be ready." He accentuated his point with the grill fork before turning back to check the steaks.

"Hey, how are those steaks coming?" Jodi called out from the glass slider.

Both Jim and Sam jumped, much like two kids caught up to no good, and they began to laugh. Jim stabbed a steak again and called over his shoulder back up to the house. "They should be done in just a minute."

Jodi leaned back inside, shouted something to her mom, and then strolled slowly down the deck, stepping up behind Sam and wrapping her arms tightly around her waist. "So, what have you two been talking about out here?"

Sam threw her arm around Jodi as they stood beside the grill, watching Jim fuss with the steaks. "Oh, your dad is really interested in having me do his website. We're going to hammer out the details next week."

"Hey, that's great." Jodi pulled her closer and gave her a tender kiss on the cheek.

"Mmmm." Sam closed her eyes, savoring the feel of Jodi's warm, soft lips on her skin. When she finally opened her eyes, she bent in close and whispered in Jodi's ear. "Thanks, by the way."

Jodi pulled back, still holding her by the waist. "For what?"

"For recommending me to your dad. I probably would never have had a chance like this without your help." After the chat with Jim, she was definitely looking forward to working with him. Now if she could only win over Diane.

While she stood by the grill with Jodi, their arms lazily around each other's waist, she continued working the plans for the website in her head. So many possibilities, she wished she had her computer right there. Still, she wouldn't want to give up having Jodi's arm around her.

Jim stabbed a steak and flipped it, carefully surveying the juice bubbling up. "Oh, good, they're done." He then picked up a plate and slid the charred T-bone off the grill. Jodi and Sam each took a plate and waited while Jim pulled the other steaks from the fire.

Sam held the plate under her nose and breathed in the steam rising up. "Oh, God, this smells so good."

With a plate in each hand, Jodi ran one under her nose. "Mmmm. You're right. You really outdid yourself this time, Dad."

With the last plate in his hand, he puffed up his chest. "I'm glad you think so."

"You know what would go perfectly with this?" Jodi raised her eyebrows in anticipation. "A Guinness."

Sam quickly covered her mouth, hiding the smile on her lips. Jodi was so predictable. Give her a Guinness and she was happy as can be.

"Sorry, but you know your mom. No beer for dinner." Jim then leaned in closer and gave Jodi a wink. "Maybe later."

"Ahhhh." Jodi grumbled and stomped a few steps like an unruly toddler before she glanced over at Sam and started giggling.

"Holy cow." Sam stared wide-eyed with her mouth hanging open. "Was that a Guinness tantrum?"

"Yeah, something like that."

Jim watched Jodi and Sam's antics, a smile on his face. "Well, come on, girls. Let's get these inside so we can eat."

She hadn't had a father growing up and for the most part, she had never missed that. Her mom was great. But hearing Jim include her as if she were also a part of the family really touched her, more than she had thought possible. His kindness and caring made her feel completely welcome. She could easily see that maybe someday she could come to think of him as the father she never had.

Diane met them at the slider, taking the extra plate out of Jodi's hand. "This looks delicious, dear."

"We aim to please." Jim stood up tall and strutted, a huge schoolboy grin lifting his lips.

"Everything's ready so let's gather around." Diane led the way to the large mahogany table in the dining room overlooking the cove on the lake. A rustic dark ceiling fan slowly paddled overhead.

Sam slipped in between Jodi and Jim. Soon, the sounds of clanking plates and silverware rose from the table as everyone grabbed dishes, doled out a serving onto their plates and passed it along to the next. Just as she reached for the vinaigrette dressing for her salad, she noticed the full wineglass in front of her. She glanced quickly across the table to be met with a bright smile from Diane.

"Yes, and we have Sam to thank for the lovely wine. You are very thoughtful and generous." Diane lifted her glass and tilted it toward Sam. "We are glad to have you here with us today."

"Um, you're welcome." Try as she might, Sam couldn't quite hide the surprise from her face. Could this be the same woman who had drilled her with question after question? What on earth had happened while she was outside? She then caught the gentle smile on Jodi's lips and she knew. Jodi must have said something to her mom while she was outside talking to Jim. Whatever it was, it had seemed to work. Returning Jodi's smile, she mouthed, "Thank you."

* * *

After dinner, Jodi stepped into the upstairs guest bathroom to change into her bathing suit. Her dad always liked to go out on the boat after Sunday dinner and the best way to enjoy the ride fully was to lounge on the bow of the boat. Right now, Sam was using the bathroom downstairs off the family room to change. Jodi wouldn't have minded sharing the bathroom with her but even if she had promised not to peek, that would only be a lie. She wouldn't be able to avert her eyes from Sam's naked body.

She quickly slipped into her swimsuit and tied a wrap around her waist to hide the good six inches of deep rippled scar still visible on her left hip. She must have tried on fifty different suits until she found one that covered her scars—or at least most of them. At least this side cutout one-piece on her long, slender frame gave the impression that she actually had a waist, which looked good with her small breasts. She wouldn't be caught in one of those frilly bikinis, probably in pink no less, that took five times more chest than she had to fill. Those just made her look like a very tall, scrawny ten-year-old. With one last peek into the mirror, she ruffled her short hair with her fingers and kicked open the door to find Sam.

When she got downstairs, the bathroom door hung open and Sam was nowhere in sight. With a towel slung over her shoulder, she strolled out on the deck and draped her long arms over the railing, looking down at the lake. Sam stood on the dock, talking to her dad as he prepped the boat. Just then, her mom, already lounging on the deck of the boat, rolled her head back and laughed at something Sam had said. It had been a rough start but her mom seemed to be warming up to Sam nicely. She didn't have to worry about her dad. He was completely taken with Sam, which she could completely understand. There was something about Sam, something infectious, something she certainly couldn't resist.

Jodi quickly trotted down the long series of steps to the dock. She was dying to see Sam in her bathing suit, but as she bounced up beside her, she was apparently going to have to wait a bit longer since Sam had a light wrap around her shoulders, covering everything. "Hey, I looked for you in the house."

"Oh, yeah. I got changed and decided to wander down here. Your dad has been filling me in on boating." Her eyes traveled up and down Jodi as she spoke.

At Sam's intense gaze, she tried not to blush. It had been a long time since anyone had looked at her like that. "Well, I hope Dad hasn't been boring you too much." She let out a nervous giggle.

Sam finally tore her eyes from Jodi, but not before biting her lower lip and sucking in a slow breath. "Not at all. It's really fascinating. I never knew there was so much to it."

"Wow. Dad's going to love you. He'll have someone to share all his boating knowledge with who will actually listen."

"I heard that." Without looking up, Jim was busy checking the engine.

"Sorry, Dad." They both burst out laughing like a couple of teenage girls at a slumber party.

Diane sat on the boat, smiling as she watched the two.

Jodi then leaned in, her lips softly brushing Sam's ear. "So, when do I get to see what you're wearing?"

Sam raised her eyebrows, giving Jodi a sly grin. "Just be patient."

"Oh, come on."

"Mmmm. But I haven't finished checking you out yet." Sam once again slowly ogled her up and down, a deep hunger in her eyes.

This time she wasn't able to keep from blushing. She had never had anyone make her feel as desirable as Sam did, even before her accident. Sam also made her feel as if her accident had never happened.

"Are you girls ready to get onboard?" Jim stood in the boat and held a hand out.

Sam took Jim's hand, stepping carefully from the dock into the boat. Jodi quickly followed. She grabbed Sam by the hand and led the way to the front of the boat where they sat up on the deck. Jim and Diane sat together behind the wheel, Diane with her head on Jim's shoulder. After starting the boat, he hollered out. "Are my girls ready up there?"

"Yep, we're ready, Dad." Jodi squeezed Sam's hand. "How about you?"

"Almost." Sam slipped out of the wrap, revealing a small emerald green string bikini clinging to her taut body. The color accented Sam's fiery red hair. "Well, I hope you like." She then bit her bottom lip, completing the image.

Jodi took in all of Sam, the adorable way she bit her lip when unsure, her slightly freckled pale skin, her perky full breasts straining against the thin fabric, her firm nipples two erect points in the light lake breeze. The string bikini bottom clung tightly to the swell of her hips. And to top it off, she was becoming aroused, more aroused than she had been in a long time. She tried to sit still but as her arousal built, she squirmed in her seat. Finally, she shook her head, bringing herself back to reality. Barely more than a whisper, all she could utter was, "Wow."

"So, you do like it, right?"

Her mouth now gaping open, Jodi slowly bobbed her head up and down. "Uh-huh. I definitely like."

With a wide grin, Sam leaned closer. "Good. I'm glad. I was nervous at first to wear this, especially around your parents for the first time."

Jodi quickly glanced over her shoulder. Here she had been so mesmerized by Sam, taking in every inch of her firm, smooth body, she had completely forgotten her parents were right behind them. "Well, you look absolutely gorgeous. It was definitely worth the wait."

"You know what they say—good things come to those who wait." Sam slid in closer and slipped her arm around Jodi's waist, her head against Jodi's shoulder.

With Sam pressed tightly to her body and the shoreline slowly pulling away, Jodi leaned down and softly kissed the top of her head. Never in a million years would she have thought someone could warm her heart as much as Sam. Even as they picked up speed, the cool mist spraying up over the bow did little to dampen the heat building inside her. Yes, good things *did* come to those who wait.

CHAPTER NINE

Jodi sat in her studio, wearing only a pair of denim cutoffs and a baggy black tank top, the sun streaming through the windows. With her eyes closed, she turned her face to the light, the warmth softly caressing her skin, and played her new purple Paul Reed Smith guitar, a super slow howling solo. Anything to take her mind off Sam. All morning, she had been fighting the urge to call her. Every few minutes, she would pick up the phone then put it down. She had even dialed Sam's number once before she pushed the phone away. Normally, it wouldn't be a big deal. She could call Sam anytime and it was an odd day if they didn't talk at least three times. But today, Sam was meeting her dad and she was keen to know how it went. She was sure everything would go well. Sam was brilliant when it came to computers and her dad was able to see when something would benefit his business. Still, her stomach fluttered as she stared at the phone, willing it to ring.

Finally, she set the guitar in the stand. It was no use. She needed to move on before she went totally batty. She jumped up from her stool and marched over to behind her piano and dragged out another guitar case. With a deep breath, she opened the lid and pulled out her Jose Ramirez Elite Classical guitar, the same guitar she had played at Juilliard. She hadn't played it much since then, and not once since her accident.

Slowly, she ran her fingers over the wide-spaced nylon strings and then lifted the guitar to her chest. With her left hand, she tuned each string as she gently plucked it by the bridge with her right. She began fingerpicking a simple classical warm-up exercise she always used in college, a series of chords and scales up and down the neck. Over the next hour, she played through most of her classical numbers, the warm, rich sound filling her studio, each note flowing into the next. To say she was out of practice was a gross understatement. The soft nylon strings rolled beneath her fingers unlike the steel strings on her Paul Reed Smith electric guitars or even her Ovation acoustic. However, as she played, she fell back into the groove and her playing improved quickly.

For some reason, the classical guitar reminded her more of her loss than any other guitar. Maybe that was because she had studied voice at the same time she studied classical guitar. Whatever the reason, that guitar had sat in its case all this time, out of sight, out of mind.

She continued slowly fretting different chords, her eyes half-closed, when the phone rang, echoing throughout her studio. She sprang up so fast to grab the phone, she nearly spilled her guitar onto the floor. With her pulse now racing, she crossed her fingers. Please let it be Sam this time. One more telemarketer and she'd scream.

"Jodi Price, you're the absolute best." Sam nearly shouted into the phone.

"I take it the meeting with Dad went okay." She had to work hard not to laugh. The excitement in Sam's voice was obvious.

"I don't want to get into the details at the moment. All I'm going to say is that it went really well. How about I meet you for dinner and I can fill you in?"

She could picture Sam on the other end, smiling from ear to ear. "That sounds great. What do you have in mind?"

"Hmmm." Sam paused. "I'm not really sure. Would you want to eat out *or* fix an intimate dinner in, maybe a little pasta, a little garlic bread, a little wine?"

"Oh, that's a tough call." She smiled at Sam's not-so-subtle suggestion. "Given the choices, I'd have to say an intimate dinner in sounds very nice. That is as long as there's garlic bread."

Sam burst out laughing. "Oh, I see. It's the garlic bread that's the dealmaker, huh?"

Totally deadpanning it now, Jodi continued to play along. "Oh, definitely. You've got to have garlic bread or what's the point?"

"Well, I think that can be arranged. Is there anything else that sounds good?"

"Only you." The thought of Sam, running her hands over her body, kissing her full lips and down her neck, sent a violent shudder through her body and she bit down hard on the side of her hand, trying her best to stifle the low moan rising up her throat.

"Mmmm. Jodi Price, like I said earlier, you're the absolute best. How fast can you get here?"

"How about thirty minutes?"

"Uh, that long? I'm not sure I'll be able to survive that long."

"Okay, I'm on my way." She sprinted to her bedroom, pulling the baggy tank top over her head as she went. She flung it behind her as she ran up the hallway. When she rounded the corner, she kicked off the denim cutoffs, sending them flying halfway across her bedroom. Standing naked in the door, she quickly glanced around for something to wear. Granted, Sam probably wouldn't mind if she showed up naked, but getting across town might prove difficult. Still laughing at the thought, she slid into a pair of her favorite jeans and tugged a black spaghetti strap top over her head. One quick ruffle of her hair with her fingers and she grabbed her keys and sandals then dashed out the door. All down the walkway, she skipped along on one foot while trying to slip a sandal on the other. After nearly falling headfirst into the begonias, she flung the sandals into the passenger seat of her Escape. Who needed them anyway? She didn't imagine Sam would complain. Now, her heart thundering, she jumped behind the wheel and with a loud chirping from her tires, she quickly backed out of her driveway.

* * *

Sam ripped back the blinds on her front door window for the third time in five minutes but still no Jodi. She didn't know how much longer she could hold it all in. The meeting with Jim had gone far better than she could have hoped. The moment she walked out of the boardroom, a smile permanently plastered on her face, she wanted to call Jodi and spill everything to her, every detail, every word, everything. But the more she thought about it, she wanted to share it with her face-to-face, even if that meant that she had to wait another half hour while she paced back and forth from her kitchen to the living room.

Finally, she peeked out the window once again and hopped up and down as Jodi pulled up in front of her house. She tore open her front door, banging it hard against the wall—drywall be damned—and ran down her cobblestone walk. Before Jodi could even get out of her car, she yanked her out of her seat and with a hand on each side of her face, quickly silenced Jodi's startled gasp with her lips. When she finally pulled back, her breathing ragged, she stared deep into Jodi's bright eyes. "I'm so glad you're here."

Jodi also fought to catch her breath. "Wow, I'm glad I'm here too."

She took Jodi by the hand, intertwining their fingers, and led the way back up the walk to the house, this time much slower than when she had run out to meet Jodi. "By the way, I owe you a big thanks. I have never had a job this big before. I've done corporate websites, but nothing compared to this one."

"Obviously Dad really liked what you had in mind."

"That and the fact that I can save him at least twenty percent on web hosting. He didn't even bat an eye when I gave him the figure for writing the site. He just leaned back in his chair, grumbled a bit, and said he'd paid more than that back when they designed the site he has now." She leaned in close and lowered her voice. "Don't tell him this but I think he got ripped off."

Jodi quickly shook her head. "Oh, believe me, I won't tell him. He'd just fume about that for the next six months."

"A lot of people got ripped off in those days. It was all the rage for businesses to have a web presence. If you didn't have a website, you were losing money. At least that was what they wanted you to believe. They charged a fortune and the sites were really simple. Look at the dot com craze. A lot of people paid a lot of money for nothing." At the look of utter bewilderment on Jodi's face, she stopped and took a deep breath. "Sorry about that. I get carried away sometimes."

"That's quite okay, Sam. I love seeing you get carried away." Jodi gently squeezed her hand as they walked. "Sounds impressive though. I'm really happy for you."

Sam pulled Jodi around, peering directly into her eyes. "I can't say it enough, Jodi—thanks." She then hopped up on her tiptoes, pressing her lips to Jodi's.

Her eyes closed, Jodi returned Sam's kiss, her hands slowly sliding down Sam's sides until they rested on her hips. She then leaned back, Sam still in her arms. "So, if I remember right, there's supposed to be garlic bread with this deal."

Sam burst out laughing. "Yes, I do remember something like that. Come on." She pulled Jodi toward the house.

"Great. I haven't had anything to eat today."

"What? You haven't eaten at all today? Good God, it's nearly six, Jodi. No wonder you're so thin."

Jodi simply shrugged. "It's no biggie. I was practicing guitar and forgot."

"Good grief. I don't think it's possible for me to forget to eat. I get really cranky if I don't eat regularly. I inherited my mom's low blood sugar. Thanks, Mom." She rolled her eyes.

"Oh, that sucks. Maybe we should hurry up with dinner then. We wouldn't want you to get cranky."

Sam elbowed Jodi in the ribs. "Oh, you're really funny. And it wouldn't have anything to do with wanting garlic bread, huh?"

"What? Are you saying all I'm concerned with is garlic bread?" Jodi slapped her hand to her chest, doing her best to look innocent. "Well, okay, maybe you're right."

"In that case, we'd better hurry then." She nearly tugged Jodi off her feet and together they ran the rest of the way to the door. Once inside, she waved to the living room. "Go ahead and make yourself at home while I quickly get dinner going."

Jodi followed her to the kitchen. "I can help."

"You sure? I can get it."

"Sam, don't be silly. Just tell me what you need me to do. Want me to cut up veggies for the sauce or something?"

"Well, that's just it." Sam spun around with a sheepish grin, a jar of pasta sauce in her hands. "All I have is canned."

For a second, they simply stared at each other until they both burst out laughing. Jodi shook her finger at Sam. "So that's why you didn't want me to come in the kitchen and help."

"Sorry. It's not fancy. Just canned sauce, pasta and frozen garlic bread." She glanced down at the jar of sauce in her hands.

Jodi stepped forward and covered Sam's hands with hers. "Sounds perfect to me."

Together, they fixed dinner. Jodi poured the sauce in a bowl and placed it in the microwave. Sam slid the garlic bread into the oven and dumped the pasta into the boiling water. They both stood, side by side, in front of the stove, watching the pasta boil. Jodi leaned her head over until she nearly touched Sam's. "So, tell me all about the meeting with Dad."

Sam blew out a long whistle. "Oh, where to begin? At first, I was so nervous. I walked in and here was this room filled with a ton of people. I thought it would be only your dad and maybe a couple of others but it looked like the whole dealership was there. Your dad just sat up at the head of the table and told me to dazzle them."

"Yep, that sounds like Dad. He probably *did* have every free person in there."

"Yeah, so I ran through some of the ideas I had—mostly things your dad and I had talked about on Sunday. Then when I was done, the room was dead silent." She let out a soft chuckle.

"I looked around and thought, oh shit, they all hate it but then your dad clapped and everyone joined in. Then they all started asking questions."

"Dad can be really intimidating sometimes. I've sat in on a few meetings before and even I was nervous." Jodi rubbed Sam's shoulder.

"Oh, God, Jodi. I could have used that during the meeting. Mmmm." She leaned into Jodi's hand, the tension draining from her muscles. It didn't help that her new client was her girlfriend's dad either. If he hated what she did for his business, it could really make a mess out of her relationship with his daughter. Then again, if something happened between her and Jodi, that could really make a mess out of the business dealings with her father. There was a lot at stake. But Jodi's strong fingers against her back were really doing the trick. With that, she could get through anything. "After the meeting, some woman came up to me and whispered that it was about time your dad got rid of that horrible website they've had for nearly ten years."

"Oh, yeah? What did she look like?"

"She was about this tall—" Sam waved her hand a couple of inches above her head. "Short silver hair, blouse with a string tie."

"Oh, that would be Marie Carbonelli, Vice President of Sales. She's not afraid to tell it how it is either."

"I could tell. I wouldn't want to mess with her."

"She's actually very sweet. Also, she's family." Jodi gave her a wink.

It took her a minute before she got it. "Oh, you mean she's gay too?"

"Yep. There's several gay people at the dealership. I think Dad actually goes out of his way to hire a diverse staff since I came out. It's his way of being supportive."

"That's really cool. Too often people are worried that having someone gay on staff will drive away business."

"Yeah, it can be like that in the music business too." Jodi then bumped her hip against her. "You know, Sam, I'm very proud of you."

"Proud of *me*? I just *got* the job. Now the real work begins. With all the features I'm thinking about, it will take at least several weeks to get it up and running."

"You're in heaven, aren't you?" Jodi smiled as she watched her.

"Is it that obvious?"

"Yep." Jodi now wrapped her arm around her waist. "I love seeing you like this."

"I love seeing you like this too."

Jodi leaned back. "How? Old jeans and a black top?"

"Well, yeah. That too. But I meant so happy." She watched the soft smile lifting Jodi's lips. Jodi had certainly known more than her share of pain and loss but she wasn't the cold woman she had first seen up on stage playing guitar who would never speak to anyone. She leaned forward, closer and closer, only inches now separating them. But just as their lips were about to touch, the buzzer blared on the stove and they both jumped. Sam laughed and grabbed the oven mitt. "Well, looks like the garlic bread is done."

"Oh, goodie." Jodi bounced about while Sam pulled the bread from the oven.

Next, they both loaded up plates of pasta overflowing with sauce. Jodi piled four huge hunks of garlic bread carefully around the edge of her plate. When Sam glanced over, she nearly gasped. "Good God, Jodi. Got enough garlic bread?"

Jodi stared down at her plate. "You can never have *too* much garlic bread."

While they ate, Sam filled Jodi in on more of the job details, everything from searching the online inventory to scheduling an appointment with the service department. As she mopped up the last of the sauce with a chunk of garlic bread, Sam sat up straight, her eyes wide. "Oh, yeah. I almost forgot. My mom invited us to dinner this weekend if you're not busy. She would really like to meet you."

With her glass to her lips, Jodi nearly spilled her drink. Covering her mouth with her left hand, she coughed several times.

"Don't worry. You'll be fine. Besides, it's only fair. I had dinner with your family."

"I know. Fair's fair." Jodi groaned. "I just hope she doesn't hate me."

"Oh, please." Sam grabbed her by the shoulders and planted a firm kiss on her cheek. "She's going to love you like I do."

* * *

Jodi spent the rest of the week replaying Sam's comment—*she's going to love you like I do*—through her head. Was Sam actually saying she loved her? Or was it only something someone would say to a friend? Then again, how did she feel about Sam? She had to admit that she was really falling for her. But could she also be in love with her? The more time passed, the more she felt that was a definite possibility.

By Sunday morning, she was about to tear her short black spiky hair out as she waited for Sam to pick her up. She had tried playing guitar—that usually settled her nerves—but she couldn't concentrate. Dozens of questions spun around inside her head. What would happen if Sam's mom didn't like her? Would her voice freak her out? Most people were uncomfortable when they first heard her speak. Or what if Sam's mom didn't think she was good enough? She was the dean of a college after all and her daughter was a successful computer programmer. Would she be okay with her daughter dating a musician? She finally let out a long ragged groan. This was worse than the anxiety before a big show—much worse.

In her big heavy boots, she clopped a good half-dozen more laps through her house. Maybe she should just call Sam and cancel. She could say she was sick. That wouldn't be too much of a lie. But she really did want to see her. *She's going to love you as much as I do*. The words tickled her thoughts again. If her mom was anything like Sam, then what did she have to worry about? Still—

When the doorbell finally rang, she nearly knocked over her recliner in her haste to get to the door. She ran across the room, skidding to a stop in front of the door and wrinkling up the throw rug.

"Good God, Jodi. It sounded like an elephant running through your house." Eyebrows raised, Sam stepped forward and wrapped her arms firmly around her.

"I was just glad you were finally here." Her face now beaming red, she pulled Sam tight to her body, her breathing still coming in gasps.

"Wow, I *guess*." Sam leaned back with her arms still around Jodi's waist. "Well, in that case, I feel honored."

Now that she had Sam in her arms, she didn't feel nearly as nervous. As long as Sam was with her, she could get through anything, even if Sam's mom hated her.

They stood on the porch, not moving an inch until Sam finally sighed. "So, should we get going?"

Should we get going? A simple enough question so it would seem. But again, a maelstrom of horrific visions—everything that could possibly go wrong—flashed through her head and Jodi gasped. "Ah, yeah, I…I guess."

Sam stepped back and peered directly into Jodi's eyes, gently cradling her face in her hands while she stroked her cheeks with her thumbs. "Hey, hon. Are you all right? You're not yourself."

Jodi tried to laugh, hoping that would reassure Sam, but it sounded more like a sick hiccup. "Yeah. I'm okay. Just a little nervous."

Now looking even more concerned, Sam pulled her in until their foreheads touched. "Jodi, believe me, there's nothing to be nervous about. Mom's going to love you."

Jodi finally managed a small smile. "I hope so." How could she explain to Sam—Sam who had never once raised a single eyebrow because of her voice—how much she worried about how her mom might react when she heard her speak?

"Trust me, Jodi. Mom's dying to meet you." Sam then grasped Jodi by the shoulders and gave her a gentle shake to emphasize each word. "It—will—be—fine."

Jodi tried her best to relax as she walked with Sam toward her Volkswagen, failing miserably. Her stomach felt as if it were twisted in knots. Her breath rasped as she tried to breathe. If only she could spend the day alone with Sam. Maybe find a place where Sam could wear that skimpy little green bikini. But instead of lounging on the bow of the boat, here she was standing beside Sam's car, feeling decidedly sick. She swallowed hard and spun around to face Sam. "So, were you nervous to meet my parents?"

Sam took in a deep breath and gave a firm nod. "Scared shitless."

They both then broke out laughing.

"Good. So it's not just me."

"No, Jodi, it's not just you."

While Jodi slipped into the passenger's seat, Sam dashed around the front of her Jetta and jumped in, but before starting her car, she spun around, fixing Jodi with her eyes. "I really do appreciate this, hon. I know how nervous it makes you to be around new people. And maybe later, we can have a little alone time with just us." She then brushed Jodi's cheek with her lips.

Jodi held her hand to her cheek, her skin still tingling from Sam's kiss. She could get through this—if only for Sam.

Twenty short minutes later, Sam pulled up in front of a large two-story colonial in Heritage Hill. Jodi sat staring out the window, wringing her hands in her lap. Oh, if only she were anywhere else. It wasn't too late, was it? Maybe she should just tell Sam she felt sick. That certainly wouldn't be *that* much of a lie.

"Well, we're here." At Jodi's deer-in-the-headlights look, Sam reached over and pulled Jodi's left hand to her chest, placing it over her heart. "Remember, hon, I'll be right here with you."

"Okay, I think I'm ready."

Sam took Jodi's hand and lifted it to her lips. With a warm, reassuring smile, she led the way up to the large oak door set between two wide sidelights and without knocking, walked right in, still holding Jodi's hand.

Once in the entryway, Sam called out. "Hey, Mom, we're here."

A reply drifted through the house. "I'm in the kitchen."

Sam turned to Jodi and gave her hand a reassuring squeeze. "You're going to like dinner. Mom said she was working on something special."

Jodi could already smell whatever was cooking. Although she hadn't felt hungry all morning, her stomach now growled loudly.

Sam lowered her ear to Jodi's stomach and giggled. "Sounds like you've forgotten to eat again, huh?"

"You know me." She hadn't eaten anything all day or even most of yesterday either. Granted it wasn't so much that she had forgotten to eat this time. Just the thought of food had made her stomach churn. But with the deliciously pungent aromas, her appetite had returned despite her anxiety.

Sam led the way through the house to the large tiled kitchen. Standing in front of the stove, Sam's mom, Sharon, dressed in a wine bottle print apron, stirred a simmering sauce. Sharon lifted her head from the bubbling pot, dropped the ladle onto the countertop, and trotted right over. "So, you must be the Jodi I've heard so much about. It's finally such a pleasure to put a face to the name."

"Um, it's good to meet you too." Sam's mom certainly wasn't how she had pictured. She had been expecting more of a stiff intellectual type instead of the bubbly, open woman that stood in front of her.

Sharon turned to Sam and gave her a warm hug. "You're just in time. I could use a little help with the wine. It's over on the countertop." She then scurried back to the stove and picked up the ladle again. "Oh, and there's Guinness in the fridge for you Jodi. Sam's told me you're an Irish beer lover."

"Wow, thanks." She nearly tripped over her feet. This certainly wasn't going to be as bad as she thought. So, while Sam opened a bottle of St. Julian Braganini Reserve Traminette, she pulled a cold Guinness from the refrigerator. Sharon had chilled an entire six-pack, not that she would drink more than a bottle or two. After all, she was meeting her for the first time. She didn't want to come across as a total lush.

Sam spun around on her heel, wine bottle in one hand, empty glass in the other. "Hey, hon, did you want any?"

With a wide grin, she held up her bottle of Guinness. "I think I'll be okay."

"I figured you'd feel more comfortable with your favorite beer so I suggested it to Mom."

"Thank you. You're the best." She gave Sam a pat in the center of her back and followed her as she walked over to her mom with a glass in each hand.

"So, Jodi, I hope you're hungry. I'm fixing a baked whitefish and pasta alfredo." Sharon raised the glass Sam offered to her lips and sipped the wine while stirring the sauce with her other hand.

"Yes, ma'am. It smells delicious." She fidgeted with the beer bottle in her hands. If she weren't careful, she'd probably end up causing it to foam all over the kitchen floor.

Sharon laughed and shook her head. "Oh, please. Call me Sharon. Ma'am seems too formal, like I'm talking to one of my students."

"Oh, okay Sharon." She dashed a glance to Sam and winced. Calling Sam's mom Sharon felt weird, not that she didn't feel weird already.

Sam wrapped her arm around Jodi's waist, lifting her lips to her ear. "Now you know how I felt when your dad kept telling me to call him Jim."

With her attention back on the stove, Sharon called over her shoulder. "Sam, dear. Why don't you take Jodi into the dining room and set the table while I finish up here. We'll be eating in just a couple of minutes."

"Okay, Mom." Sam grabbed Jodi by the hand and quickly tugged her out the door.

Once in the dining room, Jodi let out a low whistle. A large, intricately carved antique cherry dining table took up the center of the room. Along the back wall, a huge cherry china cabinet housed the flatware and plates. Throughout the rest of the room, rich cherry furniture and cabinets made up the décor. She spun slowly in one spot. The only thing she could compare it to was some old restored Victorian on *This Old House*. "Wow, this place reminds me of an old mansion."

"It's a little too dark and gloomy for my taste. That's why I chose my place—bright and open." With a half shrug, Sam took Jodi by the hand. Together, they quickly laid out the place settings and flatware. Sam then rolled up three linen napkins to complete the table. When she finished, she wrapped her arms tightly around Jodi's waist. "So, how's my baby surviving?"

"I must admit, your mom's totally different to how I imagined."

"See, I told you. You don't have anything to worry about. Mom's really cool." Sam rubbed her hand against the small of her back. "And she's really fascinated by you."

Jodi nearly tipped over the chair in front of her. What could Sharon possibly find fascinating with her? It wouldn't be because of her screwed up voice or her accident, would it? Oh God, Sharon wasn't that type, was she—wanting her to relive the most tragic moments of her life as some ghastly *Twilight Zone* version of a dinner and a show? But just as she opened her mouth, trying to form words from the jumble in her head, a voice drifted out of the kitchen.

"Dinner's ready you two."

Jodi closed her mouth, stifling a sigh. Once again her stomach began to churn. What could she do? She couldn't very well tell Sam's mom to mind her own business. How rude would that be? Especially after she had spent most of the morning preparing such a fabulous meal. She turned to Sam and tried her best to smile, if only for her sake, and then followed her back into the kitchen.

With a pair of oven mitts that matched the wine motif of her apron, Sharon pulled the fish from the oven. "Sam, be a darling and grab the pasta and sauce for me." Sharon quickly hustled out of the kitchen to the dining room, tendrils of steam from the baking dish trailing behind her.

Sam grabbed the bowl of alfredo sauce. "Could you get the pasta, babe?"

"Sure." Jodi grabbed the pasta bowl and followed Sam back in the dining room. She forced herself to focus on the food and not the torrent of thoughts rushing through her mind. Sometimes she just wanted to jump up and scream, "Yes, I was in a bad car accident and my voice is totally screwed up. Can we get over it and move on?" That at least would clear the air, but from her experience, people couldn't leave it alone. They had to ask question upon question. They wanted to know every agonizing detail and the more painful it seemed, the more they wanted to know about it.

Once in the dining room, she tucked the pasta beside the sauce. Sharon pulled out the chair at the head of the table and gestured to the chairs on each side of her. "Well, why don't we eat before this all gets cold?"

Jodi slipped into the chair to the left of Sharon and peered across the table at Sam. She was met with a wide, warm smile.

Sharon reached out and patted both Sam and Jodi on their arms. "Now, Jodi dear, why don't you get us started off with the pasta."

Not needing to be told twice, Jodi dished out some pasta and then helped herself to a huge serving of the broiled whitefish. Her stomach growled loud enough that Sam peeked up from across the table. With a shy smile, she shrugged and lifted a heaping forkful of the whitefish to her lips. When the taste flooded her mouth, she leaned back in her chair and let out a soft moan.

"This is really good, Mom." Sam held up a forkful of whitefish to Sharon.

With her mouth full, Jodi bobbed her head. She then quickly swallowed, covering her mouth. "Yes, very good." Hopefully, she didn't come across as too much of a glutton but the food was so good. Bite after bite, she savored each flavor. She paused only long enough to take a long sip from her Guinness. Probably not the most sophisticated drink for the rich dinner but she liked the combination.

"There's more in the fridge if you need it, Jodi. Don't be shy." Sharon reached over and lightly patted her arm.

"Thanks. I'm good for now." She couldn't help but smile. Her mom would have a fit if she saw her drinking beer at dinner, let alone leaving the table to get a second bottle.

"So, Jodi." Sharon turned sideways in her chair. "Sam tells me you're quite an accomplished musician."

Jodi choked on her beer and quickly covered her mouth. "Well, sort of. I play guitar a bit in a band."

"Sort of? Don't be so modest, Jodi." Sam gently toed her with her foot under the table before rounding on her mom. "She's absolutely amazing, Mom."

Blushing profusely, Jodi dropped her eyes to the table.

"Well, Sam's told me all about you. Your academic credentials are quite impressive. Interlochen and Juilliard?" Sharon nodded her head as she spoke. "Have you ever thought about teaching?"

Jodi jerked up. "Teaching? I…I…honestly, I've never really considered that." Many students from Juilliard did go on to teach, especially if they had been through the graduate program like she had, but for now, she preferred playing in her band. Besides, if she were to teach, she'd have to talk to a whole room and she could just imagine how that would go with her screwed-up voice.

"You should someday. It's really a wonderful experience." Sharon sipped from her wineglass then tilted it toward Jodi to emphasize her point. "I think sometimes the thing I miss the most about being an administrator is the classroom. What was your area of study anyway?"

Oh, great—a discussion of her college career. Just what she didn't need, especially since part of what she studied was voice. All that would do is lead to a lot of uncomfortable and painful questions. "Um…"

"Mom, Jodi's our guest. Let's not drill her on her academic history."

Sharon let out a laugh. "Sam's absolutely right. You'll have to forgive me. It's just the dean in me."

She silently thanked Sam. Whether a quick joke or a gentle reminder, Sam always seemed to know just what to say to make everything better. She flashed her a warm smile before she turned back to Sharon. "That's okay. Mostly I learned classic guitar and piano. Nothing too spectacular."

"Nothing too spectacular? Oh, please." Sam rolled her eyes. "You should hear her, Mom. Jodi does things on the guitar that

I didn't even think were possible. And I almost cried when she played the piano for me."

Jodi simply gaped at Sam, a lump rising in her throat. So, Sam had almost cried when she heard her play piano? Just hearing *that* was about enough to make *her* cry. No one had ever said that about her playing before. Truly, it had to be the best compliment she had ever received.

They finished dinner talking about different types of music and Sam filled her mom in on what she was doing with the J.P. Motors job. When Sam poured a second glass of wine for her and Sharon, Jodi helped herself to another bottle of Guinness. Finally, Sharon stood with her plate in one hand and the leftover fish in the other.

"I'll help you, Mom."

Sharon waved off Sam's offer. "You just sit here with Jodi while I clear the table and bring a little surprise for dessert."

After Sharon disappeared into the kitchen, carrying the last of the dishes, Jodi leaned closer to Sam. "By the way, thanks."

Sam lowered her eyebrows. "For what?"

"For…for…" She didn't know what to say. Gee, Sam, thanks for steering your mom away from the uncomfortable line of questioning? Thanks once again for making me feel normal? Finally, she gave Sam a soft smile. "For just being you."

"Well, Jodi, thank you for just being you too." Sam lightly ran her toe up Jodi's leg.

They leaned closer. Jodi reached out and took Sam's hand in hers. She wanted to tell Sam how much she appreciated her treating her as if she were normal, as if there was nothing wrong with her. But just as she opened her mouth, Sharon stepped through the door carrying three large Depression glass dessert cups filled with old-fashioned peach cobbler and ice cream.

"Here we go. My grandma's recipe." With a flourish, Sharon set a cup in front of Jodi then Sam.

Jodi held Sam's gaze as she peered back, a lopsided smile on her lips. Finally, she tore her eyes away. The moment had passed. She glanced down at the dessert in front of her and licked her lips.

Sam dug in a spoon and took a quick bite. "This is great, Mom."

With the spoon almost to her lips, Jodi met Sam's eyes across the table as she licked away an ice cream mustache. "Yes, this is great."

CHAPTER TEN

Jodi sat on her large amp in Lynn and Kat's garage, tuning her new electric guitar. She had just put on a new set of strings. When she finished with the last string, she hit three heavy chords, the sound blasting. Dragging her long guitar cable behind her, she hopped over beside Lynn and Terra as they stood in front of Kat's drum set. "Hey, I was thinking, maybe we should start out with 'Tease Me, Please Me' for the music fest. That way we could start with a bang and then go into the ballad, 'In Your Arms.'"

Lynn threw an arm around her shoulder. "Yeah, that sounds great to me."

"I agree. That will get everyone really pumped up." Kat stomped a quick thundering roll on her double bass pedals.

Terra gave a big thumbs-up. "Works for me."

"Great. I've got a new solo worked out too." Jodi ran through a short scale struggling to hold back her excitement. This next show was a big deal. They would be playing downtown Grand Rapids during the Festival of the Arts. Unlike their typical venues at Pride and women's festivals, they would be playing for a mainstream audience. She hadn't done that since before her accident when she headlined her own band.

Kat stood up behind her drums, peering over the top of her cymbals. "Hey, are you going to ask Sam to come?"

"I was planning on it." Actually, she had been more than planning to ask her. She had created entire conversations in her head.

"Great." Kat jabbed her sticks at her. "You know, Jodi, that Sam is pretty damn amazing. Just yesterday I was talking to her about the new website—adding a few more pictures—and she had a great idea. We should not only announce the website during the set, but also put the web address on the CDs. It will increase the number of hits and hopefully increase online sales."

"Holy shit. Now that's an excellent idea." Leave it to Sam to come up with such a good marketing plan. And to top it all off, she wouldn't accept any money for it. She just said it was her contribution to the band. One more reason she was falling hard for her.

"That girlfriend of yours is really something, Jodi." Lynn patted her on the shoulder as she walked by.

Terra slung the strap for her bass over her head. "She sure is. We need to make her a part of the band. Maybe she can be our roadie or something."

A slow grin lifted her lips. She had been planning to ask Sam to at least come to their show but make her a roadie? She didn't want Sam to feel obligated to help. Granted, as far as she was concerned, the website had already made her a member of the band, in an even bigger way. Still, she should probably give her a call after practice and run it by her. If nothing more, it would be a good excuse to call, not that she needed an excuse. She fought the urge a dozen times a day not to grab the phone and dial her up or given Sam's influence, splurge on a smartphone so they could text whenever they wanted or at least more than the one or two word replies she did now on what Sam liked to call her "dumb phone."

Over the next two hours, they ran through their entire set. The new changes to "Tease Me, Please Me" worked very well. One of the great things about playing with Lynn, Terra and Kat was they were very tolerant of her improvised guitar playing. Although she wrote all the songs, she knew how hard it could be to play together when there was a change, but Terra on bass and Kat on the drums were solid together, not to mention Lynn with her strong vocals, so that gave her the freedom to have some creative fun.

Finally, sweat trickling from her forehead, she dropped her guitar back in its stand and grabbed a bottle of Guinness from the cooler. "I think we've got everything pretty well down."

Twirling her sticks, Kat fetched a cold bottle of Killian's. "Yeah, I missed the changeup in 'Little Miss Innocent' but other than that, it went good."

Lynn laughed. "Yeah, Kat, you screwed me with that one. I just sort of slurred the line."

Kat stuck her tongue out at Lynn.

Terra sat back, kicking up her feet. "I did like that new solo of yours, Jodi. It's a bit easier to keep a beat through."

"Good, I'll definitely include it then." She had taken a bit of a risk with it but it had paid off. And with a little more practice, it would be perfect. She then chucked a ball of paper towel over Terra's head at Lynn and Kat as they poked at each other like a couple of unruly children. "Hey you two, quit screwing around for a minute. How about we practice again tomorrow?"

Lynn stopped in midswing as she was about to flick Kat with a tie-dyed bandana. "Yeah, that works for me." She tried her best not to smile.

Kat stood up straight, hiding a wild smirk behind her hand. "That shouldn't be a problem."

"How about you, Terra?"

"Just so it's after five, Jodi. I've got to help out at the bookstore tomorrow afternoon."

"That will work." They all tried to be flexible with everyone's schedule. If it weren't for her parents' financial support, she couldn't spend as much time on her music as she did.

After their break, they ran through a few of their trickier songs, ironing out the snags. Finally satisfied, they exchanged a round of high fives and began to pack up. Jodi glanced at her watch. She now had the rest of the afternoon. Maybe she could give Sam a call and see what she was doing later. Maybe, if she was lucky, they could even get together. She hopped up, grabbed her case and flashed a wave to the other women as they stood around gabbing in front of Kat's drum set. "Hey, I'll catch you later."

Both Lynn and Terra, who were deep in a heated conversation, glanced up and quickly waved. Kat smiled and wiggled her fingers at Jodi. "Give Sam my best." With a wicked grin, she leaned forward and gave her a wink. "And don't do anything I wouldn't do."

"Yeah, yeah, don't worry, I won't." She could always count on Kat to make her laugh with her anything-but-subtle teasing. With one last glance over her shoulder, she shook her head and quickly walked to her Escape where she slid her guitar case in the back.

After she backed out of Lynn and Kat's driveway, she picked up her cell phone. It had been a couple of days and she was really missing Sam. Actually, she missed Sam anytime they were apart. If it were up to her, she'd spend every night with her. Even picturing Sam now, she could feel her body respond. She knew they were taking it slowly—she suspected mostly for her benefit. But it was getting more difficult not to just rip Sam's clothes off when she was with her. A deep heat boiled up in her and she squirmed in her seat. Yes, it was getting harder and harder. She quickly dialed Sam's cell, drumming her fingers against the steering wheel as it rang. When Sam answered, her breath caught in her throat until she realized it was only her voice mail. She then dialed Sam's home number but again only got her voice mail.

"Hey babe…um, yeah…it's just me, calling you. Seeing what you were doing. I guess I'll talk to you later." She hung up and thumped the phone against her forehead. She hated leaving messages. And now Sam was going to think she was an idiot after *that* message. Why did she have to sound like such a dork? With nothing more to do, she slumped back in her seat, a long sigh spilling over her lips, and drove home.

* * *

"Hey, Sandy, come check this out." Sam called out the door of her office to her assistant. She had been working for hours on the Price project. The main page was beginning to come together and she wanted another opinion.

"What's up, boss?" Sandy slipped through the doorway.

"I wanted you to take a look at the J.P. Motors website. I want your take on it." She scooted her chair back so Sandy had a better view of the screen.

"No problem." Sandy leaned in and squinted as she peered at the monitor, bobbing her head with her chin in her hand. "Ah, I like the background graphics."

"Yeah, I was pretty happy with that too. I blended a picture of the dealership with one of the showroom and one of the staff."

"It's good." Sandy continued to scan over the page. "It looks really good, boss."

"Do you see anything I might have missed? I've been staring at it so long now I need a fresh set of eyes."

"Hmmm. Let's see. You have the business name, the logo, the slogan." Sandy ticked off the items on her fingers. "You've got the hours, the phone number…wait, where's the address?"

"What? I forgot the address? You've got to be shitting me." How could she have forgotten that? But sure enough, no address anywhere. "Damn, I can't believe I forgot that."

Sandy laughed. "It's easy to do."

"Not by me it's not." How could she have forgotten something so simple? That was a rookie mistake. Then again, she couldn't get Jodi out of her mind. Even now as she pictured her full, soft lips, her insides began to stir. That probably had a bit to do with her lack of concentration right there.

Sandy patted her on the shoulder. "Other than that, it looks excellent."

"Thanks, Sandy. That was a good catch." Again, she leaned back over her keyboard and focused so intently on the screen, she didn't even notice when Sandy left. She added the address and carefully scanned the page for any other omissions or errors. She certainly didn't want to make some amateur mistake.

It would be bad enough if it happened to any client but it simply could not happen with *this* website. It needed to be perfect.

With the main page as a template, she plugged away on other pages, slowly checking them off the legal pad she had used to outline the structure. She hadn't realized how late it was until Sandy popped her head in hours later.

"I'm taking off boss."

Sam glanced up at the clock on the wall. Well past six. She spun around in her chair. "Okay, Sandy. I'll see you tomorrow."

"Sure thing boss. Have a great night." Sandy gave her a sly wink before scurrying out the door and down the hall.

Sam continued clacking away at her computer. Her eyes burned but she wanted to at least complete the page she was on—the service department—then she'd wrap it up for the day. She had been hoping to hear from Jodi, though. She could almost count on a surprise call sometime during the day. And that didn't include their deep conversations every night, some of which lasted for hours. She had grown accustomed to crawling in bed with the phone and talking until she could barely hold her eyes open anymore. It was the next best thing to curling up with Jodi. If it were up to her, she wouldn't mind curling up in Jodi's arms every night, feeling her heart beat next to her and breathing in her hair as she fell asleep. Finally, she blinked her eyes and glanced up again at the wall clock. Another twenty minutes had blown by while she had been daydreaming. Since it was obvious her mind wasn't on what it should be, she shut down for the night. Still, she wished Jodi had called. Maybe they could have gotten together tonight.

Locking up, she pulled out her cell phone and punched in Jodi's number. Without even ringing, it went to voice mail. Great. "Hey, it's me. Hope to talk to you later. Love you." She froze in midstride, nearly falling over. Had she really just told Jodi she loved her? What had she been thinking? It just popped out—*love you*. Yes, she was pretty sure she had fallen deeply in love with Jodi but she didn't want to scare her away. Oh, God, now what? She pulled her cell phone back out and was halfway through dialing Jodi's number again to leave another message but what would she say? All she'd end up doing is sounding like a total nutjob. Why had she blurted that out? With a low groan, she slowly lowered her phone and slumped to her car.

Sam walked into her house and tossed her keys and phone on the kitchen counter. She trudged off to her bedroom and stripped out of her blouse, throwing it beside her bed along with her bra. Next, she collapsed on the edge of her bed, stretched, and kicking up her legs, slipped her black slacks off. In only her green string panties, she flopped back and closed her eyes. It felt good to finally relax. She had been in front of her computer all day and her eyes were burning. If only Jodi were there. She began to smile. Yes, if only Jodi *were* there. She was naked except for her skimpy panties and those wouldn't be much of an issue. With her eyes still closed, she pictured Jodi running her hands over her naked skin, kissing her warm flesh with her full, inviting lips, sliding her body over hers. As she continued to picture Jodi slowly caressing every tender part of her eager, willing body, she slowly slid her hand down her stomach until it rested over her panties. Feeling the warmth, she let out a low, guttural gasp. She pulled her hand up slightly, feeling the soft whisper of silk against her skin, and just as the tips of her fingers slipped under the waistband, the phone rang. "Christ Almighty!" With her heart thundering, she ran into the dining room for the cordless phone.

Skidding to a halt and nearly falling on her butt, Sam grabbed the phone on the fourth ring, hoping to catch it before the answering machine. Gasping, she answered. "Hello." With her hand to her chest, she tried to catch her breath.

"Hey, what's up?" Jodi chuckled on the other end. "You sound like you just got done running a marathon."

Oh, crap. She couldn't very well tell Jodi what she had been up to *or* what she had been thinking about at the time. How would that go? Hey babe, I was just diddling myself while thinking of you. Yeah, that wouldn't be awkward at all, would it? She tried to giggle but it sounded more like a cat yakking a hairball on the carpet. "Sorry, I was trying to get the phone before the answering machine picked up so I was running then I slipped but I got it so here I am." Great, now she was babbling.

"Wow, Sam, you sure you're okay." Jodi continued to chuckle.

"Yeah, I'm okay." Sam sprawled across her recliner with her legs over the arm. "Hey, I tried to call you earlier."

"You did?"

"Yep, about forty-five minutes ago when I got out of work. I left a message on your voice mail. I was seeing if you wanted to do something."

"That's weird. I've been here all afternoon. Hold on, I'll check."

Sam snapped bolt upright. "Wait, Jodi. Don't. I sounded like a total dweeb—" But it was too late. Jodi was listening to her message.

When she came back on, her voice was soft. "You didn't sound like a dweeb. Not at all."

Sam blew out a quiet whistle. Jodi must not have even noticed it. Or maybe she just took it as something a friend would say to a friend—hey, you know, love you. Thing was, she didn't just love Jodi, she was in love with her and falling more all the time. "Well, thanks. I always hate leaving messages."

"Me too. I probably didn't sound any better when I left a message for you earlier."

"What? You did?" Her pulse quickened. So, Jodi did try to call.

"Yeah, I tried your cell phone first then I left a message at your house."

Sam piled out of the recliner and marched over to her answering machine. Sure enough, there on top the light was blinking and when she pushed the button, Jodi's voice poured out. "Hey babe…um, yeah…it's just me. Seeing what you were doing. I guess I'll talk to you later." Silently kicking herself, she turned back to the phone in her hand. If only she had heard it earlier. "You didn't sound bad at all. When did you call?"

"Oh, it was early this afternoon, just after getting out of band practice."

"Early this afternoon?" A sickening feeling settled in Sam's stomach. She quickly stomped into the kitchen, grabbed her cell phone and slapped herself on the forehead. Damn. If she'd received the message, they could have met. She didn't have to work as late as she did. Trying not to sound too disappointed, she cleared her throat. "Shoot, my cell was set to go directly to voice mail. You should have called me at my business."

"I didn't want to bother you at work."

Sam burst out laughing. "Jodi, hon. I'm the owner and boss. You can call me at work anytime."

"I'll have to remember that from now on."

"Now that we have that all cleared up, what's going on there?" She walked back to her recliner and flopped down in it sideways again.

Jodi paused before answering. "Hmmm. Not too much. I did need to talk to you about something but I'd rather do it in person."

"Oh. Nothing bad I hope." Sam quickly spun around in her chair. Had she relaxed too soon? Had her message actually freaked Jodi out more than she had thought? Maybe Jodi had finally picked up on her feelings and now wanted to put a little distance between them.

"No, no, nothing bad. That's why I was hoping to get together maybe today."

Sam glanced at her watch. It was just before eight. It wasn't *that* late. Besides, she wouldn't be able to sleep at all until she found out what Jodi wanted to talk to her about. "Well, we could still get together tonight. It's really not that late." She held her breath, hoping she didn't sound too eager, especially if Jodi was already feeling she was pushing things too quickly.

"You sure?" Jodi paused, her voice rising. "You've got to work tomorrow, right? I don't want to keep you up too late."

"It's quite okay. Believe me." She nearly pleaded with the last word.

Jodi chuckled loudly. "Wow, I do."

"So, you want me to come over there?" Sam bit her lip.

"Hmmm. I've got a better idea. Why don't I come over there? That way you won't have to drive back to your place and you can get to sleep sooner."

"Okay, that sounds good if you're fine with it." It didn't matter to her where they met as long as she could find out what Jodi wanted to talk about, what could only be said in person.

"Really, it's no problem. I don't have to get up quite as early."

"In that case, I'll let you go while I go get dressed." Sam sat up in her chair about to say goodbye.

"Oh, you need to go get dressed, do you?" The surprise in Jodi's voice was obvious. She then lowered her voice. "So, what have you been wearing all this time while we've been talking?"

"Um." Now what was she going to say? "Well…you see…"

"You're naked, aren't you?" Jodi was giggling.

Sam could feel her cheeks now burning. "Not entirely. I do have panties on."

"Damn, maybe I should have just stopped over without calling. Next time I'll have to do that."

"Ahhhh…" Now she really didn't know what to think. Jodi wouldn't say that if she was upset with her, would she? Was she blowing this all up in her head like she tended to do? Or was she just so scared that the proverbial shoe would drop as it had with her ex that she was seeing it everywhere?

Before she could respond, Jodi continued. "Hey, I'll be there in a bit. *See* you soon." She let out another wild chuckle.

"Okay, see you soon." Sam stared at the phone. What could it be that Jodi wanted to talk about in person? If it had been something bad, she wouldn't be joking around with her, would she? Of course not. Jumping up from her chair, she ran into her bedroom and pulled on a pair of shorts and a tank top. Jodi may have joked about it but meeting her at the door naked might be a bit much. Still, just the thought of that made her entire body tingle again.

* * *

Jodi screeched to a halt in front of Sam's house, threw open her door and sprinted up the cobblestone walk. The door flung open and Sam stood in front of her in a pair of shorts and a tank top, biting her bottom lip, a trait Jodi found adorable. Her knees grew weak. Finally, she peeled her eyes away—she couldn't very well stand there on the porch all night gawking—and with a dramatic shrug, stuffed her hands in her pockets. "Hey, I made it."

"You made it." A wide grin curled Sam's lips. "Come on in."

Jodi stole a quick kiss—and a nibble on Sam's earlobe—as she stepped past. But it wasn't until she had flopped down on the couch, kicking out her long legs, that she noticed something was up. Sam sat opposite, chewing on her lip almost to draw blood. "Hey, Sam, are you all right? You're about to bite a hole right through your lip."

"Yeah, I'm fine. Why wouldn't I be?" Sam let out a nervous laugh.

"Seriously, Sam, you don't seem fine." She scooted closer and lifted Sam's chin with her fingers until their eyes met. "What's up? Did I say something wrong earlier?" Was Sam upset with her little joke about stopping by instead of calling in hopes of catching her naked? She had thought they were moving toward that type of relationship. Had she read that wrongly? Maybe Sam had no desire in letting her ever see her naked much less anything like making love.

"No, it's nothing like that." Sam gave a great sigh, her shoulders falling. "I guess I'm just a little scared about why you needed to talk to me in person. I mean, whatever it is, I understand this may be going too fast and things have been said but I hope we can still be friends because I really like being around you and I can't imagine not being able to get together and talk, you know, like we do." She gasped for breath as she finished.

"Whoa. Slow down, hon." Where had all this come from? She certainly hadn't meant for Sam to feel things were going too fast. She should never have teased her about seeing her naked. What was she thinking? "Sam, I just wanted to ask you if you'd like to go with me and the band to this big gig at the Festival of the Arts and be our roadie."

"You wanted to ask me to go with you to a gig?" Sam cocked her head to the side, slowly taking in the words. "You—wanted—to—ask—me—to—go—with—you—to—a—gig?" She then began to laugh, quietly at first then building.

Jodi stared at Sam as she now laughed wildly, snorting each time she took a breath. She wasn't sure what was so funny but it was better than seeing Sam eat her lip. "Um, yeah, that's what I wanted to talk to you about in person. I mean, you don't have to go if you don't want to."

Sam leaped forward and threw her arms around Jodi's neck, planting a kiss firmly on her cheek. "Oh, yes, Jodi. Yes, I'd love to."

"Great." Jodi finally smiled and slid her fingers down Sam's arms until she covered her hands. "Hey, I'm sorry if I said something wrong earlier."

"No, it's just me. I got nervous when you said you needed to talk to me in person about something. And with my freaky message earlier, I guess my imagination got the better of me." With a wry smile, Sam slowly shook her head. "Sorry."

"Don't worry, it wasn't you. I wanted it to be a surprise but I should have just told you over the phone." That and she really wanted to see Sam in the flesh.

"I'm glad." Sam took Jodi's hands in hers and squeezed tightly. "Well, since we've got that all cleared up, tell me about this gig of yours."

"Oh, it's going to be great. We'll be hitting a much broader mainstream audience than we usually do, which might be a good thing or a bad thing."

"Why would that be bad? It seems like it would only be a good thing."

"You never know. I had some group protesting a show several years ago with a bullhorn saying we're all going to hell." She cringed. "Hopefully, we won't get too many nuts."

"Wow. Seriously, you had someone do that?"

"Oh, yeah. Made for a real fun show, let me tell you."

"I can imagine. That would suck." Sam wrinkled her nose. "So, when is this gig of yours?"

"Two weeks from this weekend."

Sam bounced on the couch. "Oh, that will be great. I should have your dad's website up and running by then. That way I can kick back and relax. That is after I've performed my roadie duties, of course."

"You know, you don't have to help out if you don't want to, Sam. If you want to relax, that's fine too. I'd be happy if you just come to the show no matter what."

"Don't be silly." Sam swatted her lightly on the arm. "I'd be happy to help. Makes me feel like I'm part of the band."

"Oh, that reminds me, Kat told me your marketing ideas for the band at the show. I would never have thought of that stuff. You're just awesome, Sam."

"So are you, Jodi." Her voice no more than a whisper, Sam lowered her head, a blush rising on her pale skin.

Jodi pulled her in tight, slowly stroking her fingers through Sam's hair, the silky strands tickling her skin. She then leaned down and planted a soft kiss on top of her forehead. "You know, I'm glad I did get to see you tonight. I've missed you."

Sam rolled her head up against Jodi's shoulder. "Mmmm. Me too. I was hoping all day you'd call."

"Really? I thought you'd be so busy, I'd be the last thing on your mind."

"To be honest, that's usually how I am. When I get going on a new project, nothing else matters. I don't think about eating, drinking, sleeping, nothing. But since I've met you, you're always in my thoughts. You've had quite an effect on me, Jodi Price."

"Wow. I hope that's a good thing."

"Yes, that's a very good thing, silly. Well, maybe not a very good thing for business. My mind keeps wandering."

"Oh, I know what you mean. I found myself thinking about dinner with you at your mom's last Sunday during a guitar solo today at practice. I really flubbed up a couple of bars." She mimed messing up on her guitar. "You should have seen the look Lynn gave me."

"What? Jodi the great guitar goddess screwed up a solo? I can't believe it. I didn't think you ever made mistakes." Sam poked her in the ribs.

Now laughing, she poked Sam back. "It's all your fault for distracting me."

"Hey, that's not fair. I wasn't even there."

"You might not have been there in person, but you were definitely there in my thoughts." She didn't dare tell Sam that she had actually been picturing running her lips over every inch of her soft warm body.

Sam spun sideways and threw her legs over Jodi's. "Well, you weren't any better with me at work today. You distracted me so much I kept going over the same coding for a web page a good ten minutes before I realized I'd already completed it."

Jodi squeezed her knee. "So, tell me, little Miss Computer Genius. What was I doing in your thoughts that was such a distraction?"

Sam choked and began coughing, her cheeks turning deep red. "Um…well…yeah, I'm sure I don't remember now."

"Oh, come on, Sam. You can't leave it like that. What were you thinking about?"

Sam dropped her eyes to her lap. When she finally opened her mouth, her words were no more than a whisper. "Actually, I was thinking about running my hands over your entire body."

Jodi swallowed hard, her breath caught in her throat. Whatever she had been expecting, it wasn't that. Maybe the dinner at her mom's or riding on the boat, but not that. Although they had shared some deeply passionate kisses, they still remained chaste in many ways. She hadn't wanted to push anything with her. She wasn't sure Sam was ready for that. Then again, she wasn't sure *she* was ready for that. "Um, wow, I see."

Still looking down, Sam let out a nervous laugh. "I hope I didn't freak you out."

Freaked out wasn't the word. More pleasantly surprised. She swallowed again. "I must admit, I was thinking about the same thing too. I just don't want to go too fast if you know what I mean."

"Yeah, I feel the same way." Sam stared back at her, nodding. "Let's take it slow. The last thing I want to do is screw everything up." As she spoke, she leaned even closer.

Jodi met her intense, hungry gaze. Their eyes locked and she leaned forward, slowly, running her hand up Sam's thigh to her taut, flat belly, their lips now only inches apart. Sam bit her bottom lip and that was all she could take. She quickly closed the distance and their lips met, each kiss more demanding. Together, they gasped, their intermixed breath now ragged. Sam parted her lips, accepting Jodi's tongue. She lost all track of time. A minute, an hour? It was all a blur. They kissed, hands flying over each other, over every eager, pleading inch, each moment more intense, more passionate, more frantic.

When Jodi finally pulled up, her heart thundering and gasping for breath, the room had grown dark, the full moon shining through the windows the only light. She took in all of Sam, the flush on her skin evident even in the soft moonlight. She wanted nothing more than to make love to her right there, to take her in her arms and tear her clothes off, but she forced herself to sit up. "I should probably get going. You need to get to bed."

Sam lifted Jodi's hand to her lips, staring deep into her eyes. "Please, stay." Her voice nearly pleaded.

Her entire body cried for her to obey Sam. What would it hurt? But now wasn't the time. She hopped up, smoothing her shirt back over her bare skin. If she didn't leave right then, she wouldn't be able to. "Sam, I really should go. I'll…I'll talk to you tomorrow."

Sam slid off the couch and took Jodi by the hand, quietly walking with her to the door but just as Jodi was about to step out on the porch, she pulled her back. "You know, Jodi, you could stay."

"I know—believe me I know." She pulled Sam into a tight embrace, breathing in the slightly floral scent of her hair. Was that lilac? Strawberry? Damn, she wanted to stay. She wanted nothing more than to stay, but she just couldn't—not yet. Finally, pushing back the lump in her throat, she leaned down, her lips barely brushing Sam's ear. "Soon, I promise."

CHAPTER ELEVEN

Sam pulled aside the curtain and peered out at the empty street once again. Still, no Jodi. For over two weeks, she had been looking forward to today, the big concert. Actually, it had given her a greater incentive to finish up the website for Jodi's dad, not that she wouldn't have worked hard on it anyway. She had toiled nearly nonstop, even over the past two weekends. She'd have much rather spent the time with Jodi, but instead continued slaving away and as of eight last night, had put on the finishing touches, uploaded all the files and done one final error check. It had gone live.

That *is* when Jodi got there. She stomped over and flung herself sideways onto her recliner, shaking her right foot furiously. The clock ticked on the wall. Somewhere a dog barked. Then a light knock—holy shit, Jodi was there—and she sprang up and dashed across the living room, tearing open the door. Jodi stood there in her typical jeans, black spaghetti strap tank and the same big clunky black leather boots she had worn the first time she had seen her at Pride. She jumped out onto the porch into Jodi's arms. After a long, deep kiss, she stepped back, a bright smile still on her face. "I'm so glad you're here."

"Wow. I couldn't have guessed." Jodi gaped wide-eyed, still trying to catch her breath.

Her cheeks now blazing red, Sam gave a quick little shrug. "What can I say? I've missed you lately."

"I've missed you too. You up and disappeared on me the past couple weeks."

Sam now cringed. "Oh, geez, I'm really sorry, Jodi. I didn't mean for you to feel like I was avoiding you. I was working really hard on the website for your dad and I wanted to finish it before today so I could relax and spend the day with you without worrying about that and I—"

Jodi pressed her finger to Sam's lips, silencing her. "Baby, it's okay. I completely understand, you've been really busy. I was just giving you a hard time."

Sam now tucked in her chin, a guilty sparkle in her eyes. Jodi pulled her in tight, lifting her quickly off her feet before letting her go. "So, did you get everything finished then?"

"Yep." Sam gave a firm nod.

"Wow. That's great. Dad's going to be ecstatic." Jodi lowered her voice and leaned closer. "Between you and me, he's been like a kid waiting for Christmas although he'll never admit that."

"Seriously? I didn't know your dad was that excited."

"If you ask me, I think he's more excited that *you're* doing it than the website itself. He seems to have really taken a liking to you. You impressed him deeply and believe me, he doesn't impress easily."

Sam began biting her bottom lip again. "Geez, I hope I did a good enough job then."

"Oh, don't worry about it. Trust me, whatever you did, he's going to love it."

She sure hoped so. Until she got the final okay from a client, she was always nervous. Still, she crossed her fingers.

"Well, we'd better get going. Trust me, it's going to be a madhouse trying to get through the crowd and close enough to unload the equipment."

Sam pushed out any thoughts of websites and computers. All she wanted to think about today was Jodi. "Okay, I'm ready." Quickly closing the door behind her, and holding hands with Jodi, she clopped down to the Escape.

As they pulled away from the curb, Sam leaned over, tracing her fingers up Jodi's arm. "So when's your show again?"

"Our set starts at two but we've got to get the equipment there before noon." Jodi groaned. "That's the worse part—getting everything ready before the show and tearing it all down after." She then patted Sam's wandering and now misbehaving fingers with her free hand. "And thanks again for helping, Sam. It really does mean a lot."

"Believe me, Jodi, it's my pleasure. I wouldn't miss it for the world." She then stared directly at Jodi, trading a smile for her best at seriousness. "There's only one thing though."

Still concentrating on the road, Jodi raised her eyebrows and leaned her head closer. "Oh, and what's that?"

"I think I should get a T-shirt that says I'm a roadie for Blind Pariah."

"Wow, you had me scared there for a minute." Jodi nudged Sam with her elbow. "A T-shirt, huh? Well, we might have to do something about that. We could always make you a permanent member of the band."

Forget the lousy T-shirt. Here Jodi was talking about making her a permanent member of the band. That was much better. Even though she couldn't play an instrument and the only time she even approached sounding the least bit pleasing while singing was in the shower, she wanted somehow to be a part of Jodi's world. Jennifer had never included her in anything she did. She thought it was best that they kept most parts of their lives separate. That way they wouldn't get bored with each other, or so she said. As it turned out, that was just an excuse so she could cheat on her with everyone she met. So, having Jodi include her meant a lot. She never wanted to feel abandoned like that again.

When they arrived downtown, Sam gaped out the window. Jodi hadn't been kidding. It *was* chaotic—people bustling everywhere, cars blocking the streets and vendors running back and forth setting up their stalls. Jodi pulled up to a barricade and jumped out of the car. Sam watched as she talked to two security guards, pointing wildly at the street behind them. Finally, she ran back to her Escape and slid behind the wheel. "Typical. No one knows what's going on. The bands are supposed to be able to drive up and park on the back streets behind the stages so we can unload. Of course security hasn't heard anything about that." She gave Sam a wry smile.

With a scowl, the security guard on the left, a guy with a deeply-cratered face and a flattop, grudgingly pulled back the barricade and Jodi threw her car in gear. At little more than a crawl, they puttered their way through the crowd, stopping every few feet for people to step aside, until they pulled up behind Clock Tower Stage where the band would be performing. "Damn, there's a ton of people here already."

Jodi snorted. "Yeah, it sure would've sucked to have to carry all the equipment several blocks through *that* crowd."

"I bet. Just remember though, you now have a roadie for that." She smiled brightly and stuck out her chest.

Jodi laughed and threw an arm around her. "I wouldn't want to wear you out. You might decide to quit on me."

"What, me quit on you? Never. You've got me no matter what."

"Really?" Jodi lifted her eyebrows. "I'll have to remember that."

Just then, Kat appeared around the corner, stomping along with Terra and Lynn struggling to keep up. When she got close enough to hear, she raised her arms and pointed around at all the people roaming by. "What do you think of this?" She was clearly pissed.

With a wry smirk, Jodi let out a loud snort through her nose. "Figures. Where's the security?"

Out of breath, Terra laughed. "Oh, don't worry. They'll be here in a bit. Kat made *sure* of that."

Lynn jabbed a finger at Kat. "Yeah, for a minute, I thought security was going to be needed *on* Kat. We got here and she saw all these people and blew a gasket."

"What?" Kat crossed her arms in front of her chest. "This is unacceptable."

Lynn patted her on the back. "Yes, I know, hon, just like security and everyone within fifty feet knows."

"Damn right." Kat nodded her head firmly.

Jodi jumped back a step. "Wow, Kat. Remind me to never piss you off."

Sam also nodded vigorously, watching Kat continue to huff about the security.

Within minutes, six security personnel showed up and quickly began roping off the area. Jodi turned to Kat. "What did you say?"

"Oh, don't ask." Lynn quickly shook her head. "I thought for a moment she was going to make one of those big burly security guys cry."

"Hey, I wasn't that bad." Kat leaned back with a hand on her hip.

"Sure, babe." Lynn rolled her eyes behind Kat's back. "Whatever you say."

Kat grumbled under her breath sending everyone into fits of laughter. Sam never thought it possible, but this was so much better than being stuck in front of a computer all day.

* * *

Jodi sat on the fender of the trailer with her arm around Sam, her head tilted back and her eyes closed. The worst part of any show was always the waiting. But today she didn't care—she had Sam sitting beside her. She could wait all day.

"So, how much longer before we need to set up?" Sam bounced as she sat there.

Lynn burst out laughing and nudged Jodi's free arm with her elbow. "Wow, Jodi, she can't wait to be put to work. Better hold on to this one."

Kat and Terra quickly joined in as Sam's cheeks flamed red and Jodi pulled her in tight. "You know, Sam, you don't have to do this if you don't want to." She then leaned closer, her lips nearly brushing Sam's ear. "Just having you here is enough for me."

"Jodi, you're such a sweetheart. But seriously, I really do want to help out. It's just...I don't know..." She gave a small, one-shouldered shrug. "I guess it makes me feel a part of what you love and I want to share that with you."

No one had ever taken such an interest in what she did before. "Well, I really appreciate that but I don't want you to ever feel like you have to."

"I know that, Jodi. And I don't feel that way at all. I'm really excited to help out any way I can."

Before Jodi could respond, the crowd began to clap and several musicians came running around the back of the stage. Her heart immediately went into overdrive and she closed her eyes, slowly breathing in and out, in and out. It wouldn't be long now. The band quickly cleared the stage, shuttling a steady stream of equipment past. Finally, the tall, long-haired guy in spandex and lace who looked as if he had just walked straight out of a hair-metal band video from the eighties wheeled a guitar amp down the ramp and gave them a small salute as he passed. "It's all yours."

"Well, looks like we're up. Now the real fun begins." Jodi grabbed Sam by the hand and bustled to the back of the trailer.

Lynn flung open the door, dove in and returned with a tangle of microphone cables, draping them over Sam's right shoulder. "Here you go, roadie."

Kat stepped out of the back of the trailer and threw an octopus of cables over Sam's left shoulder. "There. Wouldn't want you lopsided." She gave Sam a devilish wink before ducking back into the trailer.

As Terra hobbled past, heaving her bass amp toward the stage, she laughed. "Hey, Sam, you might be getting more than you bargained for."

Jodi couldn't help but laugh as she shuffled across the pavement, pushing her amp. Sam sure seemed to be enjoying her new position in the band. She had never met anyone so thrilled to be a human cable cart.

For the next ten minutes they hauled the equipment from the trailer onto the stage, running back and forth like a strange musical relay race. At last, Jodi grabbed one end of Kat's drum set while Kat and Sam lifted the other. She let out a loud grunt. "Damn, and I thought my amp was heavy."

Kat began giggling, her entire body shaking. "You know, Jodi, you say that every time."

"Yeah, well, it's true. These things weigh a ton." She mumbled through gritted teeth, her arms trembling as she shuffled her feet backward up the ramp.

As soon as they had the drums in place, Kat began plugging in the cables she had Sam carry up earlier. Sam glanced out at the crowd milling around in between the music sets and gulped. "Oh my God, Jodi. How can you be up on stage with all those people out there? My stomach is queasy just looking out at the crowd and all I'm doing is helping carry stuff up here."

"I guess I don't really think about it much anymore. I mean yeah, I'm nervous before every show but once I'm on that stage, nothing matters but playing guitar."

"God, I think I'd end up puking."

Jodi poked her in the side. "Well, that would be memorable."

"Oh, yeah. Very memorable." Sam wrinkled her nose. "I think I'll watch from up front where it's safe."

"No thank you. Give me the stage any day. That's easy. But to be out in the crowd with all those people standing around..." she shuddered. "Yeah, now that would make me puke."

After running back down the ramp yet again, Jodi popped open the rear hatch and began pulling her guitars out of their cases. She handed her purple Paul Reed Smith to Sam. "Here, how about you carry this one for me?"

Sucking in a quick breath, Sam bit her lip. "Oh geez, Jodi, you sure?"

"Of course. I trust you." With her blue Paul Reed Smith in one hand and her Ovation in the other, she leaned forward, her eyes locking on Sam's, their lips only inches apart. The thundering of Kat's drums as she did a sound check broke the moment. "Well, apparently that's my cue." With a soft smile, she hustled up the ramp while Sam waited at the edge of the stage.

She slipped the two guitars she was carrying in the stand and ran back to Sam, grabbing her Pride Purple guitar from her and throwing the strap over her head.

Sam bobbed up on her toes. "Break a leg, babe."

"Thanks, hon." Jodi wrapped her free hand behind Sam's head, pulling her in until her mouth closed over Sam's. Her legs grew weak as Sam's hot, full lips began to part and a soft, hungry moan rose up her throat. Screw the concert. They could run away right then. Kat and the others could handle it. Finally, mustering all her strength, she tore herself away. She reached out and gently stroked Sam's cheek, peering once again into those deep green eyes. She then bit down hard on her lip, turned and skipped across the stage with her guitar.

* * *

Sam floated down the ramp, her lips still tingling from Jodi's passionate kiss. She wished they could have kept kissing, maybe even run away somewhere, it didn't matter where, and spend the rest of the day together. But as Jodi began the first song, jumping off her amp with a high kick, she smiled. "That's my girl."

She hustled out in front of the stage for a better view and leaned against the yellow and black striped barricade separating the crowd from the stage area. Since she was with the band, she had the privilege of standing inside the barrier, only about ten feet away. But even that was almost too far. And after that last kiss, all she wanted was to have Jodi wrapped tightly in her arms.

A large crowd had formed with people rocking out to the music. Jodi leaped around the stage, slinging her guitar back and forth, and working the crowd. She then ran up to the edge of the stage directly in front of Sam. Their eyes met and Jodi smiled, giving her a huge wink before going into a wild solo, whipping her guitar around in a blur. But when Jodi flipped her guitar upside down above her head, Sam began to laugh. The difference in Jodi since Pride in Lansing was astonishing. Jodi was a completely different person, smiling out at the crowd and running all over the stage, not at all the cold woman in her own little guitar-playing world.

At the hand on her shoulder, Sam whirled around to find Cheryl and Angi standing behind her. "Hey, you guys made it." She threw her arms out, giving each a hug over the barricade.

Cheryl patted her on the back. "Yep, wouldn't miss it."

Angi leaned forward and cupped her hand to her mouth, trying to raise her voice over the band. "Sorry we're late. Parking sucks."

With one arm still around Sam, Cheryl pulled her tight, the barricade pressed between them. "Gee, look how you rate. You've got your own private spot for the show."

"What can I say? Helps to know someone."

"Look." Angi frantically smacked Cheryl on the shoulder, pointing up at the stage with her mouth hanging wide open. "Holy shit, I can't believe it. Look at Jodi."

Sam whipped around and immediately burst out laughing. Jodi had her back to Terra and they were both dancing while playing their guitars. There was no denying, this Jodi was certainly a different woman. Cheryl dropped a hand on each of Sam's shoulders. "I don't know what you've done to Jodi but this is a fucking miracle." She emphasized each word she spoke with a small shake.

"I…I…" What could she say? She couldn't take credit for Jodi's transformation. She hadn't done anything. It had just happened. But it made her heart soar to see her like this now. "Seriously, Cheryl, it wasn't me."

"Well, whatever it was, I still say it's a fucking miracle." Cheryl squeezed Sam's shoulders one more time.

Before Sam could respond again, the band moved into a slow ballad. Angi hopped up and down. "Oh, oh, oh, I love this song."

"Yeah, I do too." Sam nodded, not taking her eyes off Jodi for a second. Of all the slow songs the band played, she liked this one the most. However, it wasn't quite as good as having Jodi play it for her privately in her studio. Nothing could compare to that.

With her arms wrapped around in a self-embrace, she swayed to the gentle beat, losing herself in the notes. She could almost feel Jodi's hands caressing her as she listened to the soulful cry of her guitar. The song continued to build. As it reached the crescendo leading into the solo, Jodi slowly stepped to the edge of the stage where she knelt, her eyes locking with Sam's.

Her legs growing weaker with every note, Sam leaned hard against the barricade to support herself. There may have been several hundred crowded in front of the stage, but at that moment, Jodi played only for her. No one else existed.

Cheryl patted her on the back. "Damn, Sam. You are one lucky girl."

"Uh-huh." She absently nodded, her eyes still glued on Jodi. She didn't even dare to blink. She didn't want to miss a single moment.

When Jodi finally finished up the long solo, she leaned forward, gave a small nod and mouthed out three words.

Sam gasped. She hadn't just seen that, had she? Or was it only wishful thinking? Jodi could have said, "Sky of blue," for all she knew. But as Jodi jumped up, gave her a wink and blew a kiss at her, she knew she wasn't mistaken at all. Jodi had whispered in front of all these people, the one thing above all else that she had been hoping to hear, praying to hear the most. Without a sound, Jodi had mouthed, "I love you."

The crowd began to cheer and clap. Several whistles pierced the air. Sam wasn't sure if they were cheering because of Jodi's mind-blowing guitar playing or for what had silently passed between them. But what did it matter? They may only be cheering because of Jodi's talent but for her, she'd just as soon think it was because Jodi had picked that moment, that sweet intimate moment, to declare her love for her.

Angi threw an arm around her. "Holy crap, Sam. I'm so jealous. That has to be the most romantic thing I've ever seen."

"What? I can be romantic too." Cheryl wrinkled up her nose on one side and stuck her tongue out at Angi.

"Honey, you're romantic too, but this was like..." Angi stomped her foot twice on the ground and fanned herself. "This was like, oh my God, wow."

"Maybe I should get up there and play guitar for you." Now a devilish grin lit up Cheryl's face.

Snorting out a laugh, Angi shook her head. "Oh, no, no, no. That wouldn't be romantic. That would be just plain frightening."

Cheryl pulled Angi in, giving her a passionate kiss on the neck. "How about a private show later?"

Tilting her head to the side, Angi raised her eyebrows. "Oh, really? You're going to give me a private guitar show later?"

Cheryl gave a playful nibble on her earlobe. "Who said anything about a guitar?"

Cheryl's amorous antics amused Sam greatly. Seeing the ease and comfort that Angi and Cheryl shared, Sam realized that it was what she had always wanted with someone. She had almost given up all hope of ever finding it. Maybe she was just destined to always be lonely. But now it appeared that her wildest dreams had come true. She had Jodi.

With Cheryl's arms still wrapped around her, Angi turned back to Sam. "Girl, seriously, I don't know what you've done with Jodi but I never in a million years thought I'd ever see her happy and smiling again."

"I didn't do anything, Angi, seriously. I was just a friend." Her hand on her chest, Sam protested. Angi had it all wrong. If anything, Jodi should be getting the praise. If it weren't for her, she'd be huddled in front of her computers, a can of Diet Coke in one hand, a mouse in the other, miserable and lonely.

Cheryl reached over and clapped Sam firmly on the shoulder. "So, aren't you glad now I dragged you kicking and screaming to Pride?"

"Yes, yes, you were right." She couldn't keep the silly grin off her face. She owed Cheryl and Angi big-time. All too quickly, the band finished their last song. It certainly hadn't felt like an hour and a half. More like a few minutes. Up on stage, Terra had taken Lynn's left hand. With her guitar held high in her free hand, Jodi grabbed Lynn's right hand and together, they all took a deep bow as the crowd roared with applause. Sam jumped in place, clapping wildly. Jodi usually walked straight off the stage without a backward glance, but not today. With one final thrust of her guitar in the air, Jodi smiled out at the crowd and then turned to Sam, giving her a wink.

"Well, that's my cue. Time to do my roadie duties." With a quick wave, she darted off for the stage.

* * *

Jodi bounded down the ramp beside the stage, holding her guitar high over her right shoulder. She couldn't remember a better show. The crowd was alive, clapping and cheering. Also, no flying supersized drinks to duck or bigots with bullhorns. And then there was Sam. Despite the large adoring crowd, she had played only for her. And she certainly hoped she had been able to read her lips at the end of the solo in her song, "Forever, You." From the look on her face, she figured she had—a mixture of surprise and jubilation. The best part, she hadn't even planned it. She was just finishing the solo, her eyes locked with Sam's, and it seemed the perfect moment. Although they had been separated by a stage and an exuberant crowd surrounded them, none of that mattered. At that moment, she wanted Sam to know, needed her to know, that she had fallen deeply in love with her.

Sam met her at the bottom of the ramp, gasping for breath, and flung her arms tight around her waist, nearly taking her off her feet. "You were *awesome*, baby."

Still holding her guitar in her right hand, Jodi slipped her free hand behind Sam's neck, pulled her quickly in, and planted her lips firmly against Sam's, feeling the soft fullness of her mouth against hers. Her heart still hammered, whether from having Sam in her arms or the excitement of the show or both she wasn't sure. She had to fight the urge not to sweep Sam up, spinning around so fast that her feet flew out. "Oh my God, thanks, Sam. That was such a blast. Did you see that crowd?"

"Yeah, it was unbelievable. You were a huge hit."

Just then Lynn ran down the ramp, carrying several microphones. As she passed, she clapped Jodi on the back. "Hey, you two. No kissy kissy until we get the stage cleared."

Jodi and Sam looked at each other and laughed. "I guess I've been neglecting my roadie duties. Hope I don't get fired."

"Hmmm. Well, we wouldn't want that, would we?" Jodi raised her left eyebrow and then held out her purple Paul Reed Smith guitar. "Here, why don't you take this over and put it in its case while I run back up and grab the others?" Before turning back up the ramp, she watched as Sam walked away, her guitar cradled in her arms as if it were a newborn baby. The show may have been great but it wasn't nearly as good as having Sam there with her. Sam had changed everything.

After packing away her guitars, Jodi joined Kat on stage with Sam. Lynn ran up to join them and with one on each corner, they heaved Kat's drums. Jodi let out a loud grunt. "Damn, give me my guitar amp any day." She winked at Sam across from her.

Kat merely shook her head. "Always the same with you, Jodi. Always the same."

"I swear to God, Kat, someday I'm going to put wheels on these."

"Well, that way I can chase you around stage while we're playing, Jodi."

Lynn chimed in. "Yeah, holy crap, Jodi. What did you do, chug a dozen espressos or something before the show?"

"What? I just felt really fired up."

Kat giggled. "I guess."

"Well, it was an awesome show." Lynn gave a firm nod.

After they shuffled Kat's drums down the ramp to the trailer, Lynn hooked a finger over her shoulder. "Hey, I'm going to go help Terra sell albums. Catch you guys in a bit." With a wave, she trotted off around the side of the stage.

With Jodi on the front and Kat and Sam pushing from behind, they slid Kat's drums into the trailer. Once in, they quickly packed equipment around the drums.

Kat wiped her forehead with the back of her hand. "So, what's left?"

"Just my amp and effects pedalboard." Jodi threw her arm around Sam, pulling her under her arm. "Sam and I can get that, can't we, Sam?"

"You bet."

"Okay, great." Kat patted Jodi in the center of her back. "I'm going to go help Lynn and Terra sign some CDs."

Jodi grabbed Sam by the hand and they bounded up the ramp. With the next act up in less than fifteen minutes, they hustled across the stage. Jodi quickly unplugged her amp and wound up the cord. "Hey, I'll grab my pedalboard, if you get this behemoth." She pointed to her amp.

"Uh…uh…" Sam glanced from Jodi to the amp, her mouth struggling to form words. "You want me to *what*?"

Jodi began to laugh and quickly pulled her into a one-armed hug. "I'm only kidding, but you should have seen your face."

"Oh, thank God. I wasn't sure what I'd do."

"No, I'll grab the amp if you can get my pedalboard."

Once they had stowed all the equipment in the trailer, Jodi hopped out and locked the door. She turned her face up to the beating sun and ran her fingers through her short black hair before turning to Sam. "Hey, thanks for all the help."

Jodi reached out and clutched Sam's hand in hers. Part of her wanted nothing more than to wrap her arms tightly around her, feeling Sam's body pressed against hers, their lips teasing. Or maybe run away and find a quiet place for just the two of them, not another person anywhere around. She could pull Sam in close, her hot breath against Sam's neck, and whisper those three words again. No show could compare to that. Finally, she forced herself to step back. "Say, why don't we go see how they're all doing with the CDs?"

* * *

Go see how they're doing with the CDs? She must have misheard Jodi. She never approached the fans. She did everything she could to avoid the fans. "So, you want *me* to go see how they're doing selling CDs?"

"No, I thought I'd come along." Jodi waved her hand beside her head and marched off toward the table where the others were signing CDs for the large crowd that had lined up. She glanced back at Sam. "I'm curious to see how the advertisement for the website is going."

Sam stared at Jodi with her mouth hanging open. "Okay… um, that sounds good." What else could she say? This really *was* a whole new Jodi.

Jodi walked up to the table, pulled out a chair and sat down beside Terra where she picked up a pen, opened up a CD case and began signing the inner sleeve as if she had done it a million times before. Sam stood back, her fist pressed to her mouth as Kat, Lynn and Terra each whipped around, one after the other, all gawking down the table at Jodi, looking much like the Three Wise Monkeys—see no evil, hear no evil, speak no evil.

Kat found her voice first. "Holy shit."

Jodi lifted her eyes and met the stares of her bandmates. "Hi guys. So, how's it going?"

Terra blinked. "Ah…well, good. We're selling quite a few."

"Wow, that's great!" Jodi bobbed her head as if talking about the weather and turned back to the young woman standing in front of her, flipping open another album to sign.

Slowly, the three women dragged their eyes away and turned back to the queue in front of them. From the way Kat kept shooting glances out of the corner of her eye down the table, Sam knew exactly what she was thinking. Who is this woman and what did she do with our Jodi? She felt the same way, but whatever had happened, she wasn't complaining. She stepped up beside Jodi and lightly tickled her fingers over her shoulder.

Jodi reached up, covering Sam's hand for a moment, and then brushed her lips over her fingers before turning back to a young woman, no more than sixteen, with green dreadlocks and a tie-dyed orange skirt, holding out an album for her to sign.

"I just wanted to say, you're like…I mean totally wow." The young woman fought to catch her breath.

Jodi let out a soft laugh. "Why thanks. I hope you liked the show." Her voice was low and breathy, a sound Sam had come to love.

The young woman started, her eyes flying wide, before she quickly recovered. "Oh, yeah. I certainly did." She quickly nodded, her vibrant hair whirling about her head.

"That's great." Jodi flipped open the case and with a quick scrawl, signed her name followed by, "Rock on."

"Hey, thanks." With the CD in her hands, the young woman skipped off.

Sam pulled up another chair beside Jodi. It was all she could do not to reach out and wrap her arms around her. She had talked to a fan, actually *talked* to her. In a way, that was even more surprising than the message she had whispered to her during the show. If she hadn't already totally fallen for Jodi, she certainly would at that moment. With her heart pounding, she leaned her lips close to Jodi's ear. "So, you doing okay, babe?"

Jodi shot her a bright grin. "Yeah, actually I am." Their eyes connected for a second before Jodi turned back to the line in front of her.

Half an hour later the crowd had finally dwindled down. Jodi talked with a teenage girl with bubblegum-pink spiky hair about playing guitar as she signed a CD for her. "Hey, keep it up and you can do anything you set your mind to."

Terra and Lynn were packing up the remaining CDs while Kat stood up and stretched. With her fists in the small of her back, she groaned. "Oh my God, I don't think we've ever sold that many CDs."

"No kidding. I thought we were going to run out." Terra rattled the box in her arms. "We've only got about a dozen left."

Jodi bounced up from the chair as if launched by a spring. "Wow, only a dozen? That's unbelievable."

Kat spun around on the spot. "Speaking of unbelievable—"

From behind Jodi, Sam waved her hand across her neck furiously, shaking her head. "No, no, no." She mouthed the words.

Kat's eyes flew wide and she quickly changed direction. "Um, the weather turned out good." Meeting Sam's eyes, she shrugged.

Jodi continued on, missing the exchange between Sam and Kat. "Hey, let's all get out of here and head back to your house and grab a few beers."

On the walk back to the car, Sam held Jodi's hand as they bounced along. She had never seen her so excited before, not even the day when she bought her new guitar. Kat trotted up beside her and leaned in, lowering her voice to barely a whisper. "Hey, Sam, what's up with Jodi?"

Sam turned to Jodi, watching for a moment as she rocked her head back and barked out a loud laugh at something Terra said. The transformation in Jodi was nothing short of miraculous. Finally, she leaned over to Kat, fighting back tears. "I don't know, Kat, but whatever it is, I certainly don't want to jinx it."

CHAPTER TWELVE

Jodi pulled up in front of Kat and Lynn's house with the trailer. It had taken over an hour and a half to get out of downtown Grand Rapids. Although they had access to the side streets, the huge crowds prevented them from driving any faster than a crawl, but she wasn't going to let that put her in a bad mood. Not today. Not after the show they had. And not with Sam sitting there beside her. She threw her Escape in reverse and with a devilish grin, quickly brushed her hand up Sam's thigh as she twisted around in her seat to peer out the rear window. "Oops."

Sam spun sideways in her seat. "Oops, huh? Yeah, I bet."

Jodi slapped her hand to her chest, her best who-me-couldn't-be expression on her face. "What?"

Sam jabbed her in the ribs. "Jodi Price, I don't think you've ever been innocent."

"Oh, and what about you? I could barely drive through Grand Rapids with your hands wandering up and down my leg."

"Well, I had to amuse myself somehow."

"Oh, really?" Jodi leaned in, pressing her lips to Sam's until a car horn blasted, making her jump.

Behind them, Kat and Lynn were waiting to pull in. Lynn blasted the horn again while Kat hung out the passenger window. "Hey, you two, get a room or something. You're blocking the street."

Jodi laughed, rolling her eyes as she watched Kat sitting on the edge of the car door, her entire upper body out the window with her hands held palms up beside her. "Maybe we should finish pulling in, huh?"

Sam wiped her mouth with the back of her hand. "Yeah, maybe that's a good idea before Kat and Lynn really start teasing us."

"Yeah, well, it's probably too late for that." Jodi quickly spun the wheel around, backing the trailer perfectly into the driveway. She was nearly halfway up when the trailer veered off to the right and she stomped down hard on the brakes. "Damn it. Every—single—time." Shaking her head, she emphasized each word. "I swear I'm going to fix that pothole myself one of these days."

Sam hid a grin as Jodi pulled forward to straighten out the trailer. "I'm sure that's it, hon."

Jodi couldn't help but smile. Not even that pothole could put a damper on her day. She straightened the trailer back out and quickly reversed the rest of the way up the drive. Terra dashed up the drive having just pulled up in front of the house in her car. Together, they hustled to unload the equipment from the trailer, forming a sort of production line. Sweat trickled down Jodi's face as they finished with the last of the equipment and she locked up the back of the trailer. She leaned back and wiped her forehead. "Wow, after this, I could use a Guinness."

Sam snorted. "When couldn't you use a Guinness, Jodi?"

Kat joined in, patting Jodi on the back. "She's got you figured out, my friend."

"That she does." Jodi leaned forward, her chin resting on top of Sam's head. She had spent far too long pushing everyone away. Now she wanted nothing more than Sam to figure out everything there was to her.

They all walked around the back of the house to the deck. Lynn slipped through the slider to fetch drinks while Kat and Terra pulled up a couple of lounge chairs. Jodi flopped back in the porch swing with Sam, rocking back and forth. She closed her eyes and breathed in the humid evening air. What a day. Her entire body still tingled. Even though almost every muscle ached in some fashion, she could barely sit still. Give her a stage and her guitar and she had no doubt she could easily put on another hour and a half show, maybe two. Finally, she reached over and squeezed Sam's hand. "Hey, thanks again for coming today."

Sam tightened her grip on Jodi's fingers. "Wouldn't have missed it for the world."

Lynn trudged back through the slider with a cooler filled with drinks, pushing the door open with her hip. Jodi leaped up, grabbing Sam by the hand and sending the swing rocking, and quickly snatched a bottle of Guinness from the ice, popping the top off with the opener attached to the side of the house. After today, nothing would hit the spot better.

Sam finally settled on a Killian's Irish Red while the others each grabbed their favorite drinks. For a few minutes, everyone sat in silence relaxing, sipping their beverages, the sun peeking through the tall elms surrounding the backyard.

Kat scooted forward, her beer bottle resting on one knee. "Hey, Jodi, what was that dance you were doing during 'Tease Me, Please Me'?"

"You liked that?" Jodi jumped up and began hopping across the deck on one foot, pretending to play guitar and slopping Guinness with each step. When she reached the end of the deck, she whirled around. "Ta-da."

Sam dried her eyes as she rolled in the porch swing with laughter. Terra snorted beer out of her nose while Kat doubled up laughing, her head in Lynn's lap. Lynn dabbed the corners of her eyes with the back of Kat's shirt.

Lynn found her voice first. "Oh my God, Jodi. I think you just made me pee myself."

A new round of laughter exploded from the deck. Jodi merely shrugged. "At least I didn't try lying down and running in circles on my side while playing guitar."

Terra pointed her beer bottle at Jodi. "I'm not sure any of us would have made it through that."

Kat sat back up. "Yeah, I was waiting for Jodi to jump off the stage and try crowd surfing."

"Oh, I can just picture that." Jodi held her arms out as if she were about to do a swan dive off the deck. "Here I go flying off the stage and everyone jumps to the side. Splat."

Sam laughed so much the entire swing shook. "Well, babe, I'd try to catch you."

"Now then, that would definitely be worth it." Jodi plopped down beside Sam, wrapping her arm around her shoulders. She certainly didn't need a stage to want to jump into Sam's arms. No, she didn't need any excuse at all for that. She pulled Sam closer, brushing her lips lightly against Sam's ear. "Believe me, you can catch me anytime."

* * *

Kat tossed her empty beer bottle in the recycle bin beside her on the deck and flipped open the lid on the cooler. Her shoulders fell. "Oh damn, we need more drinks." She grumbled as she heaved herself up from the lounge chair.

Lynn hopped up beside her. "Here, I'll help you, hon."

Kat scooped up the cooler in her arms and shook her head. "No, Sam wants to help, don't you Sam?"

Her beer bottle almost to her lips, Sam froze. "Um, yeah sure." She wasn't sure what Kat had in mind but from the look on her face, filling the cooler with fresh drinks was probably the least of it. She nudged Jodi beside her who was talking rapidly with Terra. "I'll be right back, babe."

Jodi stopped midsentence and flashed her a bright smile. "Okay, I'll be right here."

With her beer bottle clutched tightly in her fist, Sam followed Kat in the house. It was obvious that Kat had something she wanted to talk about. Hopefully she hadn't wrecked something on her drums. With each step, her chest tightened. Something about Kat's stance, her stiff shoulders or maybe the way she tossed around the cooler, said she meant business.

Kat heaved the cooler up onto the center island in the kitchen and then whirled around, jabbing a finger at Sam. "I just want to know one thing—what the hell happened to Jodi?"

Stunned, Sam fought hard not to laugh. She had been wondering the same thing all day. What the hell *did* happen to Jodi? All she knew was she certainly didn't have anything to do with it. Jodi was just different, better. She couldn't explain it any better than that. Finally, she shook her head. "That's just it, Kat. Honestly, I have no idea."

"You mean you didn't have anything to do with her coming up to the table and signing CDs for the fans?"

"I swear I had nothing to do with that. I was just as shocked as everyone when she walked up there."

Kat finally slumped back against the countertop. "You never saw Jodi perform before…well, you know." She cringed.

Without speaking, Sam quickly shook her head.

"I didn't think so." Kat paused for a moment. "Well, I have. I've known Jodi for a long time. And that was the old Jodi up onstage today." She nodded to the patio door leading out to the deck. "That's the old Jodi out there tonight. I never thought I'd see her like this again. After her accident, so much of her died. I still can't believe it. Whatever you've done, Sam, this is all because of you."

"Seriously, Kat, I haven't done anything. I've only tried to be a good friend. I swear, that's it." Sam turned and watched Jodi through the patio door, her head thrown back and laughing with Terra and Lynn about something. Still staring, she let out a long, low breath. "Amazing."

"Yes, you are."

Sam tore her eyes away to find Kat staring directly at her, her elbows slung back against the counter as she slowly appraised her. Her amazing? How could Kat think that about her? It was Jodi who had changed so much. She opened her mouth to protest but Kat held up her finger.

"Look, Sam. I know you don't think you did anything and all that but from my standpoint, you are nothing short of a miracle. Trust me, you are just what she needed. Jodi has pushed away everyone in her life since that accident. God, I was probably the closest to her and even I couldn't get past that tall, cold wall she put up. I kept telling her that her voice didn't matter to me, her scars didn't matter, but her eyes would glaze over and she was a million miles away. I know Lynn and Terra feel the same way but we couldn't convince Jodi of that. I didn't hear her once mention her voice or scars today, did you?"

"Actually, Kat, Jodi's never said anything to me about her voice or her scars. I know it bothers her a lot, I'd have to be blind not to see that, but it's just something we've never talked about. I figured someday when she was ready to talk about it, then she would."

"Seriously, Sam? You've never talked to Jodi about her accident? You truly *are* amazing. There're not many people who would let something like that go. You really are perfect for Jodi."

Still running Kat's words through her head, Sam stepped over beside her, grabbing a couple of bottles of Guinness from the fridge while Kat plucked several Coronas from the door. Although she could see how Kat might think she was perfect for Jodi, it was actually the other way around—Jodi was perfect for her. If it hadn't been for her, she would never have let herself get close to someone again. But still, there seemed to be a wall with their closeness, a point where Jodi would pull away. Lord knows, it was probably something she was doing wrong. She had messed up every relationship she had ever had—just look at the Jennifer disaster—but she didn't want that with Jodi. With Jodi, she wanted not only a relationship but forever. Waking up when they were eighty and trying to remember where they put their teeth, laughing at each new wrinkle, each new gray hair, going to bed each night holding each other's liver-spotted hand. Nothing less than forever. She just didn't know what to do. Finally, she stood up. "Say, Kat, I have a question."

"Oh, what's up?" She looked up with a Killian's in her hands.

Sam tried to clear her throat. If there were ever a time she could use a drink it was now. Her mouth felt as if it were filled with dry sand. "Well, things have been going really well between us. I mean like today during the concert, Jodi mouthed out 'I love you' during one of her guitar solos."

"She *did*?"

"Yeah, I about fell over."

Kat let out a soft whistle. "Wow."

"Tell me about it. She will stay at my house or I will stay at her house. Yet it seems to get to a certain point and then there's this awkwardness. I'm not sure if it's just me or what."

"Hmm. I wouldn't worry about it, Sam. I see how Jodi looks at you." Kat leaned in and lowered her voice to barely a whisper. "She's probably worried about her scars. You know, they're not only on her neck."

Sam thought about it for a moment. That would explain the one-piece bathing suit with the wrap Jodi had tied around her waist, not that she hadn't found it extremely alluring, but it would hide those scars. And her jeans with the black tank top tucked in. How many other things did Jodi do, big and small, every day to hide her scars? "You know, Kat, I bet you're right. I know I'm probably being silly but I don't want to mess everything up."

Kat grabbed her by the shoulders and spun her around quickly, facing the patio door and the deck beyond where Jodi was slapping her thigh and laughing. She pointed. "Look at that. Whatever you've been doing, Sam, just keep doing it." She gave Sam a small shake. "And relax. Everything will be okay. Now, what do you say we get this cooler out there before they begin to wonder what happened to us?"

"Sounds good." Sam grabbed one end of the cooler while Kat grabbed the other. As they walked back out on the deck, Kat's words whirled about in her head. *Whatever you've been doing, just keep doing it. Whatever you've been doing, just keep doing it.* But that was just it. She didn't really know what she had been doing. She simply tried to be a good friend, perhaps even help take away some of the pain in Jodi's life that she lived with every day. That's all. And then somewhere along the way, she had fallen in love with her—totally and helplessly in love.

* * *

Jodi gave Kat, Lynn and Terra each a hug for the second time as they got ready to leave. The entire day still felt like a dream—a very good dream, not like the usual Technicolor nightmares she had of her car crash—crunching metal and busting glass. This was the closest she had been to what it was like before her accident. The crowd was great. The music had all come together. It didn't seem as if she could play a wrong note. And then there was Sam. She had to be the best part of all. Still, she couldn't quite shake the feeling that at any moment, she would open her eyes and find herself lying alone in her bed. She forced herself to refrain from yet another round of hugs—it had just been one of those days that called for hugging—and threw an arm around Sam's shoulders, pulling her in tight. "Well, we should probably be going."

"Hey, now you two have a *good* night." Kat leaned in and gave an exaggerated wink, sending a new bout of laughter around the deck.

"Yeah, yeah." Jodi rolled her eyes, accepting Kat's good-natured ribbing. Actually, she didn't mind being teased about her relationship with Sam. Quite the opposite, she welcomed it. She had someone in her life that saw her merely for her. She looked down at Sam, tucked tightly under her arm. For a moment, the moonlight caught in Sam's eyes and it was all she could do not to lay her back right there and slowly, methodically remove each piece of her clothing, savoring the moment as the pale soft light illuminated her body. She didn't care who else was standing there—it would be only Sam she would see.

"Don't worry, Kat, I'm sure we will." Sam leaned forward and twisted her face up in an extremely exaggerated wink.

After another round of quick goodbyes and *another* round of hugs, Jodi sauntered with Sam tucked under her arm to her car, slowly swaying back and forth, neither of them speaking. They rode in silence. She had wanted to pinch herself several times to make sure it wasn't a dream. Even if it were a dream, she didn't mind. Headlights whizzed past on the darkened streets, the sound of her tires softly howling against the pavement. She glanced over at Sam slouched back in her seat, her eyes half closed and a look of utter contentment obvious in the darkness.

Sam rolled her head toward Jodi, a lazy smile curling her lips. "Some day, huh?"

"Yeah, you can say that again." Jodi giggled, a low musical riff like one of her slow solos.

"Some day." Sam joined her giggle—two instruments playing in unison.

As they passed under the streetlights, the inside of the car pulsed like a slow heartbeat. Or more like slow, rhythmic breathing. Jodi continued to peer out of the corner of her eye at Sam as the street lights illuminated her fine features, breathing color into her flame-orange hair before fading back to gray. Maybe it was coming off the adrenaline high or maybe she was just tired, but watching Sam seemed to add to the dreamlike feeling—one of those where you never wanted to wake up. That's exactly how she felt right then—if this was a dream then she never wanted to wake up. She nearly jumped at the touch of warm fingers on her arm. Pulled back to reality, she turned to find Sam leaning forward and staring at her, her head cocked slightly to the side.

"You okay, hon?" Sam slowly walked her fingers up Jodi's bare skin.

"Yes, yes. I'm fine." She swallowed. She was anything but fine. Any moment now she was probably going to hyperventilate. She could feel each hair on her arm standing up as if static flowed over her body. If she had any question whether this was only a dream, the feel of Sam's hand against her tingling flesh certainly dispelled that. Each light caress sent jolts coursing through her like small electric shocks. Sam leaned her head over, resting it on Jodi's shoulder, continuing to trace her fingertips lightly over Jodi's skin.

Jodi now shivered, goose pimples rising not only under the warm pressure of Sam's fingers but over her entire body. Even when she turned onto Sam's street, her house halfway up the block on the right, she had a wild urge to slam down the accelerator and just keep driving. They could drive all night—didn't matter where. Maybe end up on the lakeshore and watch the sun rise. But a heavy lump settled deep in her throat when she threw her Escape into park and shut off the engine. Finally, her voice low and husky, she leaned her lips against the side of Sam's head. "Well." Not so much a question or a statement but a little of both.

"Well." Sam echoed back, her voice barely a whisper.

Jodi let out a long labored breath. "We're here."

"Yes, we're here." Sam again began tracing her fingertips lightly up and down her arm, working higher and higher up to her bare shoulder.

In the darkness, Jodi closed her eyes, her skin burning. "I guess I should walk you up to your house."

Still teasing her flesh, Sam ran her fingers across her shoulder to the side of her face. "I guess you should walk me up to my house."

With a soft sigh, Jodi pressed her lips to the side of Sam's face. She then threw open her door and quickly hopped out before she could change her mind. The temperature had fallen but the air was still heavy, making each breath difficult. At least she thought it was the air. Her feet felt as if they weighed a ton as she trudged around the front of the car where she met Sam already standing on her cobblestone walk. Without a word, Sam nestled in under her arm, pressing her body against hers and wrapping her arms tight around Jodi's waist. Together, they slowly walked up to Sam's door. Although she wanted nothing more than to stay the night, to curl tight into Sam's waiting arms, she didn't trust herself, not after today. When they stepped up on the porch, Sam slid out from under her arm and stood in front of her, holding a hand in each of hers and looking up directly into her eyes. Small pinpricks of light reflected in her eyes, either from the streetlights or the stars, she didn't know which. "It's been such a great day today, Sam, I wish it didn't have to end."

Sam leaned closer, standing up on her tiptoes and continuing to stare directly into her eyes. "It doesn't have to end you know."

Jodi opened her mouth—if she didn't leave right then, she wouldn't be able to—but a soft finger silenced her protest. She stared deep into Sam's eyes, past the pinpricks of light, searching.

With her hands tightly wrapped around her arms, Sam took one step back, then another, and yet another. Now backing through the doorway, Sam pulled her in tight, her lips to her ear. "It—doesn't—have—to—end."

* * *

Sam leaned forward and placed her finger to Jodi's lips as they glistened in the moonlight, the same lips that had uttered soundlessly the words, "I love you," just hours before. There was no way she was going to let Jodi take off, not tonight, not after those words. With her heart thundering, beating the inside of her chest so hard she could barely catch her breath, she pulled Jodi in tight, her lips to her ear. "It—doesn't—have—to—end."

She took another step back into the pale glow of the streetlight flooding in through the window, the only light filling the room. With Jodi still in her arms, she laid her chin softly on her shoulder and toed the door shut behind them, the clack of the latch echoing through the quiet house until it finally faded, leaving only the swishing of her own heartbeat rushing in her ears. Or was it Jodi's? She wasn't sure. She wasn't even sure if it was her pulse or Jodi's that beat against her cheek as she hugged her tight. Or did it even matter? Under the soft light, she leaned back, peering up at Jodi. Whatever she had expected, it certainly wasn't what she saw on Jodi's face, a cross between terror and nausea.

Her chest suddenly tight, Sam stepped back, biting her lip. Had she just made a huge mistake? Was she pushing Jodi too much? After such a great day for Jodi, had she gone and ruined it? She had to say something, make some excuse, any excuse, but Kat's advice again popped back into her head—*relax and everything will be okay*. Like she had said, Jodi was probably terrified at the thought of someone seeing the scars on her body. If it were her, she'd most likely feel the same way, wondering how Jodi would look at her if she had scars covering her body. Granted, she wasn't exactly the picture of self-confidence herself. Just look at how her last relationship had turned out with her ex. She'd let her run all over her. This time round, she was going to have to be the strong one, the one to make the first move. For a long moment, she simply held Jodi tight in her arms, no expectations, no pressure, rubbing her fingers up and down her spine, doing her best to comfort her while she trembled. If nothing more, she could be a good friend.

At last, Jodi took a deep breath and slowly let it out. She leaned her lips down to Sam's ear. "Are you sure this is what you want?"

Sam pulled back so she could look directly into Jodi's eyes. "Oh, yes." At that moment, there wasn't anything else in the world she wanted more. She wanted all of Jodi. She wanted Jodi to have all of her. Yes, she was definitely sure this was what she wanted, what she needed. As if to reinforce the point, she threw her arms around Jodi's neck and standing on her tiptoes, covered Jodi's warm full lips with hers, pressing her body firmly against her.

They started slowly but with each gasp, each caress, each deep moan, their kissing became more passionate, more urgent. Sam lifted her hands to the side of Jodi's face. When the tip of Jodi's tongue touched hers, her knees buckled and she fought to hold herself up. She kissed Jodi faster and faster. She wanted her, needed her, every bit of her. Her entire body felt as if it were on fire as she pressed it against Jodi's. The growing excitement between her legs began to ache, dull at first then building to a damp, hot throbbing. Oh God, she couldn't ever remember feeling this aroused. Any moment, just the feel of Jodi's hungry lips against hers might send her over the edge.

Finally, she tore away from Jodi's mouth, gasping for breath. The room spun slowly as her heart tore at the inside of her chest. "I've been waiting all day to do that."

"You've been waiting all day to do *that*? Wow." Jodi blew out a low whistle through her teeth.

"Yeah, all day. And more." Much, much more. Sam giggled softly, barely making a sound. She twined her fingers through

Jodi's then took a tentative step toward her bedroom. This time, Jodi followed with no resistance. With each step, they picked up speed—or was it just her imagination—as she led Jodi through the dark house. Without letting go, she flipped on the light, a momentary explosion of brightness, which she quickly dimmed to a soft glow. She then turned back to Jodi and slowly closed the distance between them until their hips again touched. She had lived this moment in her dreams what, a hundred times, a thousand times? And now it was happening. Here was Jodi right in front of her, her small chest heaving with each deep breath, her nipples straining against the black spaghetti strap tank.

Still peering deep into Jodi's eyes, Sam slowly reached down, hooking her fingers into the hem of her shirt, her arms crisscrossed, then lifting, inch by inch, over her flat stomach, over her ribs, over the bottom of her breasts, gradually exposing first one hard erect nipple followed by the other. She eased her shirt up over her face and then quickly yanked it the rest of the way off. She wasn't sure what made her do it—nervousness or silliness or some combination of the two—but she slowly whipped her shirt through the air in great circles over her head like a cowgirl with a lariat—the only thing missing was a good ole yeehaw—then tossed it on the floor beside her bed. Now standing in the dim light of her bedroom, she gave a small shrug, waiting. The moment drew out, still Jodi said nothing. Sam swallowed, her mouth suddenly dry. Why didn't Jodi say something? Did she think her goofy little cowgirl up display was stupid? Or worse, did she simply not like what she was seeing? She could hear the clock ticking on the wall like small explosions blasting through the silence. By now, she'd settle for any comment—a hey, not bad, or even gee, better than expected—anything.

Jodi stared back, wide-eyed, barely moving except for her eyes that traveled up and down Sam's body. "Um, wow." She covered her mouth with her hand and slowly shook her head, again seemingly taking in all of Sam. "Wow."

Sam stood there, now the one at a loss for words. No one had ever stared at her with such intensity before, as if trying to take in every single aspect of her. She had always thought of herself as just little miss plain Jane computer geek. But that look from Jodi, that hunger in her eyes, that craving on her lips, made her feel beautiful, sensual, sexy, desirable, all wrapped up together. She had never before felt so wanted, so complete.

With her eyes still boring into Sam, Jodi quickly stepped back and in one swift motion, tugged her black tank top over her head much the same way someone rips off a Band-Aid. With her shoulders slumped and her arms wrapped around her naked chest, she now glued her eyes to the floor in front of her.

Even in the dim light, even with Jodi wrapping her arms around herself, Sam could still see the deep scars which dug into the side of her body, starting under her left armpit, running down behind her left breast, and disappearing into the waistband of her jeans over her left hip. Sam nearly gasped but quickly slammed her mouth shut. Sure, she had known Jodi had some scars on her body. Even Kat had told her they were pretty bad, but good God she wasn't prepared for this. No one could be. It looked as if someone had gone in and carved the flesh from her body, leaving a deep jagged white trench in its place. Sam swallowed, tears threatening. No wonder Jodi was self-conscious. Having her body torn up by someone else, a drunken nobody, and to feel all that pain, she couldn't begin to imagine. Even as she continued staring at Jodi, she quickly blotted away a tear that spilled over her eyelid. It would do no good if she started crying in front of Jodi, so swallowing again, doing her best to force down the lump in her throat that was nearly choking her, Sam shuffled forward, taking Jodi's hands in hers. With a gentle reassuring squeeze, she pulled Jodi's arms wider, slowly opening up the view of her chest. Jodi's small breasts lifted with each ragged breath. Her slightly upturned dark nipples stood out like two hard points. Even with the scars, Sam had never seen anyone as beautiful. Finally catching her breath, she let out a low, soft whistle. "My God, Jodi, you're absolutely gorgeous."

Jodi lifted her eyes, tentatively at first as if daring, hoping, pleading. Without saying a word, Sam could read a dozen questions racing across her face. Could what she thought she heard be true? Could Sam have meant what she said? Could she possibly believe it? Slowly, her face relaxed, a small smile curling her lips. "Thanks, Sam. You're the best."

Sam closed the remaining distance between them and wrapped her arms around Jodi, their naked skin pressed together. She could feel the heat from Jodi's small firm breasts against hers. Her nipples burned as if seared by fire as they brushed up against Jodi's smooth skin. Her knees growing weaker and weaker, Sam teetered forward, hanging her chin on Jodi's shoulder, her lips less than an inch from her ear. "So are you, Jodi."

Their arms tangled, they simply held each other. Sam counted Jodi's heartbeats—one, two, three—as they beat against hers. If nothing else happened, this would be enough, only holding each other, not sure whose heartbeat was strongest, Jodi's or hers. Slowly, she began to slide her fingers over Jodi's naked back, tracing over each bump in her spine.

Eyes closed, Jodi arched her back in Sam's arms, her bottom lip rolled over her teeth. A small sigh escaped her throat. "Ohhh."

Sam inhaled quickly. That small sigh had sent tingles like small lightning bolts through her body, bouncing along the surface of her skin while she continued to caress up and down Jodi's back, with each pass to her sides inching closer and closer to Jodi's waiting breasts. She steadied herself, she was almost there now, just a little farther, but just as she was about to make one final pass, Jodi threw up her hands and in one smooth motion, enfolded Sam's throbbing breasts, lifting them, gently kneading them, working from her chest to her burning, aching nipples, where she rolled each hard raised point under her thumbs. Oh, God. Sam wasn't sure she could take it but just as she was about to cry out, Jodi covered her mouth with hers, and when their tongues touched, she let out a long, low whimper.

She groaned, a deep low sound swallowed by Jodi as she teased her nipples, softly flicking the hard, raised peaks. Jodi then squeezed harder, gently tugging, and Sam gasped, her mouth snapping shut as every muscle from her mouth to her toes tensed. If she weren't careful, she'd end up accidentally biting Jodi as they kissed. But then Jodi lowered her lips to

Sam's burning right nipple, and she threw her head back, all thought erased.

Each time Jodi captured her nipples lightly between her teeth, tickling the tip with the point of her tongue, Sam let out a tiny cry. The sensation was unbelievable, shooting spasms throughout her entire body. Never before had she ever had anything so intense. Her very center pulsed as the warmth continued to build between her legs. Pulsing and throbbing, throbbing and pulsing, each beat of her heart, each breath she took, each tug on her nipples, sending a new surge through her womanhood.

She continued to run her hands over Jodi's bare skin, exploring, searching, and when she finally felt the small swell of Jodi's right breast and her rock-hard nipple, she wanted to yell out in triumph. She ran the nipple through her fingertips, back and forth, lightly circling it as it grew even more. Jodi bent her head back, a loud gasp escaping her shining moist lips, and using the moment of distraction, she ducked down to Jodi's awaiting breast, sucking in her dark, jutting nipple. Jodi began to teeter, and Sam wrapped her arms around Jodi's bare torso. She wouldn't let her fall. She worked at one breast, flicking the tip of her tongue around the hard, excited nipple, teasing it, then jumped to the other. Each time, Jodi shuddered in her arms. Each time, her own arousal grew even more. She didn't know she could feel such intensity. If someone had asked her only that afternoon, she would have said it was impossible. She may have been with others before, but this was the first time she felt fully sexually and sensually alive, as if a blindfold had been ripped off.

With one last taunt of Jodi's nipple with the tip of her tongue, Sam slowly began working her way down, kissing a trail from Jodi's breasts to her belly button, until she knelt in front of her, her face only inches away from Jodi's center. Even through her jeans, she could smell her excitement, a scent that increased her own arousal. She wanted nothing more than to get to the source of that sweet fragrance, to bury her tongue into the deepest depths of Jodi. With her fingers now shaking, she fumbled with Jodi's belt, the ends finally falling to each side.

Next, she focused on the button on Jodi's jeans, but no matter what she tried, she couldn't get it, her fingers seemed to be tied in knots. She gritted her teeth. This was ridiculous. Why couldn't she get it?

Just then, Jodi covered Sam's hands with hers, quickly slipping the button on her jeans. With Sam's fingers still entwined with hers, Jodi reached up, hooking her thumbs in her belt loops, working her jeans gradually lower over her hips, first this way and then that, each time exposing a little more bare skin.

Sam closed her eyes, her breath catching in her chest in great gasps. This was what she had been waiting for, dreaming of since that first night they had met. Finally, she could feel Jodi's jeans fall free and with one great deep breath, she opened her eyes. Whatever she had envisioned, whatever she had dreamed of, it was nothing compared to the beauty in front of her, the small dark neatly trimmed racing stripe leading to Jodi's full awaiting lips. Still, she couldn't help but notice the deep scar along the side of Jodi's body continued over the front of her hipbone, stopping near her inner thigh. She couldn't seem to tear her eyes away from that scar, that deep jagged gash that gleamed white in the dim light of her bedroom. Once again, her heart went out to Jodi.

Sam once again focused on the very center of Jodi. She wanted her, wanted her now, to inhale her sweet musky scent, to bury her tongue into her deep recesses. But just as she leaned forward, only an inch away now, Jodi pulled back. Sam nearly screamed. She had been so close.

Jodi pointed down at her jeans wrapped around her legs just above her knees. "Sorry, hon, but I need to get these off. I'm about to fall over."

"Oh, okay." Sam giggled. It wouldn't be good if their first night together ended with a trip to the emergency room. She then leaned forward and lowered her voice. "Just so you don't go too far away. I'm not done with you yet."

Jodi sat on the edge of the bed, unlacing those big black leather boots. "Believe me, you don't have to worry. I'm not going anywhere." A loud clunk accented the point as one of the boots fell to the floor.

Sam flopped down beside Jodi and quickly kicked off her own shoes, flinging them kitty-corner across the room where they bounced off the walls. By the time Jodi's second boot hit the floor, she already had her jeans unbuttoned.

Jodi then slid her jeans the rest of the way off in a whisper of fabric. Now completely naked, she leaned back on one arm, her long lean body stretched out in the soft light, her left arm strategically covering most of the scar running down the side of her body.

Sam turned and gawked, her fingers still hooked in her own jeans now forgotten. But this time, she wasn't staring at that scar. All she saw were those long, long legs. She knew Jodi was tall. She topped her by a good four inches. But as she lay there, her legs just went on forever. Sam swallowed. "Wow."

Jodi grinned as she nodded to Sam. "But what about you?"

"Oh, yeah." Sam blinked. Here she had been so focused on Jodi's gorgeous naked body, she had completely forgotten about undressing. With her hands still on the waistband of her jeans, she rocked back on the bed and lifted her butt. In one quick motion, she slipped her jeans over her hips and down her thighs. She then kicked her feet up in the air, scissoring her legs until her jeans finally flew close to the ceiling before landing in a heap on the floor.

"Holy crap, Sam. Now *that* was a show."

Sam giggled with a small shrug. She was beginning to feel silly, like she could laugh hysterically at any moment. Maybe she just needed to break the tension. She had been so worried about this moment but she wasn't uncomfortable in the least. Quite the opposite. "So, you like?"

Jodi tucked her chin down, her eyes boring into Sam. "Uh-huh."

From the way Jodi was staring at her, intense, piercing, Sam had a feeling she wasn't talking about her little show anymore. Her skin burned as Jodi raked over her with those deep pools of blue. And there was no denying she liked Jodi staring at her that way.

Slowly, she leaned in, cupping Jodi's face in her hand while she gently stroked her thumb along Jodi's soft, warm cheek. As Jodi closed her eyes, nestling her head into her hand, Sam dipped down, brushing Jodi's lips with hers, once, twice, pulling back slightly only to dive in again, each time closer, she needed to be closer. Any distance was too much.

Her heart once again pounded as if she were being kicked with one of Jodi's big heavy boots from the inside out—or maybe even both of them for all she knew. Blood rushed like an ocean in her ears. Pins and needles shot up her leg as Jodi slid her hand over her inner thigh and she raised her hips to meet it. Oh, yes. This was it. This was what she wanted, what she needed. Every muscle in her abdomen tensed and then Jodi's fingers met her hot, wet center. She tore her mouth away, her back arched, her head nearly rolling under her. She bit her lip as she let out a low throaty moan. Rocking her hips, she matched Jodi's stroking, rising and falling, rising and falling, slow at first then building.

Almost immediately, she could feel the beginning of an orgasm, a deep surging flood of visceral need building within her, starting from her center and radiating outward throughout her body. Biting down even harder on her lower lip, she gasped breath after breath. Oh, God. It was building so fast. The smell of her excitement intermingled with Jodi's scent and she hadn't even begun to touch her, to return the favor.

Sam lightly slid her hand down Jodi's smooth skin, over her flat stomach, searching for the source of that rich heady fragrance, all the while still rolling her hips to the rhythm of Jodi's hand. Only a couple of inches now and she'd be there, right where she needed to be. With each gasp, her breath burned in her lungs. Finally, her fingers brushed the top of Jodi's small racing stripe and she nearly cheered. Now all she had to do was follow those soft tickling curls to that which waited below.

Her hand now shaking so badly she wasn't sure she'd even find where she was going, Sam closed her eyes and held her breath. Quickly, she shifted her hand, slipping down. Almost there. Almost there. And then her fingers met Jodi's center, passing through her warm, slippery folds, and she echoed Jodi's deep moan. The heat was astonishing, almost like the flame from a candle. Being inside Jodi, feeling her slickness as her fingers passed in and out, sent her own arousal into overdrive. She began thrusting her hips quicker and quicker, feeling Jodi's fingers passing faster and faster into her center. With each thrust, Jodi's thumb teased her engorged clitoris and she dug her toes into the covers. "Oh God, Jodi. Yes, yes, yes." Her voice increased in intensity as the sensations, starting from her very center and rising into her stomach, spreading slowly, then quicker and quicker, spreading throughout her entire body— arms, legs, fingers, neck, breasts, clitoris—all cried out. Like an explosion ripping through her very being, her orgasm hit, sending convulsions through her body. She tore her head back as wave after wave of pleasure washed over her. "Oh, God. Oh, God. Oh, God. YEEEEESSSS."

Even as she bucked her hips against her, Jodi caught her earlobe between her teeth, blasting her searing hot breath against her neck. She moaned, her voice low, airy. "Oh Sam, oh Sam, I'm coming."

Jodi gasping her name sent a second round of pleasure shooting through her body. Her lungs burned as she fought for breath. If anyone had told her before now that her body was capable of feeling this intensity of pleasure, she would have called them a liar. With one last fierce spasm, she collapsed back onto the pillow. "Holy shit, Jodi. That was unbelievable!"

"You can say that again." Jodi brushed Sam's hair back from her eyes.

"Holy shit, that was unbelievable!" Sam giggled, sweat trickling down the side of her face. As she lay there, she could feel the energy draining from her body as if she had just run a marathon, or maybe even two. Granted, this was definitely more fun than running a marathon or anything else that she could think of. Much more fun.

Sweat now running off the tip of her nose, she rolled over on her side, taking in all of Jodi, every inch. She blinked, half afraid that she'd open her eyes and Jodi wouldn't be there. But this wasn't a dream—this was real. This had really happened. She was here in Jodi's arms, just having made the most intense love of her life. Slowly, she brushed the back of her fingers over

Jodi's skin, the weight of her body sinking deeper and deeper into the bed.

"God, you are so beautiful…" Sam stared down at the ghostly white gash gouged deep into Jodi's throat, the very spot that had cost Jodi her voice. In slow circles, she traced along that gnarled fissure, the flesh puckered and rippled like a shiny pale burn. Jodi's heartbeat drummed a quick staccato under her fingertips, and she swallowed. So much pain. So much loss. But still, so beautiful. There were so many things she wanted to say, needed to say, but with each second, sleep was pulling her further away, down and down. She opened her mouth, her voice thick, distant, hollow.

"…so very beautiful…"

She blinked slowly once, then twice, her fingers to Jodi's neck.

"…just wish…you didn't…have…these…scars…"

* * *

With only her heartbeat breaking the silence, Jodi lay frozen, Sam's arm draped over her chest. She gasped, unable to fill her lungs, bile searing her throat as her stomach twisted and churned. What the hell had just happened? She couldn't possibly have heard Sam right, could she? No, Sam wouldn't have said that. Not Sam, who was so different from everyone else, who had never once mentioned a single thing about her scars. Sam's voice still echoed through her head, piercing through her like feedback from her amplifier—*just wish you didn't have these scars, just wish you didn't have these scars*—over and over. What had she been thinking? All this time, ever since she had met Sam, she had been waiting for the proverbial shoe to fall. Each day, she waited and waited and damn it, she had almost let herself believe, if for one very small second, that it wouldn't ever be an issue, not with Sam.

Her entire body now shaking, she bit down hard on her lower lip, her eyes beginning to burn with those all too familiar tears. After everything, why now? They had just made love. It had been as Sam had said, unbelievable. She had never thought she would find someone to be with like that again. Who would be able to deal with her grotesque disfiguration? She had thought that would be Sam. But even she couldn't deal with it in the end. The warm taste of copper and salt trickled into her mouth as she continued to bite down on her lip, harder and harder.

By now, her lungs were on fire. The weight of Sam's arm slung over her seemed more like a grand piano across her chest, crushing the breath out of her. Still fighting back the tears, she stared at Sam as she lay beside her, breathing softly, a peaceful smile across her lips. This was all her fault. She should never have let anyone get that close to her. Sooner or later, her scars always became an issue. *Always*. It wasn't fair. Up and down her body, nothing but goddamned scars, leaving a deep ragged white slash and stealing her voice, her goddamned *voice* for Christ's sake. If only she could dig her fingernails into her flesh and rend those scars from her body but she couldn't. No, they would always be there—for the rest of her damned life.

With her heart thundering in her throat, she slid out from under Sam's arm, careful not to wake her. The entire room spun around her as she sat on the edge of the bed, digging her fingers into her hair. How could she have been so stupid? She had sworn she would never let anyone close to her. Finally, she slid off the bed to the floor and swept up her clothes and boots. She then stood, completely naked, clutching her clothes to her chest. As second after second ticked away, she peered down at Sam, that sweet, peaceful smile still on her face. The tears that had threatened all this time now spilled down the sides of her face.

Still grasping her clothes, her arms wrapped tightly around her stomach, she slowly stumbled out of Sam's bedroom. In the living room, she quickly tugged on her jeans and jerked her tank top over her head. She then slipped into her boots, not bothering to tie the laces, and tucked her socks and panties into her back pocket. Again, she wrapped her arms around her stomach, bending nearly in half, tears now freely pouring.

With the glow from the streetlight, she hobbled into Sam's kitchen as quietly as she could in her big clunky boots and glanced around, looking for something to write on. She couldn't just run out. Sam deserved better than that. Besides, this wasn't Sam's fault—it was her fault for letting anyone get that close in the first place. Finally, she spotted a notepad on top of the microwave and quickly scribbled out a note while roughly swiping tears from her eyes. When she finished, she shuffled back to the door, glancing over her shoulder one last time toward Sam's bedroom. Why had she been so stupid? No one could possibly love her with all those scars on her body. No one. *Just wish you didn't have these scars*. That said it all. With those words screaming in her head, she opened the door and ran into the heavy, humid night.

CHAPTER THIRTEEN

The next morning, Sam woke with a smile still on her lips. Without opening her eyes, she moaned softly and reached out for Jodi. She couldn't believe that she had slept so soundly after making the most passionate love of her life. She had even fallen asleep before she got a chance to echo the words Jodi had mouthed to her during the concert. Even now, she could picture it—taking Jodi's face between both her hands, looking directly into her eyes, and telling her how much she loved her. Well, she could still do it. What could be a better way to wake her up? With her eyes still closed, she reached out farther only to find the sheets cold.

She rolled over and propped herself up with her arm against her face, gazing at the empty bed beside her. "Huh?" Well, there was nothing stopping her from jumping out of bed, finding Jodi, wrapping her naked body around her, and with her lips less than an inch from her ear, breathing out the three words above all else that she was dying to tell her. Just thinking about it now aroused her. Hey babe, I love you. I love you with all my heart.

A deep burning flush now racing over her body, she threw off the blankets and hopped out of bed. Her clothes were still flung across her room. She laughed at the large dark smudge on the wall. She must have kicked off her shoes a little harder than she thought. Oh, well. It was certainly worth it, even if she might have to repaint her bedroom. But as she sat there on the edge of the bed, her smile slowly faded. Where were Jodi's clothes? Even her boots were gone. Every trace of her was gone.

Sam poked her head out into the living room. She had been half expecting to see Jodi with her feet kicked up on the end of the couch, doing her best to flip through one of her computer magazines. She would run over, throw a leg over each side of her, and deeply kiss her good morning before she even got a chance to open her mouth. But the house was silent. "Hey, Jodi, you out here?" Her soft voice echoed in the quiet room.

Sam peered back over her shoulder. She wasn't sure what she was looking for. Maybe she was hoping that somehow she had made a mistake and Jodi was still back in there, curled up under the covers, a little whistle coming out of her mouth as she slept. But the bed was just as she had left it.

She turned back to her living room, her stomach now churning. "Hey Jodi, where you at?" She called out a bit louder only to get more silence. Had Jodi mentioned that she had plans today? Was there somewhere she had to go? She couldn't remember anything but then again, she wasn't really thinking about that last night. She hadn't really been thinking of much of anything last night. Jodi could have told her she had to get up early to go rob the 7-Eleven and she wouldn't have known the difference.

With a giggle, she shook her head—just more of her inherent insecurities. Of course, Jodi had something she had to do early this morning. She just didn't want to wake her up. Jodi probably woke up and couldn't bring herself to wake her. Now feeling a bit more relieved, she bounced through her living room. She'd probably even get a phone call any minute from Jodi asking if she'd slept well. But when she stepped through the doorway to her kitchen, she froze. One of her notebooks was lying open on the dining table. Even from across the room, she could make out Jodi's handwriting. It was probably only a note saying she had to meet her parents for an early brunch or some such. But as she continued to stare at the open pages, transfixed by the scroll print on the paper, her stomach twisted. Suddenly, all she wanted was to crawl back in bed and pull the covers over her head. It wasn't a small tender note—"Hey hon, had to run, see you later, I love you, Jodi." No, it wasn't some sweet little missive. She just knew.

She forced herself, step by step, over to the table. The last note like this had been from Jennifer, and that had totally destroyed her world. She couldn't go through that again. For one wild second, she almost grabbed the notebook and pitched it without even looking at it. If she didn't read it then it wouldn't be bad. But with her eyes closed, she reached out and slid the notebook into her hands, holding it at arm's length.

She took a deep breath, her entire body quivering, and opened her eyes. At the first line, her knees buckled. "I'm sorry but last night was a huge mistake." Oh, God. She stared at the words as they slowly sunk in. *Last night was a huge mistake.* How could that be? She had thought they had a great time. Had it really been that horrible? As she stood there, her hands trembling, her ex's voice filled her head. "If you weren't such a terrible fuck, I wouldn't have had to find it elsewhere." Was that what had happened? Was she such a terrible lover that Jodi couldn't bear to be with her?

Although her knees had buckled when she read those words, nothing could have prepared her for what she read next. "We've only been kidding ourselves with this. We shouldn't see each other anymore." Her breath seized in her throat and she collapsed to the kitchen floor. She closed her fist over the paper in her hand. This was Jennifer all over again. How could she have let this happen? Still clutching the crumpled letter in her hand, she curled up naked on the cold tile floor and began to cry, her chest heaving in great spasms. How could she have let this happen?

* * *

After nearly a half an hour crying on the kitchen floor, Sam finally heaved herself up and shuffled to her bedroom where she grabbed a loose pair of sweats and a baggy T-shirt. She looked at the bed, the sheets still rumpled from last night. She wanted nothing more than to curl up and try to forget about what had just happened, but as she stared at her bed, she nearly retched. That was the last place she wanted to be at the moment. Not after last night. Not after making love to Jodi in that bed. She staggered out to her living room where she threw herself hard onto the couch.

For once, she wished her house wasn't bright and airy. It should be dark like a cave, someplace she could crawl into and forget everything. Even as she lay there, the bright sunlight burned red through her eyelids. She tried draping her arm over her face with little success. Finally, she slammed her arm against the couch and flopped over so she faced the back. At least that was a bit better. At least she didn't have to focus on anything. Maybe she could go to sleep and when she woke up, she'd find this had all been a nightmare. She would still be in bed with Jodi, her arms wrapped around her.

She didn't remember drifting off until she woke to the knock on her front door. For one crazy moment, her heart jumped—Jodi had come back. But then she let out a low groan. It wasn't Jodi. Her letter had made that perfectly clear. *Last night was a huge mistake—we shouldn't see each other anymore.* You couldn't get any clearer than that. But whoever it was, they could just go away—she didn't want to see anyone.

"Knock, knock." With another rap on the now open door, Cheryl called into the house. "Hey, Sam. You decent in here." She let out a giggle.

Leave it to Cheryl to stop by. Anyone else would have gone away, but not Cheryl. They had been friends so long they could walk into each other's house uninvited. Usually it wasn't a big deal. But there was no getting around it now. She sat up, waiting for Cheryl to come in.

"Hey, there you are." Cheryl peeked around the corner with a wide grin. "So, late night?"

"Something like that." Sam hung her head in her hands. If only she had locked the front door. She wanted nothing more than to curl up and try to forget everything, not spend the afternoon reliving what happened.

Cheryl bounded across the room and flopped down beside her. "Do tell." She could barely sit still. "I didn't get to see you after the concert but I told Angi you were in for a wild night."

With her head still in her hands, Sam shook it back and forth, fighting back a fresh round of tears.

Cheryl stopped bouncing and took a close look at Sam. "Hey, sweetie, what's wrong?"

Sam lifted her head and as tears began to trickle down her cheeks, she stared up at the ceiling. "Nothing—everything—I don't know."

"Whoa, whoa. What happened?" Cheryl leaned in, her mouth hanging wide open. "The last time I saw you, you were on cloud nine."

Sam took a deep breath. She didn't even know what had happened herself. Here she had fallen asleep in Jodi's arms after the most intense sex she had ever had and woken to find her entire world had gone to shit. She whipped around to face Cheryl, her voice now cracking. "Oh, God, Cheryl. I don't know what happened. I really don't." She began to cry harder, gulping in great gasps of air.

Cheryl jumped up and pulled her in close, stroking the back of her head. "Shhh. Shhh. It'll be all right."

Sam shook her head. How could it be all right? Like Jodi said, apparently, they had only been kidding themselves and it had all been a huge mistake. And here she had thought it had been something special. When she finally regained a bit of control, she pulled back from Cheryl, drying her eyes with the back of her hand.

Cheryl now knelt in front of Sam, pulling her hands into hers. She leaned in, looking more serious than Sam had ever seen her. "Sam, sweetie, what happened?"

Sam sniffed, her nose dripping, and turned toward the window. She just couldn't meet Cheryl's eyes. "I honestly don't know. Everything was going great. We came back here last night. Everything was perfect." Her chin quivered.

"Did you…?" Cheryl lifted one eyebrow.

"Yeah." Sam lowered her head. "And it was amazing. At least *I* thought it was amazing."

"That's great, Sam. Then what's wrong?"

"Hell, all I know is I fell asleep in Jodi's arms and woke to find her gone and a letter in her place."

"*What?*" Cheryl snapped up straight, her body now rigid. "Where is it? What did it say?"

Her eyes still glued to the window, Sam lifted a shaking finger and pointed to the kitchen, to the wrinkled sheet of paper still on the floor in the middle of the room.

Cheryl marched into the kitchen and snagged the paper from the floor. The more she read, the more her hands shook until her whole body seemed to vibrate. She wrinkled the note in her hands, her face turning a bright scarlet. "That goddamn Jodi. When I see her next, I'm going to let her have it. Who the *hell* does she think she is?" Cheryl stomped her foot. "No, forget that, I'm going to go let her have it now. This is *bullshit*. She can't do this to my best friend."

"No, Cheryl, don't. It's not worth it." Sam finally cracked a small smile as Cheryl thundered around her living room in a towering rage. She was lucky to have such a good friend, one who was willing to go right out and let Jodi have it for hurting her.

Still breathing hard, Cheryl regained some semblance of calm and flopped down again beside her. "I'm so sorry about this, Sam. I never should have pushed you into meeting Jodi. Believe me, I never thought she'd do something like *this*."

"It's not your fault." Sam shrugged her shoulders. "Maybe I'm just a terrible lover."

Cheryl grabbed Sam by the chin and jerked her face around, staring directly into her eyes. "Don't you be saying that."

Sam dropped her eyes to her hands in her lap. "Well, maybe it's true. First Jennifer and now Jodi."

"Fuck Jennifer. She was a self-centered bitch." Cheryl gave Sam's chin a little shake. "And forget Jodi too. Neither of them knows what they're talking about. I'm sure you're a great lover."

Sam couldn't help but smile at the earnestness in Cheryl's wide eyes as she bobbed her head emphatically. Cheryl certainly meant the best. However, it was just as likely that she *was* a terrible lover. And the worse part of it all, she had actually thought last night had been very special. The term mind-blowing came to mind. But maybe she was just that pathetic. What she thought was mind-blowing turned out to be humdrum at best and repulsive at worst. Still, she couldn't bring herself to say what she was really thinking, that she had to be such a miserable excuse for a lover that she sent women running. It was bad enough *being* that without having to argue the point with her best friend as well. "Thanks, Cheryl. You're too sweet."

"Naw." Cheryl grabbed her around the shoulder one-armed and pulled her close. "I can still go give Jodi what for if you want me to." She puffed herself up.

This time she did manage a laugh. "No, that's okay. I'd just rather forget about everything."

Cheryl slowly stood. "Okay, sweetie, but I'm here for you. If you want, I can stay with you today. Maybe we can watch some chick flicks and pig out on Häagen-Dazs."

"Gee, Cheryl. As tempting as that sounds, I'd rather just be alone." Sam twisted the drawstring from her sweats around her finger, not meeting Cheryl's eyes.

Cheryl threw a hand on her hip and stared down at Sam, her shoulders set. "Now you're not going to disappear into those computers of yours, are you?"

Actually, that was exactly what she had planned on doing. She could sit in front of the monitors, tinkering with bits of code, maybe a new application or two, and forget about everything. She could pour herself into her computers and push out the world. That was what she had done after Jennifer.

Cheryl finally let out a deep breath. "Well, at least don't shut out everyone, Sam. Angi and I are here for you and we don't want to lose you. Angi will want to see you for dinner at least once a week." She then leaned forward and cupped a hand to the side of her mouth. "And you can't abandon me when it comes to Angi's new culinary experiments."

"Okay, I'll try." Cheryl was trying to cheer her up and for that, she was thankful. But right now, what she'd *really* like was to be with her computers. At least they were predictable. Or at least more predicable than people.

Finally, Cheryl bent forward and folded her hands around Sam's, pulling her up from the couch and wrapping her arms around her in a tight bear hug. She held her for a long moment, not saying anything, and then pulled back, staring directly into Sam's eyes. "Now if you need anything…"

"I know. I know. You'll be the first I'll call."

"Day or night." With a firm nod, Cheryl sidled over to the door and whipped back around. "Oh, and you're better than all them, Sam. Remember that."

Sam swallowed hard and fought back the threatening fresh tears. "Thanks again, Cheryl…for…for everything."

With a quick wave, Cheryl left and Sam flopped down again on her couch, staring into the quiet space, not focusing on anything. Even with Cheryl's sweet words of encouragement, she still couldn't shake the feeling that this had been her fault. Her own inadequacies as a lover had made Jodi want nothing more to do with her. She should never have opened herself up like that. After Jennifer, she had said never again. Well, she did and look how it turned out. Never again.

With her resolve firm, Sam leaped up from the couch and walked into her home office. Three large flat-screen monitors lined her wide cherry U-shaped desk. Underneath on the left, a cart housed two servers. She had more computer power than many small countries. But this was her world, a world she could understand. Forget Jodi. Forget everyone else. With a smile slowly lifting her lips, she brushed her fingertips over her keyboard. "Hello, beautiful."

* * *

After a little fitful sleep, Sam arrived at the office the next morning at a little past five. It would be hours before Sandy got in so she'd have the place to herself. Although she had worked at home until nearly one in the morning, she couldn't sleep. Every time she turned over in bed, she had half-expected to see Jodi there. Finally, she ended up staring at the ceiling, working the letter Jodi had left through her head, over and over. She had it committed to memory. Since she couldn't sleep, she figured she might as well do something productive so here she was.

She settled in front of her screens, cracked open a Diet Coke and pushed everything from her head. After the weekend, she was sure she'd have a ton of business email and as she checked her account, she wasn't disappointed. Nearly two hundred messages. If anything could distract her, it was that. Some were from clients, everything from wanting updates to their websites to a couple in near panic because they had forgotten how to access their accounts. She passed up a message from Kat. Probably something about the band's website. That could wait. Next were the new software offers from a half-dozen companies to invitations to no fewer than ten computer programming conferences. A couple of those actually caught her eye. She could certainly use a vacation. Then there was the spam. She burst out laughing at the offer for ten inches of rock-hard penis. Talk about marketing that to the wrong girl. Three Diet Cokes later and she was still clearing her inbox, pushing all but work from her mind. When Sandy came in at eight, she didn't hear her.

"Hey there, boss." Sandy poked her head in Sam's office. From the bubbliness in her voice, Sandy was safely into her second espresso. "You're off to an early start."

"Just wanted to get to work. After the Price Motors job, I'm way behind." She didn't turn around. The less Sandy saw of her, the fewer questions she'd have to field. "And Sandy, I would prefer not to be disturbed if at all possible."

Sandy leaned her arm against the doorframe. "Okay, boss." She paused for a minute and then lowered her voice. "Hey, is everything all right?"

"Just got a lot to do." She watched Sandy's reflection in her computer monitor. Sandy was perceptive enough to know that she was lying but also discreet enough not to pry. That was one of the things she liked best about her. Sandy would do her job and give her space. Like she had done after the Jennifer blowup. And she would also be there if she decided to talk. But for right now, she just wanted to push everything as far from her mind as possible.

Sandy pursed her lips. She took a step forward and stopped as if she thought better of it, then without saying a word, she slowly shook her head and crept back out of Sam's office.

* * *

"Hey, Jodi, you in there?" Kat rapped on the door. "It's Wednesday. You missed practice."

Jodi sat on the floor, leaning back against her couch with a bottle of Guinness in her hand. All the blinds were pulled, throwing the room into a hazy twilight. As she brought the bottle to her lips, wincing while she took a long pull, Kat pounded hard on the door again. She didn't want to see anyone. After what had happened with Sam, she didn't care if she ever saw anyone again. They were all the same. All they looked at were her scars and her screwed up voice. That's all they saw. Oh yeah, they might pretend it didn't matter but in the end, it always did. No one saw *her* anymore. They just saw who she used to be and the grotesque scars she had become. Why couldn't they admit it? That girl they want her to be, she died in that car wreck. All she was now was a ghost, a shadow of who she had been.

Bang, bang, bang. Kat's knocking rattled the door in its frame. "Goddamn it, Jodi, open the fucking door. I know you're in there. I can hear you breathing."

Jodi closed her eyes and tipped up her bottle again. What was this, number nine or ten since this morning? She couldn't remember.

"Okay, that's it. If you're not going to open the door, I'm just coming in." Kat yelled from the other side of the door.

With her eyes still closed, Jodi leaned back against the couch, her head tilted to the ceiling, her beer bottle balanced on her leg. She was glad she had locked her door. Unless Kat was planning to break it down, her threat was empty. She might be a tough scrapper, all five-foot-two of her, but even she couldn't break down the door. At the rattle of a key in the lock, Jodi snapped her head up. How could she have been so careless? She had forgotten about the spare key under the flowerpot. But before she could stand, bright light blasted into the room. Jodi squinted and teetered back and forth, trying to brace herself. Her beer bottle slipped off her leg and wobbled across the dark cherry floor, beer foaming from the neck as it went.

"There you are." Kat stomped in, her chest heaving, a mere silhouette in the doorway. "What the hell's going on? I've been calling all afternoon."

Jodi threw her hand up, blocking the light flooding into the room. Slowly, she leaned over, ignoring Kat, and picked up what was left of her bottle from the puddle of beer on the floor, slid it onto the end table and then slumped back against the couch, her eyes again closed and her head tilted to the ceiling.

At the scene in front of her, Kat seemed to calm a bit. She let out a deep sigh, closed the door behind her, and slowly walked over to Jodi, dropping to one knee and taking a long hard look. "What's going on, Jodi." Her voice now softer, she reached out, about to lay her hand on Jodi's leg, then as if thinking the better of it, closed her fingers and pulled back. "Talk to me."

Jodi opened her eyes and stared blankly at the ceiling, watching the fan slowly paddle the thick, sticky air. She wished she hadn't left that spare key outside. Damn, she wished Kat hadn't *known* about it. All she wanted was to be left alone. She had been a fool to let people into her life—Kat, Lynn, Terra, Sam, all of them. No one could get past her scars. With a deep sigh, she rolled away from Kat. "Please, just go."

"What the hell happened?" Kat grabbed Jodi by the shoulders, yanked her around, and gave her a firm shake. "What's all this? What's...what..." She stared at Jodi, her mouth gaping. "Did something happen with Sam?"

Jodi felt her chin quivering. She still couldn't meet Kat's eyes. Slowly, she shook her head. "It's just *everything*." She spit out the last word. "I hate being me. I hate living with these god—damn—scars. I hate living with my goddamn fucked-up voice."

"Jodi, hon. Please, what happened? Where's all this coming from? You're not making any sense."

"I'm sick of living with scars up and down my body. I'm sick of my voice, having to listen to it and wanting to puke. That's all anyone sees of me. That's all I am, now—nothing but a goddamn jagged little scar." Tear after heavy tear spilled down the side of Jodi's face, following her sharp jaw, and finally pooling into the scars carved deep into her neck.

Kat tucked her legs under her and scooted around beside Jodi. She reached over and pulled Jodi in tight, cradling her head to her chest and gently rocking her like a child after a bad nightmare. "Shhh. Shhh." She brushed her fingers lightly through Jodi's short black hair.

Jodi shook in Kat's arms, her entire body rigid. Her chest heaved, once, twice, and then she let out a long, pained howl, echoing in the dark room, a sound of utter anguish. She cried. With great gasping sobs, she cried. Kat held her tight, rocking her, stroking her hair. "Shhh. Shhh." Time passed. Finally, Jodi's emotional torrent began to subside until she shuddered one last time. In a low, harsh voice, not much more than a whisper, she spat out what she had felt since the day she woke up in the hospital. "They should have let me die in that car."

Kat swallowed, her own chin quivering as she listened to Jodi's chilling words. "Jodi, hon, I can't imagine what you've gone through, what you're still going through. I can't even begin to fathom. But, sweetie, what brought all this on? What happened? Is it Sam? Did she do something?"

Jodi hung her head in her hands. "Yes, no, I don't know." She then jerked away from Kat, slamming her fists into her thighs. "I don't *know*. I just don't *know*."

"Okay, Jodi, I'm sorry." Kat winced as if she had been slapped. "I didn't mean to ask so many questions. I'm only trying to figure out what's happened. I mean, the last time I saw you, you were with Sam and you were literally bouncing off the walls. From the way the two of you were holding onto each other when you left, I figured you were in for a long fun night. What happened after that?"

"Nothing, okay. I don't want to talk about it." Jodi hung her head, staring at her hands in her lap. "I've just been really stupid, deluding myself that anyone could see beyond my scars."

"I certainly hope you don't think I'm like that." Kat rounded on her, her jaw set. "And I can tell you for sure Lynn and Terra aren't either. Neither are your mom and dad."

"Everyone sees me differently. Mom and Dad are really overprotective now. Dad keeps trying to get me into some big super-duty truck so I'll be safer. Lynn and Terra can't help but see me differently. They both have heard me before. Hell, even you played drums with me sometimes before the accident. You can't tell me that everyone doesn't see these scars." She ripped her head to the side and jabbed a finger at the deep twisted scar along her neck. "See. *See*." She then glared at Kat.

Kat again swallowed, her eyes shining and a single tear spilling down her right cheek. She took a deep breath, her shoulders slumped. "Okay, Jodi, you're right. We all *do* see that. I guess there's no way around it. That accident not only changed you but everyone around you, the way they see you, how they act around you."

"Damn it, Kat. It's not fair. It's just not fair. I wish I was *me* again."

"I know, hon." Kat slid up beside her, their legs pressed together. She cleared her throat, her voice thick. "I don't know what to say. How's Sam feel about all this?"

Once again, Jodi slumped against the couch, her chin trembling, and stared up at the ceiling, willing herself not to cry. They were back to Sam. How does Sam feel about all this? That was the magic question, wasn't it? How does Sam feel? She had made that pretty clear the night they had made love. She just wished she didn't have these scars. More than anyone since her accident, Sam had treated her as if she were any normal woman. Never once did she comment about her scars or her voice. Never once did she ask any questions. Never once did she flinch when she spoke. Sam had treated her as if her accident had never happened. And that was just it—when she was around Sam, she could almost convince herself that her accident *had* never happened. But then her true feelings came out. Sam wished she didn't have these scars. What could she say to that? All that time, Sam had really been like everyone else. She couldn't see anything but her scars either. Finally, she let out a long breath, her throat burning as if it were on fire. "I really don't want to talk about Sam."

"Jodi, is all this because of something Sam did? I can't imagine she'd do anything to hurt you."

Jodi bit her lip, her muscles tense. "Listen, Kat, I really don't want to talk about Sam, *okay?*"

"Okay, hon. I'm sorry. I didn't mean…"

Jodi grabbed for what was left of her Guinness but Kat beat her to it, snatching it away. "Hey, that's mine." She glared at her.

Kat stared right back. "Jodi, you've had enough."

"Who the hell are you to tell me I've had enough." She spat out the words, a small globule of saliva clinging to her bottom lip.

"I'm your friend, that's who." Kat stared hard at her until she finally looked away. "And I'm not leaving you." She then pulled her cell phone out and quickly fiddled through the menus. Without taking her eyes from Jodi, she lifted the phone to her ear. "Hey, Lynn. I'm here with Jodi. I'm staying with her tonight. No, no, I'll talk to you later. Love you. Bye." She gave a firm nod to Jodi. "There, I'm staying here tonight."

Jodi glanced sideways at Kat. With her arms crossed and her jaw set, she figured there was no point in arguing. She wasn't going to win. Besides, she was too exhausted to argue. She was too exhausted for anything. "You don't have to, Kat. Really, I would rather just be alone."

"I know, hon." Kat leaned close, her voice now softening. "But maybe this is one of those times it's best to have a friend with you. I'm not going anywhere."

* * *

Sam sat updating a client's website. Over the past four days, she had arrived early, well before eight, and left late, at least after ten. That gave her just enough time to quickly grab something to eat and fall asleep totally exhausted. The upside was that she was getting a lot of maintenance work done that she had been putting off for months. Hopefully, she would get a new client soon and then she could put all her focus on something else. Anything but Jodi.

With her face only inches away from her monitor, pounding away on the keyboard, she didn't even notice Sandy standing in the door. At the sound of a soft knock, she glanced over her shoulder, blinking several times. Her eyes burned from staring at the screen.

Sandy cringed and took a small tentative step into the room. "Um, boss. I know you don't really want to be disturbed but I figured you might want to know this." She flipped a pen from hand to hand as she stood there.

Sam whipped around in her chair, her jaw clenched, ready to begin ranting. She didn't care what it was, she didn't want to be bothered by anything. But then she saw Sandy, looking as if she were about to make a run for it, and she let out a sigh. Due to her perpetually rotten mood, poor Sandy had been walking on eggshells all week. That certainly wasn't fair to her. She was a great employee, always there for her no matter what. So she softened her voice and did her best to smile. "It's okay, Sandy. Come on in."

Sandy shuffled up to Sam's workstation. "I normally wouldn't have bothered you but this sounded important. Jim Price from J.P. Motors just called. He wants you to stop by at your earliest convenience. Sorry but he said it was really important."

"Oh, great." Sam kicked back in her chair and rubbed her forehead. It couldn't be anyone else. Suddenly, a horrible image popped into her head. He wouldn't be canceling the website, would he? He hadn't talked to Jodi and now that she had written her off, he was going to do the same?

Sandy raised her eyebrows as she leaned against the desk. "Is everything all right, boss?" She then held her breath.

Sam slumped her head down against her workstation and let out a deep muffled groan. After a second, she sat back up and ruffled her hair fiercely with her fingers before finally facing Sandy. "Yeah, doing great. Why do you ask?"

Sandy now stared at her with a mixture of concern and fear. "Um, I'm just a bit worried about you. You know, I'm here for you no matter what."

Sam swallowed, Sandy's words stabbing her in the chest. She really had been a nightmare all week. And it certainly wasn't Sandy's fault. Maybe she would have to think about giving her a raise sometime soon. Lord knows, she deserved it after putting up with all her crap. "I'm really sorry, Sandy. I know I've been a total bitch all week. It's nothing you've done. It's just…" Instead of finishing the sentence, she simply waved beside her head as if shooing away a fly.

"Well, if you ever want to talk." Sandy reached out and placed her hand gently on Sam's shoulder.

"Thanks, Sandy. I just might take you up on that sometime." She patted her hand on top of Sandy's. "But for now, I really don't want to."

"Sure thing, boss." Sandy gave her a bright smile and then slipped back out of Sam's office.

Once alone again, Sam kicked back in her chair, her hands locked behind her head, her eyes closed. Besides Jodi, Jim Price was probably the last person she wanted to see but she couldn't ignore him. She was going to have to suck it up and deal with whatever was coming. Finally, she opened her eyes and stood. Since there was no point in putting it off any longer, she might as well get it over with.

"See you later, Sandy." She waved over her shoulder as she marched through the door into the stuffy downtown afternoon. A few minutes later, she pulled out of the underground parking ramp. The drive across town normally took only about a half hour but today seemed to be taking forever. Or maybe it was just her reluctance to see Jodi's dad. Whatever it was, the farther she drove, the more she felt her chest tightening.

By the time she actually pulled into J.P. Motors, she was beginning to wonder if she was having a heart attack. She parked up beside the main showroom and sat behind the wheel, trying her best to calm down. Just breathe in and out, in and out. She finally gave up and kicked open the door. The sooner she got in there, the sooner it would be over.

With her satchel slung over her shoulder, Sam trudged straight across the showroom, keeping her eyes on her feet and hoping upon hope that she didn't bump into any of the employees she had spent the past several weeks working with. She rounded the corner and dashed up the stairs to Jim's office. When she stepped into the doorway, Jim looked up, phone glued to his ear, and smiled, waving her in. He then pointed to the large overstuffed leather chair across from his desk, motioning for her to sit.

Sam sat down, clutching her satchel to her chest while Jim talked on the phone. She glanced around the room, really seeing it for the first time. Before she had been too focused on work when she had been in Jim's office to notice the numerous plaques and awards. She had also missed the dozens of photographs, mostly of Jodi. She couldn't help but smile at the photo of a young Jodi—she couldn't have been more than about twelve— whaling on an electric guitar. And then did a double take at the picture of Jodi in a long simple dress, black of course, playing a classical guitar at what must have been her senior performance at Julliard. Right beside that, Jodi at an outdoor concert, her guitar raised high in the air. She was singing, her mouth only an inch from the microphone. Obviously, it had been before her accident—her throat was unblemished. But even as she sat there, the smile faded from her lips and Jodi's last words came slamming back into her head. *It had all been a huge mistake.* Slowly, she pulled her eyes from the wall and swallowed the bitter taste rising up in her throat.

Nearly five minutes had passed before Jim finally dropped the phone back in its cradle and leaned forward, his arms crossed on his desk in front of him. "Sorry about that. There was some mix-up with an order." He rolled his eyes. "The headaches of business."

Sam nodded. She wasn't sure what to say. Was she one of Jim's headaches of business? Was that why he called her down for this meeting?

With a wide smile, Jim stood. "So, is there anything I can get you—soda, coffee?"

"Ah, no thank you." Sam could feel herself beginning to sweat. Hopefully, it wouldn't be too noticeable. It certainly wouldn't look professional to sport huge pit stains.

"Okay." Jim sat down on the edge of his desk. "I suppose you're wondering why I called you down here?"

"Yes, sir." Her voice cracked and she swallowed hard. She had plenty of ideas of why he had called her down there. He didn't like the website. Or Jodi told him about last weekend and he was going to let her have it. He could be firing her. All those things flew around in her head.

Jim tipped his head back and let out a deep hearty chuckle that resounded off the walls of his office. "Please, call me Jim."

Sam began to relax a bit. He certainly wouldn't be insisting that she call him Jim if he was about to fire her. At least she didn't think he would.

"I wanted to personally congratulate you on the job you did with our website." Jim nodded his head firmly at Sam. "I've been looking it over all week and all I can say is I'm simply amazed. That's why I've decided to give you a ten percent bonus."

Sam grabbed the arms of her chair to steady herself as Jim's words sank in. The last thing she had been expecting was praise. And a *bonus* on top of that. She had never had one before. With her mouth hanging open, she simply gawked at Jim, uttering unintelligible mumbles. "I…I don't know what to say."

Jim barked out another loud laugh. "Well, you deserve it. I was expecting something good but not *that* good. And just to show you how much I really appreciate it, how about you and Jodi come up to Rose Cottage on Saturday. I'll grill some steaks."

Sam winced. Her entire chest seized at the mention of Jodi. "Um…" Quickly, she looked down. What could she say—she couldn't come because his daughter now considered her a huge mistake?

Without saying anything, Jim stood, stepped past Sam and closed his office door. He then turned back and sat on his desk directly in front of her, his elbows on his knees and his brow deeply furrowed. "What's wrong, Sam?"

Just hearing those three words—*what's wrong, Sam*—sent tears flooding down the side of her face. She wrapped her arms around her satchel, trying her best not to cry, yet the tears continued. What was she going to tell him? She wasn't really sure what had happened. All she knew was that Jodi left her a note after the first time they had made love and walked out of her life.

Jim sat quietly, waiting for her to regain her composure.

Sniffling loudly, she dried her cheeks with the back of her hand. When she was finally able to meet Jim's eyes, his concern nearly started her crying again. "Honestly, I don't know what happened. Everything was going great and then…" She slowly shook her head. "I just don't know."

Jim placed a strong hand on her shoulder, giving her a gentle squeeze. "Just start at the beginning."

Sam slid forward, her voice rising. "That's just it. We went to Jodi's big concert on Saturday. She was so wound up after that, I mean just over the moon. Then she came back to my place and we…well…" She bobbed her head side to side, a flush rising up her cheeks.

Still perched on the edge of his desk, Jim smiled behind his large hand. "And then after?"

"Well, then, I woke up the next morning to a note Jodi left saying it had all been a huge mistake and we shouldn't see each other again." Sam swallowed hard, the lump in her throat threatening to burst.

"Ah." Jim gave a single nod. "I see." He stood and paced around his office. After the second lap, he plopped back down on his desk. "Remember how I told you that there might come a time when Jodi will try to push you away?"

Sam quickly bobbed her head. How could she not remember standing beside the grill and listening as Jim shared with her a little of Jodi's heart-wrenching past? That was when she had learned how serious Jodi's accident had been and how hard it was for her afterward. She would never forget that conversation. Even now as she sat there, she could almost smell the tangy smoke from the grill. "Yeah, I remember that."

"Well, that sounds like what's happened." Jim took a deep breath and slowly shook his head. "I'm sorry to say I'm not surprised. Jodi has tried to push everyone away since that accident. But I also want you to know, I think you're good for her. And that's a lot for any father to say about someone interested in their little girl. I know Jodi really likes you. Hell, I've never seen her, not before her accident and certainly not since, as enamored of anyone." Jim leaned down. "You love her, don't you?"

Sam stared down at her satchel in her lap, twisting the strap between her fingers. When she finally spoke, it was barely more than a squeak. "Yes."

"I thought so. And I could be wrong but I'm pretty sure she feels that way about you. Father's instinct, you know."

Unable to stop it, a tear trickled down Sam's cheek. She looked up, her eyes glistening. "I just don't know what to do."

Jim lifted his hand to his brow and rubbed. "Geez, Sam. I don't know what to tell you except if this is important to you, if she's important to you, don't give up. Give her some time and she'll come around. I'd go have a talk with her but I'm afraid that would probably make things worse. Maybe I can drag her out to lunch, make sure she's okay. But if I push too much, Jodi will only see that as me meddling in things and being overprotective again and believe me, Jodi's not one to be pushed. She will withdraw instead until no one can reach her."

Now Sam didn't know what to think. Jodi's letter had such a sense of finality to it. She didn't want to see her anymore. What could she do about that? If she didn't want to see her, she didn't want to see her. She couldn't go chasing after her. She had done that with Jennifer. All that happened was that she got hurt even more in the end. She couldn't go through that again. Jodi had made her decision. She had been a huge mistake. She couldn't change her mind on that. Feeling a hand on her shoulder, she looked up.

"I, for one, hope that it works out for the two of you. That's the father in me talking." He gave a firm squeeze and then stood. "Now, the businessman in me says that no matter what happens between you and my daughter, you have a place in this company. Your work is impeccable. You're a hell of a businesswoman and I'm hoping we have a long and fruitful business relationship together."

Sam swallowed hard. "Thanks, sir—I mean, Jim. That means a lot to me. And I also hope for a long and productive business relationship together." She stood to leave.

Jim followed her to his office door. As he opened it, he quickly reached out and pulled her into a tight one-armed hug. "And I'm here if you ever need any friendly or fatherly advice." He gave her a wide smile. "Not sure how good either would be but I want you to know that we really like you, Sam."

With a quick nod, she turned and walked down the hall. She didn't dare speak. She had never had a father, but here was the first person she ever felt a fatherly connection with and it turned out his daughter wanted nothing to do with her. That was just her luck.

A lot of what Jim—Jodi's dad she corrected herself—a lot of what he said made sense. Maybe Jodi had been pushing her away, but to what end? And what was she supposed to do? Go running after her and beg her to come back? Yeah, it was horrible, absolutely horrible, what had happened to her in that accident, but she couldn't keep pursuing someone who had told her in no uncertain terms that it was over, that being with her had been a huge mistake. She had learned that hard lesson with Jennifer and she couldn't go through all that again.

Sam climbed in behind the wheel of her car and tossed her satchel into the passenger seat. It was already well past four—there was no sense going back to her office now. She wouldn't be able to do anything anyway with her mind in such a jumble. All she wanted was to go home and go to bed. So, before she could change her mind, she grabbed her cell phone. Sandy picked up on the second ring and she slumped back against her seat. "Hey, Sandy. I'm heading straight home from here. No point coming back in."

"Okay, boss. No problem."

"Thanks, Sandy. Why don't you shut everything down and close up a bit early. It certainly won't hurt anything."

"Sure thing." Sandy paused on the other line. "Hey, and boss, if there's anything you need, someone to talk to, anything, give me a call."

Sam felt the hard lump rising up her throat again. "I appreciate that, Sandy. I'll see you tomorrow."

"Goodnight, boss."

At the click on the line, Sam held out her cell and stared at it. She definitely needed to give Sandy a raise. The offer of someone to talk to didn't surprise her at all. But right now, all she wanted was to push everything out of her mind. The absolute last thing she wanted to talk about at the moment was Jodi.

CHAPTER FOURTEEN

Jodi sat naked in front of her piano, her hair still wet from the shower. Kat had finally left after spending the night. Now, she fumbled with the keys, the notes ringing throughout the room. Although she was a fantastic guitarist, she could still hold her own on piano. Striking several hard chords, she clenched her jaw. The last time she had played piano was for Sam, the first night she had come over and listened to her music. God, she should have never let that happen. She should have never opened herself to such pain. In the end, Sam had been like everyone else.

She continued to play, grinding her teeth with each note. With the muscles in her jaw flexing more and more, she stomped on the sustain pedal and hammered a rolling bass progression. Her chest reverberated from the notes as the sound pulsated from the piano. And the way she was feeling, what was more fitting than the theme to *The Phantom of the Opera*? She could certainly relate to that. All she needed was the mask and she'd be all set. The wicked irony was that the Phantom had his voice.

Halfway through the chorus, she let out a loud rasping scream and slammed her fists down on the keyboard, sending a discordant explosion across the room. It wasn't fair. Nothing about any of it was fair. She used to play this song in college. She could sing the entire part from the lows all the way to the clear piercing highs. Now, she could barely hum a few bars. Why did it have to be her? She clutched at her chest and dug her nails into her flesh. Why? Why? Why? That just about summed up her existence. Why did this have to happen to her? Why did she have to lose her voice? Why had she opened herself up and let Sam in? Yes, why. Oh, yeah, she should have known. Sam had seemed too good to be true right from the beginning. She should have listened to herself. She should have made some polite excuse and gone back to living her life without anyone close. But she had dared to let her guard down. Well, never again. Her fingers now ripping at her hair, she let out another grating howl and threw her head against the keys. Yes, never again.

* * *

At the banging on her front door, Sam stomped out into her living room, tying her bathrobe around her. "Hold on for Christ's sake." She glanced down at her watch. Who on God's green earth could be pounding on her door at nine at night? She had just wanted to come home, take a long bath and try to relax. After one of the worst weeks of her life, was it too much to ask for a little peace and quiet?

She yanked open the door only to find Kat with her fist in midswing. Before she could even open her mouth, Kat pointed directly at her. "Who the hell do you think you are treating Jodi like that?"

Sam stood there completely frozen, working the words slowly through her mind. Who the hell was she treating Jodi like that? Treating Jodi like what? Jodi had been the one who had walked out leaving only a get lost letter, not her. Who the hell was *she*? Finally finding her voice, she let go, all the frustration from the week pouring out. "What do you mean *me* treating Jodi like that? I'm not the one who snuck out of here in the middle of the night while I was sleeping. I'm not the one who left some letter saying everything was all a huge mistake. I'm not the one who told her I never wanted to see her again." Sam glared down at Kat, her chest heaving.

Kat stumbled back a step, her eyes wide. She simply stared, her mouth gaping. Slowly she lowered her finger. "Wha… *what?*"

"I don't know what Jodi's been telling you but I can assure you, I had nothing to do with anything. She's the one who left, not me." Sam could feel her face burning. Her nostrils flared. This was just the icing on the cake. After getting her heart broken by Jodi, after being told she wasn't good enough, she is blamed for it too. A perfect ending to a shitty week.

"She *left?*" Kat tilted her head, deep wrinkles across her brow.

"Goddamn right, she left." Sam stamped her foot, her entire body now shaking. "And I imagine she's probably out there having the time of her life. What's she doing, telling everyone how horrible I am? What, am I the worst fuck she's ever had?" She spat out the words.

"Whoa!" Kat waved her arms in front of her. "No one's said anything like that."

"Oh, yeah? Then why are you here? What's all this about?" Sam jabbed a finger at Kat as she stood on her porch.

Kat finally let out a long breath, seeming to deflate before her eyes. "Look, Sam. I'm not sure what happened but all I know is Jodi's completely devastated. I guess I assumed…hell, I don't know what I assumed." She ground her thumbs into her temples. "I'm sorry. May I come in?"

Sam turned and marched across her living room, leaving the door open behind her. She threw herself down on her couch, pulling her robe tightly around her, shaking her foot as she sat there.

Kat closed the door behind her and edged over to join Sam on the couch, sitting on the opposite end. After a moment, she turned to face her, not quite meeting her eyes. "Hey, look Sam, I'm sorry I flew off the handle like that. It's just when I found Jodi huddled on the floor in her house, crying and not making any sense, I guess I figured it must have been something you did."

"Something *I* did? What, didn't she tell you?" Sam sat with her arms crossed. Although her jaw was still set, she fought a lump rising up her throat. The image of Jodi huddled on the floor crying ripped at her heart. Here she had been picturing her celebrating her newfound freedom while she felt like shit. But what was going on? Why would Jodi be upset? She had been the one who had left, not her.

With her elbow on her knee, Kat leaned forward, her eyes narrowing. "Tell me what? What happened between you two?"

Sam leaped off the couch with the hem of her robe flailing behind her and stomped into the kitchen, grabbing Jodi's letter from the kitchen table. She then whipped around and flung the sheet of paper down beside Kat. "Here."

Kat's eyes widened. She scanned the letter a second time and then a third before she folded it carefully and set it on the couch beside her. "She doesn't want to see you anymore? It was all a huge mistake? That doesn't make any sense at all. Why would she say that?"

Sam threw her hands in the air palms up. "I have no idea. All I know is I woke up Sunday morning to *that*."

Kat glanced down at the letter again and tossed her head back and forth. "I tell you, this just doesn't make any sense at all. What happened before that?"

"The last thing that happened was I fell asleep in Jodi's arms. Everything was fine—better than fine. At least I thought so. And then I woke up to that letter. I swear to God, Kat, I don't have a clue what went wrong."

"I don't get it, Sam. Jodi kept going on and on about her scars and her voice, how everyone sees just that and nothing else. I mean, I haven't seen her like that since after she came home from the hospital."

"But that's not what I see."

"I know, I know. That's not what I see either. I've told Jodi over and over that she's no less a person because of her scars or her voice. I'm not sure she believes that." She let out a long sigh. "I'm not sure Jodi is capable of believing that. It's all she sees when she looks at herself or all she hears when she speaks."

Sam swallowed, fighting off more tears. "Believe me, I know, Kat. I've tried my best never to make her feel she was different. I wanted her just to be herself and not worry about any of that. God, I've seen how people look at her. I never wanted her to feel that way with me. That's why I've never brought it up. All I know about her accident and her recovery afterward is what I've heard from her dad, Cheryl and you."

Kat's eyes flew open wide. "Jim talked to you about Jodi's accident? Wow. I'm shocked. After the accident, he and Jodi's mom didn't want anyone hanging around her while she was in the hospital. Said Jodi needed her rest but I think they were just being way too protective."

"Well, that would explain the chilly reception I got from Diane the first time I met her. But as for Jim, he basically welcomed me into the family with open arms. Even today when I had a meeting with him about the new website, he told me not to give up. Said I'm good for Jodi."

"I think you're good for Jodi too." Kat reached out and patted Sam on the arm. "I'm really sorry again for beating on your door and screaming at you earlier. It's just when I saw Jodi that miserable, I was so pissed. I stayed with her all night. I figured something happened and Jodi wouldn't tell me anything so that left you."

"I don't know *what* happened. Like I said, everything was great. We came back here and…" Sam lowered her eyes, staring at her hands in her lap. She then wiped her forehead as sweat beaded on her deeply-flushed brow. "And, well, we made love for the first time."

Kat let out a low whistle. "Oh man, you guys had sex for the first time that night?" She leaned closer. "I don't mean to pry but was everything good?"

"Oh my God, Kat." The tears that had been threatening now spilled over. "It was the best thing that has ever happened to me. I mean, I was absolutely blown away."

"Wow." Kat's voice was soft.

"That's why I just don't understand what happened." Sam turned away. She didn't want to voice what was still going through her head—the possibility that although she thought it was the best thing that ever happened to her, she had been so bad at sex that it had sent Jodi running. But how could she say that to Kat? Hey Kat, maybe the problem with Jodi is that I'm such a bad lay. Certainly her ex would agree with that.

"No, it doesn't make any sense." Kat began rubbing her forehead again, kneading the flesh above her eyebrows. "Damn, I've got such a headache."

"Yeah, tell me about it. I've had one all week."

"Jodi kept going on about her scars and how that's all that people see. How'd she put it?" Kat tapped her finger to her lips. "All people see is a jagged little scar. Something like that—how sooner or later that was all everyone saw. And she just wishes she didn't have those scars."

Sam clapped her hand to her mouth and gasped as if something had hit her like a fist in the stomach. Those words. Those words sounded familiar. *She just wishes she didn't have those scars.* Hadn't she said something like that when she was lying in Jodi's arm, almost falling asleep? "Oh, dear God."

"What?" Kat slid closer, staring directly at Sam. "You look like you've seen a ghost."

Sam swallowed hard. "When you just said that, about wishing she didn't have scars, it just came back to me. I think I might have said something." She wrapped her arms around her stomach, rocking forward as she spoke. "We had just finished making love and I was lying beside Jodi. I was so tired I could barely keep my eyes open. I was running my hand over her skin and I remember telling her how beautiful she was. Then I saw her scars and I felt so bad that she had to go through all that pain. Oh God, Kat, I was thinking about that and I said something…I'm not sure…but I think I said I just wished she didn't have her scars." She now began to cry, her body hitching as she wrapped her arms tighter around herself.

"Holy crap, Sam. That's got to be it. That's why Jodi kept going on about her scars and how that's all people see."

"I swear, I didn't mean it like that. I just wish that Jodi didn't have to go through all that pain and suffering. I know how much it bothers her every day. I see how people look at her. Believe me, the last thing I ever wanted to do is cause her any more pain." Sam wiped the tears from her cheeks. "I love her, Kat. I honestly do. I was going to tell her that but I fell asleep. Then when I woke, that was going to be the first thing I said to her but by then, she'd already left."

Kat scooted over close to Sam, their legs touching. "I know you do. That's why I couldn't figure out what happened, especially after that talk we had in my kitchen. Then I saw Jodi like that. She is so sensitive when it comes to anything dealing with her scars or her voice."

Sam nodded vigorously. "Yeah, I know. Believe me, I know. I've been so careful not to mention anything or ask any questions. I even told Jodi's dad that. He couldn't believe that I hadn't asked Jodi about what had happened to her. God, I don't need to know what happened to her. I see it every time we're together and someone gives her a funny look. I see the anguish on her face when someone says something stupid about her. It breaks my heart. I never wanted to be the one to cause her any more pain. Believe me. That's why I said *I wished she didn't have those scars*. That's what I meant."

"Now it all makes sense." Kat patted Sam twice on the leg. "I can see where you were coming from. And I can see how Jodi took it, which is certainly not what you meant." She paused, tapping the side of her head with her finger. "The thing is, I'm not sure Jodi's in any state of mind to listen to anyone. All she can see at the moment is the remnants of that car accident. It's like somehow this has brought up all that again for her. I don't know, maybe if she knew this was all a misunderstanding, she'd open up again." Kat let out a deep breath. "If I were you, I'd try explaining it like that and ask for another chance."

Sam felt her chest tighten, her breath stuck in her throat. Ask for another chance? No, that was the one thing she wasn't capable of doing. She had asked for another chance with Jennifer, and then another, and another, each time being led in with a little hope and slapped down. In the end, it had become a game to her ex to see if she could pull her in one more time. She certainly hadn't meant to cause Jodi any pain. And she loved her. But to have to beg her for another chance when she hadn't intentionally done anything wrong? No, that had been what Jennifer had done to her. She couldn't do that again.

"Hey, I hope you two can work this out." Kat gave Sam's shoulder a shake. "I really do. You and Jodi are good together."

After Kat left, Sam remained on the couch, her head hung in her hands. How could everything have been so screwed up so quickly? Finally, she knotted her fingers in her hair, whipped her head back, and screamed. What was she going to do?

* * *

Friday at work was a disaster. Sam spent all day holed up in her office, trying to reconfigure her laptop and forget about Jodi, with little success at either. Finally, she had thrown up her hands and told Sandy to call it a day at four thirty. From there, she figured a nice soak in the tub might relax her, but after only a few minutes, she climbed back out and began pacing her living room. By Sunday when she showed up at her mom's for dinner, she was a complete wreck. Her hair hung limply around her face and the dark circles under her eyes looked as if she had caked on black eye shadow. Her hands were shaking so badly she could barely open the big front door. Without calling out her usual greeting, she shuffled into the kitchen.

Sharon turned around and gasped, her eyes flying wide. "Dear sweet Jesus, Sam, what's the matter with you?"

Sam opened her mouth, about to deny that anything was wrong but before she could form the words, her chin started quivering. How could she deny it, not when *everything* was wrong?

Sharon threw the large serving spoon aside on the counter and ran over to Sam, wrapping her arms tightly around her. Without a word, she rocked her, lightly caressing the back of Sam's head while cradling her to her chest.

Sam snuffled loudly and began to cry, great heaving sobs, her entire body shaking against her mom. She hadn't cried in her mother's arms like that since she was a child but as she sat there, the entire week poured out, leaving her stomach sore and her throat raw. Finally, her breath still hitching, she slowly regained control.

Sharon held her tightly, stroking the back of her head. When Sam had finally calmed, she leaned down and placed her lips to Sam's brow. "What's wrong, baby?"

Sam tried to laugh, a sound somewhere between a cough and a snort. "Everything, Mom. Everything's wrong."

"Here, come with me and let's see if we can figure this out." Sharon steered her over to the kitchen island and with Sam still under her arm, hooked her foot around a barstool leg and dragged it out. She then propped Sam up by the elbow as she climbed up on the stool. With one hand still on Sam's shoulder to steady her, Sharon scooted a second stool right up so their knees touched as she perched herself on top. She then took Sam's hands in hers. "Now, just start from the beginning."

Sam spent the next fifteen minutes pouring out everything from the concert to the get-together afterward to the night at her house to the morning after when she found the letter. She then went through her conversations with Jim and Kat. The words spilled forth like a whirlwind. Finally she finished, gasping for breath, her throat dry and raw as if she had just jogged around the block. "And I don't know what to do, Mom. I really don't."

Sharon placed her chin in her hand and gazed at Sam. She bobbed her head as if taking it all in, a trait Sam had grown up with. When she was in that state, it was no good pressuring her until she had worked everything around first in her mind. After a long pause, Sharon leaned forward, slipping her hand gently over Sam's. "Do you love her, Sam?" Her words were soft, comforting.

Biting her lip, Sam nodded, slowly at first then more vigorously, tears running freely. "Yes, Mom. I love Jodi—more than anything."

With a smile on her lips, Sharon reached up and lightly brushed away the tears from Sam's cheeks. "Well, sweetheart, that's what really matters right there. You love her. And do you think she feels the same?"

Sam nodded without saying a word.

"I figured as much. I've seen the two of you together and it's pretty obvious to anyone how she feels about you."

"Yeah, but what should I do, Mom? I mean, if Jodi doesn't want me around, what can I do?"

Sharon took a deep breath. "Well, Sam, I'll tell you, but I'm not sure you're going to like it."

"Please, just tell me. I'll do anything."

"Well, I think you're going to have to be the one to make the effort here, Sam. You're going to have to reach out to her and be the vulnerable one—take a chance and go to Jodi and ask for her back."

"Oh, no, Mom. I can't do that." Sam waved her hands in front of her. "There's no *way* I can do that. Not after what happened with Jennifer. I just can't."

Sharon scooted closer and placed Sam's hands in hers. With a gentle squeeze, she peered directly into Sam's eyes. "Baby, I know you're afraid to put yourself out there but if you love Jodi, that's exactly what you're going to have to do. You're going to have to be the one to take a chance and risk your heart here."

"Why can't Jodi—?"

Sharon quickly silenced her with a finger to her lips. "It's too far for Jodi to reach, Sam. She may want to but she can't…not after all she's been through. From the sounds of it, her entire world collapsed last Saturday. And not for the first time in her life."

"But Mom, I didn't mean—"

"I know, sweetheart. I know. But for Jodi, she risked everything to let you close to her and in her mind, when that all fell apart, it was like going through everything with that accident of hers again. Not only did she feel she lost you, but for her, she felt like she lost her voice and everything all over again.”

“But, Mom, how do you know?”

Sharon let out a soft chuckle. “Well, believe it or not, there was a time when your mom was a halfway competent counselor before becoming dean.” She raised an eyebrow.

Sam finally cracked a small smile.

Sharon wagged a finger at Sam. “Here, think of it this way. Imagine that you could no longer program computers. That’s who you are and all of a sudden, it’s gone. Then you meet someone, someone who you risked everything to let into your life, and they inadvertently said they wished you could still program computers. That’s where Jodi’s coming from, Sam. Music is her life and she lost a big part of that—more than anyone will ever know. That’s why it has to be you. She can’t take the risk because she already did once.”

Sam dropped her forehead into her hands. She was going to have to ask Jodi for another chance. That was what her mom was saying. That’s what Kat had said. But could she do that? After Jennifer, she had vowed to never do that again for anyone. She had been hurt too badly before. And would Jodi even give her another chance? Finally, she slowly lifted her head. “I’m not sure I can, Mom.”

Sharon reached out and stroked Sam’s cheek. “It all comes down to how much you love Jodi, Sam. Do you love her enough to take a risk?”

Two hours later as she drove home, Sam ground her fist into her temple. Great cannon blasts pounded through her skull. Even after talking with her mom, she was no closer to clearing her head or knowing what to do.

“Arghhhh.” With a cry that ripped at her throat, Sam slammed her fist against the steering wheel and stomped on the brakes, her tires howling as she whipped the wheel around. Her car skidded on the pavement. She then tromped on the accelerator and her engine whined, her tires searching for traction. One way or another, she was going to resolve this now.

Ten minutes later, she screeched to a halt in front of Jodi’s house, her Diet Coke leaping out of the cup holder and fizzing over the passenger floorboard. She didn't even notice. She simply gripped the steering wheel and stared out the windshield, her knuckles white.

Her hand hovered over the shifter. It wasn't too late. She could throw her car back in gear and speed off. It would be that easy. She could race home where it was safe, grab a glass of wine and work until she couldn't keep her eyes open any longer. But she had come this far. If she were ever going to do this, it had to be now—not tomorrow, not next week, but now. So before she could change her mind, she kicked open the door and jumped out.

The brisk night air met her like a slap across her face. Her head whirled and she threw a hand against the roof of her car to steady herself. It was hard to believe that it had only been a week since she had woken to Jodi's letter. Even now, she could close her eyes and see the words scrawled across the page. They had been kidding themselves. It had all been a huge mistake. But it *hadn't*—it hadn't all been a huge mistake. Nothing she had done with Jodi had been a mistake and damn it if she was going to let her say it had. No, Jodi was wrong. Her face now on fire, she stomped up the sidewalk, picking up speed. She took the porch steps two at a time and skidded to a stop in front of Jodi's door. She then hammered her fist against the wood, rattling the door in its frame. "Jodi, open up, damn it."

Sam waited, straining her ear for any sound of movement. She was certain Jodi was just on the other side of the door, only a couple of inches of wood now separating them. But still she heard nothing. As she stood there, her anger drained. Over the past week, she had bounced from despair to anger to sadness to hurt and back again. Now, all she felt was exhaustion, as if every ounce of energy she had mustered was quickly fading. She slammed her fist against the door again, this time barely making a thud. "Come on, Jodi. I know you're there, so if you won't let me in, at least listen. If I said something that hurt you, I'm really sorry. I never meant to do that. Believe me, that's the absolute last thing I ever wanted to do to you. I know you've suffered so much and it tears me up inside to know that I may have somehow added to that. Whatever I may have said or done,

I'm sorry. I'm so, so sorry. If nothing else, please believe that. I never meant to hurt you." All her strength now fading, Sam slowly sank to the porch. She leaned forward, her forehead resting against the hard door. She had been right—apparently Jodi wanted nothing to do with her. Perhaps it had all been a huge mistake after all. What more could she say? She closed her eyes and sobbed. She swung her fist one last time against the door, hardly making a sound, and whispered, her voice hoarse and raw. "Jodi, I love you."

* * *

Jodi huddled on the floor in the dark, leaning against her front door with Sam on the other side. She stared up at the ceiling, anguish twisting her every feature. Tears streamed silently and she pounded her fist against her chest, once, twice. Sure, she wanted to believe Sam, she did, but how could she? *Just wish you didn't have these scars.* She couldn't forget that. She couldn't forget those words. Sam might be telling the truth now—she hadn't meant any of it, she never wanted to hurt her. She could mean every word of it. But what would happen six weeks from now, six months from now, when the very sound of her voice grated in her ears? She couldn't take that risk. She should never have opened herself up in the first place.

"Jodi, I love you." Soft, almost pleading, Sam's words drifted through the door.

Jodi gasped. She had barely heard it yet there it was. "Jodi, I love you." She doubled over, her arms wrapped tightly around her stomach, and sobbed great burning tears. She rapped the back of her head against the door. *I love you.* The words she had longed for the most to hear from Sam. How could she turn away from that? At last, she dragged herself from in front of the door and collapsed again beside it. She slowly reached up, her arm trembling, every muscle crying out. Finger after finger, she grasped the doorknob, and with a loud clack, she threw open the catch.

The door slowly swung in on its hinges, letting out a low creak that filled the quiet living room as moonlight spilled over the threshold. Shrinking even more against the wall, Jodi pulled her legs up against her chest, her chin pressed into her knees, and stared down at the floor, afraid to look up, afraid to see Sam. *I love you*—could she dare to believe that? How could Sam love someone like her with all her scars? Was she merely kidding herself? Or could it possibly, somehow, beyond all odds, be true.

Sam carefully knelt in front of her, a whisper of fabric brushing the hardwood floor. Nothing but silence filled the room. Then, Sam softly cleared her throat. "Jodi…" Her voice cracked. "Jodi, I'm so sorry I caused you more pain. God, believe me, I know you've been through so much. I've probably messed everything up with us. I don't know what I can ever do to make it right again. I mean that night with you—it was the best night of my life. And then the next morning to find you gone—my life just stopped. I can't stand the fact that I screwed that all up and hurt you."

With her hands pressed against the sides of her face, Jodi whipped her head violently back and forth. "How can you say that? You see me like everyone else. All I am is a jagged little scar."

"That's bullshit, Jodi." Sam spun on her knee and grabbed Jodi's face in both her hands, forcing her to meet her eyes. "That's just bullshit. I don't know what other people see but I see a gorgeous, brilliant, talented young woman who stole my heart from the first time I met her."

"But my scars…my voice…" Jodi gulped in great gasps as tears streamed down her face. She desperately wanted to believe Sam. But how could she? Sam was only deluding herself. She would never be anymore than a hideous scar and who could ever love that.

"Jodi, listen. I—love—you. I love you. I think you're beautiful not in *spite* of your scars and voice. I think you're beautiful *because* of your scars and your voice—even more so." She gave Jodi a shake, emphasizing each word.

Jodi gaped at Sam. How could Sam think she was beautiful *because* of her scars and her voice? How on earth could she say that? She should have died in that car accident. The best parts of her *did* die in that accident. Her scars and voice made her beautiful? How?

Sam leaned forward, still cupping her face in her hands, brushing her cheeks softly with her thumbs. "Baby, please believe me. You're the most beautiful woman I've ever met. You play the most beautiful music that fills up parts of me I never even knew were empty. God, I know you've been through a lot and I can't even imagine what it's been like. I never will. But you simply amaze me. Every day I'm with you, you amaze me. You make my life better just by knowing you and I never want to let you go."

"But…but all people see are my scars. That's all—"

"Jodi," Sam pulled her close, their faces now only inches apart, "I see *you*…"

"But…"

"I see *you*. That's all." Two great tears spilled over Sam's eyelids.

Jodi sucked in quick, shallow breaths, her chin quivering. Could she possibly believe that anyone could see beyond her disfigurations? But as she peered deeply into Sam's eyes reflecting only earnestness and honesty, she began to cry harder, her chest hitching with each breath. How could she have ever thought Sam was like everyone else? Sam—who had always been there. Sam—who had never once treated her differently. Sam—who would wish her scars away, not because she couldn't stand looking at them but so that she, Jodi, would never have had to suffer that pain in the first place. If anyone could see her for who she was, it was Sam and she should never have doubted that.

Sam leaped forward and threw her arms tightly around her. Tears fell as she pressed her lips to her ear. "I love you, Jodi— don't you *ever* forget that."

Her face now buried against Sam, Jodi closed her eyes. "I love you too, Sam. Always."

EPILOGUE

Sam walked out in front of the stage as the band prepared for their first set of the evening. She wore the new shirt Jodi had gotten her with "Blind Pariah" across the back. Jodi had wanted it to say "Roadie" at the top but Kat had come up with the idea of putting "TECHNO GOD" on it instead. She had to admit she liked Kat's idea better. It only seemed fitting. It made her a fully-fledged member of the band. She dealt with all things technical.

She smiled and wrapped her arms around herself, watching Jodi tuning up her guitar—the purple Paul Reed Smith Custom 22. Still, it was hard to believe that only two months ago, she had thought that she had lost Jodi forever. Even now, her heart ached as she saw the deep ragged scar which carved up Jodi's neck. Not a day went by that Jodi didn't suffer the effects of that horrible car accident. She still flinched when people gave her a double take. She still grimaced when people lifted their eyebrows when she spoke. But seeing Jodi just standing up and holding her head high when Sam knew she wanted nothing more than to hide and shut the world out made her the most beautiful strong woman she had ever met. Yes, it had taken some convincing for Jodi to believe her, but those scars and her damaged voice made her even more beautiful in her eyes.

The first song started with Jodi jumping off the top of her amp with a wild leg kick and going into a blazing guitar solo. Sam smiled and shook her head. "That's my girl."

As the roar of the crowd died down—the first song had just finished up—Cheryl leaned in close and whispered in Sam's ear. "So, you two have any plans after the show?"

Sam quickly averted her eyes, her face beginning to blush. She had some plans all right—mostly of the type that would require breakfast in bed tomorrow. With a low chuckle, she quickly corrected herself—forget breakfast, maybe lunch.

The band played through their set. The fifth song was supposed to be "Tease Me, Please Me," which opened with Jodi playing another scorching solo on her electric guitar. Instead, she had walked to the back of the stage and swapped it for her Ovation acoustic. Sam shrugged, making a mental note. The band must have made a last-minute change to the playlist. She would change that on the website later. But when Jodi walked to the center of the stage, Sam stood bolt upright, her heart now racing. This was no last-minute playlist change. No, something else was going on. Jodi never played from center stage.

Lynn stepped to the side and waved one armed to Jodi. "Hey everyone, let's give it up for Ms. Jodi Price." The crowd erupted with applause and Lynn gave Jodi a small bow.

Jodi stepped up to the mic one foot at a time, her eyes on the stage in front of her, and swallowed. She then glanced out at the crowd and cleared her throat. When she finally spoke, her voice came out low and breathy, the voice Sam has fallen in love with. "This song goes out to my partner, Sam, who has taught me to both love and live again."

Jodi began playing, a slow, quiet ballad, one Sam recognized immediately from one of Jodi's early albums before her accident. She locked eyes with Sam. "Babe, there will never be anyone in my life but you…" Jodi's voice purred as she breathed out each word. She listened, her eyes locked with Jodi's, tears trickling down her cheeks. Jodi sang only for her.

When Jodi finished, Sam leaped over the gate and raced up the ramp to the stage. She dodged Lynn and ran up to Jodi, wrapping her arms tightly around her and giving her a long, deep kiss. The crowd exploded, clapping and cheering. Several whistles echoed through the club. Sam barely heard any of them. For her, there was only Jodi.

When they finally pulled back, still in each other's arms, Jodi smiled down at her. "I love you, Sam."

"I love you too, Jodi." Sam gave her a firm squeeze. "And don't you ever forget that."

www.ingramcontent.com/pod-product-compliance
Lightning Source LLC
Chambersburg PA
CBHW020402120726
47904CB00002B/668